MAY DAY!

FIORELLA DE MARIA

May Day!

A Father Gabriel Mystery

IGNATIUS PRESS SAN FRANCISCO

Cover photo illustration and
cover design by John Herreid

Photographic elements from
istockphoto.com and unsplash.com

ISBN 978-1-62164-767-6 (PB)
ISBN 978-1-64229-338-8 (eBook)
Library of Congress Control Number 2025930854
Printed in the United States of America ♾

I

Bring flow'rs of the fairest,
Bring flow'rs of the rarest,
From garden and woodland
And hillside and vale . . .

A verse from "Queen of the May" floated on the air towards Gabriel, along with the scent of freshly cut grass. Both were a happy reminder that spring had arrived, promising lengthening evenings and gardens erupting into colour, and the joyful hope of long, lazy summer days to come. Gabriel walked through the grounds of the abbey a little more slowly than usual, allowing himself the luxury of a few extra minutes to enjoy the sight of the vast carpets of bluebells and primroses that covered the orchard floor. He could feel the delicate petals of apple blossom settling on his head like snowflakes, but Gabriel made no effort to brush them away as he reached the edge of the orchard. Wildflowers and gnarled roots gave way to an impressive stretch of lawn being painstakingly mowed by Brother Gerard, the sound of the rotating blades not loud enough to drown out Gerard's desecration of Gabriel's favourite Marian hymn.

Our full hearts are swelling,
Our glad voices telling
The praise of the loveliest
Rose of the vale!

Gabriel had never been a musician like his late wife, but he had a good ear; it always astonished him how it could be possible to be tone deaf, how a man could be so completely unaware of the noises emanating from his own mouth. But young Gerard was nothing if not confident, and he stopped bawling out his off-key praises to Mother Mary only when he caught sight of Gabriel.

"Have you come to take over?" called Gerard hopefully. It was still very early, and the sun had not yet risen high enough to afford much warmth; but there were beads of sweat gathering at Gerard's temples, and he looked desperate to stop. "I don't know why the Boy Scouts can't mow their own camping ground," he continued, walking away from the mower without waiting to hear Gabriel's response. "It should be part of the bargain."

Gabriel smiled, holding out a battered metal water bottle that looked as though it had seen combat duty in France. Gerard snatched it gratefully and pulled out the stopper, taking great, noisy gulps. "It's all right, son, let me carry on here. You look fit to drop."

Gerard continued to drink greedily for several seconds, head thrown back as though he had just crawled to an oasis in the middle of a blistering desert. Gabriel heaved a sigh of relief that he had not thought to bring him a bottle of cider instead—Gerard would be nodding off to sleep by now. His thirst quenched, Gerard removed the bottle from his mouth and let out a long sigh of satisfaction. "Honestly, Gabbers, I don't know why I'm bothering. If the scouts are anything like the way my troop was, the place will be a wasteland by the time they leave. My troop even managed to set the abbey barn on fire!"

"Are you sure you weren't the one lighting the matches?" asked Gabriel, taking up his position at the mower. Gerard had done a fair job; the lawn was nearly ready. "There's no need to moan, Gerry; they work very hard in exchange for their time here. They always leave the place neat and tidy, and the scoutmaster will have them doing all sorts of jobs around the grounds before they leave."

"Just keep them away from the cider press," said Gerard, making as much space as he could between himself and the mower just in case Gabriel changed his mind. It was an ancient contraption, heavy, unwieldy, and inefficient, but it had probably mown fifty thousand acres by now and had not gone to pieces yet. "In fact, keep everyone away from the cider press. With your track record, we'll probably be pulling the scoutmaster's corpse out by the end of the camp, with you and Appleface trying to work out whodunnit."

"That's in frightfully bad taste, Gerry," said Gabriel, applying his weight to the mower and feeling the satisfying motion of the rollers moving away from him. "There's been only one murder on abbey grounds, and it was hardly my idea of a nice way to pass the time of day." Gabriel strained even harder, trying to blot out the sight of Gerard running out of the abbey cottage, white and shaking, on that terrible morning. Quite understandably, Gerard was never going to let him hear the last of that. "Haven't you some other mindless activity to be getting on with?" Gabriel asked.

Gerard chuckled, got the message, and began the walk back to the abbey, singing with all the skill of a strangled cat:

> O Mary, we crown thee with blossoms today!
> Queen of the angels and queen of the May!

Gabriel knew that he was deliberately overexerting himself—the lawn was virtually finished—but wearing himself out was the only way he could bear it. Gerard's talk of murder, however humorous, had brought everything flooding back. Gabriel could see her before his eyes, the last killer he had unmasked. There had been no acquittal for her, no mitigating factors, no wealthy relatives providing her with skilful lawyers to argue against her murder conviction. It had been only in the final hours before her execution that the bitter, emotionless woman had called for him, begging him to hear her confession so that she would not go to God unabsolved. It had taken the almost literal shadow of the noose to soften her heart in the end, but the casting off of that mask of indifference she had always worn had broken her.

Few non-Catholics appreciated how vulnerable a person became when making a confession. The act of opening the heart, the laying bare of every sin, every dark secret, was an act of healing but only in the way that cutting and draining an infected wound was an act of healing. For Florence Harding, the pain must have been almost unbearable and was quickly followed by terror at the thought of facing the hangman alone.

"I'm not afraid to stand before God now, Father," he could hear her almost pleading between her sobs, "but I cannot bear to die like that!"

Gabriel stopped resisting the memory and sat down on Gerard's newly cut lawn, taking deep breaths of fresh spring air in an effort to calm himself. Like most men of his generation, Gabriel had seen death before. He had been spared the horror of seeing his family die on the worst night of his life, but even his short sojourn on the battlefield had exposed him to the raw inhumanity of violent death. Yet that was nothing compared with the killing of Florence, her punishment carried out in cold blood. Tears had still been streaming down her face as they had strapped her arms and legs together to prevent her from struggling. Somehow or other, Gabriel had forced himself to maintain eye contact with her until the moment they put a hood over her face. In quick succession had come the crack of the trap door slamming open, the slightest gasp as Florence took her final breath, and then silence. The whole deadly pantomime had lasted under a minute.

The community had been very kind to Gabriel when he had returned, resisting the urge to ask him any questions. Only Abbot Ambrose had spoken with him about what had happened. With the wisdom of the old, the abbot knew that Gabriel needed to tell the story to someone or else spend the rest of his life replaying the memory of standing in that death chamber, knowing that he had indirectly led the condemned prisoner there—not that the conversation had fully healed him of that horror. Yes, the monks had all been kind, but Gabriel had long ago learnt that no trauma is powerful enough to stop the world from moving on. Gabriel had commended Florence's tormented soul to God and gone on with life as best he could. The sound of a door slamming shut still made Gabriel jump, but fortunately, few doors were ever slammed in the abbey.

Gabriel saw the lumbering figure of Dominic moving in his direction and immediately tried to get up, embarrassed at the thought of being found sitting on the grass like a child anticipating a picnic. It had been a great deal easier to sit down than to stand up again, and Gabriel lamented his creaking joints. He was well within Dominic's line of sight, and it had taken a painful effort to get himself onto one knee. Gabriel made a last undignified scramble and was in something resembling a standing position when Dominic reached him. "You look awful, old man," was Dominic's reassuring opening line. "I'll have to make you up a tonic."

Gabriel grimaced. "Oh, please no, it's not that bad. I don't think I could swallow another mouthful of nettle and dandelion cordial."

"I could prescribe a spoonful of cod liver oil every morning if you preferred?"

"Nettle and dandelion cordial would be splendid." Just the name "cod liver oil" evoked memories of a large glass bottle lurking on the kitchen mantelpiece and the unspeakable stink of rotten fish when Gabriel's mother removed the cork. To this day, he had no way of knowing whether that regular penance really had contributed to his good health or whether he would have been perfectly hale and hearty without it; it was one of those impenetrable mysteries of life. "I'm perfectly well," he added, "just getting a little stiff in my old age."

"Well, you'd better look sharpish," said Dominic. "I've been sent to tell you that the Boy Scouts have arrived early. They'll be wanting to set up their tents once they've taken some refreshment."

"They are keen," commented Gabriel, stumbling upon yet another mystery. He felt he ought to pretend that he had thoroughly enjoyed camping as a child, but he had never seen the point in pretending to be a refugee for a week, sheltering under leaky canvas on damp ground, only to wake up and find that a platoon of slugs had invaded. Needless to say, he had never been a Boy Scout, and not just for sectarian reasons. "I take it we're providing the refreshments?" he asked.

"Just this once; then they're doing their own thing with campfires and the like. Gerard's going to be serving lemonade and biscuits. After that, we attend only to their spiritual needs."

It was a point of pride that the Saint Augustine's Boy Scouts were the only Catholic troop in the county. Wiltshire had never been a particularly Catholic area, unlike parts of London and some of the northern cities, and what Catholics there were had the dogged determination of any minority living with a perpetual sense of isolation. Whilst boys in the other troops were expected to take part in church parades at their Anglican parishes, the Saint Augustine scouts more closely resembled their European brothers, the oath to serve His Majesty notwithstanding. During their camping trip at Saint Mary's Abbey, they would have evening prayer led by the monks and Mass first thing every morning before the boys ventured out hiking and fishing.

Gabriel's unsteady nerves were soothed by the sound of children descending in excited groups from the bus. Unlike some other members of the community, Gabriel found the presence of children hopeful rather than distracting. They were a welcome reminder that the clouds of the Second World War had dispersed and that the community outside the walls of the abbey was again growing and thriving in a time of peace. Gabriel noticed Gerard sloshing stick homemade lemonade into a row of glasses and went to help him, but he was waylaid by the scoutmaster approaching him, looking very commanding indeed in his lemon-squeezer hat.

"You must be the abbot," said the scoutmaster, giving Gabriel's hand a hearty shake. "Jack Harris, in charge of this rabble. It was frightfully kind of you to let us—"

"Oh, I'm not the abbot, Mr Harris," said Gabriel quickly, his embarrassment at interrupting outweighed by his embarrassment at being mistaken for someone important. "Dom Gabriel Milsom. How d'you do?"

Jack Harris gave a raucous laugh, exuding a peppermint odour which did little to conceal the smell of fruity tobacco on his breath. Gabriel could not help thinking that the scoutmaster had had loftier plans for his life than teaching schoolboys how to shine their own shoes and read a map. Dressed in all the regalia of the leader of such an organisation, Jack Harris looked as though he would not be out of place trekking through the jungle in search of a distant field hospital, his backpack heaving with provisions. His ruggedly handsome face even managed to be slightly sunburnt in the manner of an explorer newly home from the tropics, though where on earth Mr Harris had found enough sunshine to get burned by it was anybody's guess. "I'm terribly sorry," said Jack Harris, removing his hat to reveal a head of thick straw-coloured hair. "You look like an abbot, you see. You've got the sort of face one expects to see on a holy picture, minus the painted halo."

Gerard chuckled appreciatively, which more than made up for Gabriel's complete failure to get the joke. "You'll be wanting to see that chappie over there," said Gerard, pointing in the direction of Abbot Ambrose, who had just emerged into daylight ahead of them. Jack Harris clicked his heels together, gave a polite nod and went in search of more august company.

"What's that supposed to mean?" hissed Gabriel at Gerard, who was stifling a laugh, as soon as he was sure the scoutmaster was out of earshot. "Perhaps you could share the joke, as you seem to have found it so hilarious."

Gerard avoided the need to look at Gabriel by starting to hand out glasses to the queue of boys lined up at the table. Gabriel had to admit that they were extremely polite. Every single boy made a point of saying thank you as he took his drink and walked away. Jack Harris might have no discernment whatsoever, but he was clearly an authoritative leader who had trained his boys well in the art of good gentlemanly manners.

"Don't take it personally; he was only teasing," said Gerard. "It's just that you always look sad when you think nobody's looking. Most people see a sad face and think 'holy face,' I suppose."

"I'll fill up the jug," snapped Gabriel, snatching up the empty jug and making his way to the abbey kitchen. He had not gone far before he noticed that Jack Harris had broken away from his conversation with Abbot Ambrose and was berating a child who had already been reduced to tears. The boy in question had the rosy complexion and effortlessly handsome face that might have qualified him as a model for a public health poster promoting the benefits of eating carrots. That is, if his eyes had not been in the process of swelling with the effects of crying.

"Is anything amiss, Mr Harris?" asked Gabriel, feeling the

urge to squash the situation before it escalated. He hated seeing children in distress like that, having spent much of his own childhood having various sections of the riot act read to him. The boy had removed his cap and was using it by way of a comfort blanket, wringing it in his fists in an effort to control himself.

"It's no good making a noise like that, Nicholson," said Jack Harris relentlessly, completely ignoring Gabriel's intervention. "I distinctly remember telling you that you were banned from camp this year following your little misdemeanour."

"But Skip, I couldn't bear to tell my grandfather; he would have gone mad!" said young Nicholson between hiccups, using the cap to wipe his eyes, which only caused Jack Harris to snatch it from him indignantly. "*Please*, may I stay?"

"You should have thought about that before you played a silly prank," Jack Harris retorted. He was the sort of man who had been forced to listen to far too many children making their excuses, and he was not going to be moved by this one. "Now you'd better pull yourself together, get on your bike, and go home."

"Mr Harris, is there anything I can do to help?" asked Gabriel, unable to bear it any longer. He smiled at young Nicholson, who made a valiant attempt at returning the grin. "What's your name, son?"

"Anthony Nicholson, Father," mumbled the boy. He was well spoken, but something about the way he pronounced his Christian name suggested a foreign influence. "It's all right; I'll go."

"Is it really necessary?" asked Gabriel, searching Jack Harris' face for any sign he might relent. He found no sign. "It's quite a warm day, and the lad's only just arrived." He looked back at Anthony. "Where have you come from today?"

"Dilton Wylye," he said, holding out his hand for his cap, which was returned to him with a needless show of irritation.

"That's a fair way." Gabriel turned to Jack Harris. "It seems a bit unkind to send him packing after such a long ride."

"It's barely five miles, all downhill," Jack Harris answered impatiently, "and he knew he was not supposed to come. Master Nicholson here thought it would be a jolly jape to let off firecrackers at the back of the town hall when the good ladies of the WI were in residence. Needless to say, they failed to see the joke."

Gabriel stifled the urge to laugh. Women's Institute meetings were notoriously straitlaced affairs, conjuring up images of lengthy lectures on the benefits of tatting in this time of austerity, or the correct use of pectin in the making of damson preserve. He could see how a group of idle schoolboys (Gabriel doubted this child had acted alone) might have found it irresistible to send the worthy ladies of the WI into a flat spin. "Could he at least have a glass of lemonade before he leaves? He must have worked up a thirst after the ride."

"He has a water bottle; he will not die of thirst," said Jack coldly. "I've a few provisions to purchase in the village. I can escort him the first part of the way."

Anthony looked as though he would rather do anything—even face the wrath of an angry father—than spend another minute in the presence of the scoutmaster from hell. "It's all right, Skip, I'll go," promised Anthony, starting to move away, but Jack took him by the arm to stop him in his tracks.

"It's quite all right, Nicholson; we need to have a little talk about your behaviour."

Gabriel groaned inwardly, watching the wretched picture of the boy walking over to the place where he had dumped his bike, yanking it out of the grass by the handlebars and walking with it next to the uncompromising figure of his skipper. It seemed unduly harsh to Gabriel to deprive a child of a treat he must have been looking forward to for months over such a silly incident, but he had no jurisdiction over the scouts and knew he could not intervene. Gabriel offered up a prayer for Anthony Nicholson, that his reception at home would not be as hostile as he seemed to fear. Since the boy lived in a nearby village where Gabriel had seldom ventured, the Nicholsons were an unknown quantity, but for all he knew, Anthony's father might have a sense of humour about the whole affair. Gabriel hoped so anyway.

Moments later, Gabriel was in the kitchen, refilling the jug of lemonade and searching the pantry for a few boxes of butter biscuits to hand out. He felt an irrepressible dislike towards the scoutmaster with his petty rules and Little Hitler attitude, but he told himself he was overreacting. The child would have other treats and other outings to enjoy. One day, this would be a bitter but distant memory about which Anthony Nicholson might even feel able to laugh.

2

Gabriel was relieved that Jack Harris had left a number of subordinates in charge of the scouts, as he was gone far longer than might have been expected. It occurred to Gabriel, when Jack had not arrived back at the abbey after more than an hour, that he should perhaps have volunteered to go into the village on his behalf. Sutton Westford was a small enough village, but in the absence of local knowledge, Jack may well have got lost on his way to the village shop or found the villagers uncooperative if he had asked for directions. It was not that the villagers of Sutton Westford would have any obvious animosity towards the scouts; the movement was well loved around the country, and hardly a man in the land had not been a scout at some stage in his childhood. It was just that, if Jack had the misfortune to ask the wrong person for directions—the ever-troublesome Gordon Merriott, for example, or some urchin with nothing better to do—he might find himself being sent on a wild goose chase for the sake of it. Gabriel could almost imagine Gordon Merriott having a chuckle in the pub that night about the prank.

By the time Jack had returned, laden with paper bags heaving with what mostly looked like the vegetables no one else wanted to buy, the scouts had put up their tents and been sent on a scavenger hunt in the orchard to keep them occupied. Gabriel felt fairly sure, from the scoutmaster's flustered demeanour, which the man was desperately trying to control, that Jack had indeed been led on a wild goose chase or simply lost his way. If the latter was the case, he was never going to admit that the orienteering skills he taught the next generation were somewhat lacking in his own department. The sound of the bell ringing for chapel gave Gabriel a good reason to ignore the situation, and he processed joyfully in the direction of chanted prayers and peace.

Gabriel was sitting next to Dominic for lunch when he saw a troubling sight through the window. Anthony Nicholson had returned to the scout camp but was wise enough to avoid another confrontation with his skip and was standing alone, out of sight of the others. Gabriel could not see, from where he was sitting, what had happened to Anthony's bike, but the boy must have found some way to get himself back, assuming of course that he had gone home in the first place. It was just possible that when he had parted company with Jack in the village, Anthony had simply hidden away somewhere whilst he tried to puzzle out what to do.

Gabriel tapped Dominic on the shoulder and indicated that he needed to leave, before slipping out of the refectory. He was not quite as discreet as he had intended, as he managed to trip on the edge of a bench as he left, causing a screech like the sound effect from a 1930s ham horror film. Gabriel could almost feel the puzzled looks in his direction, but he fled with his head down and did not stop moving until he was out of the refectory and out of the building.

"Anthony!" called Gabriel from the doorway. He could

see the boy quite clearly now, and it was not a pretty sight. He stood, a dishevelled picture of dejection, his uniform untucked and grubby from a morning of hard exercise. Anthony appeared to have lost his cap altogether, and he was crying again, if he had ever entirely stopped. "What's happened?"

Anthony looked guiltily in Gabriel's direction, staring at him as though pondering whether Gabriel might be an ally in this disastrous situation. He clearly thought he might be, as he blurted out, "Father, I'm in terrible trouble! I don't know what to do!"

Gabriel signalled for Anthony to come inside, and he obeyed the order without hesitation, looking over his shoulder to ensure that there were none of his fellow scouts nearby who might report his unwelcome presence to the scoutmaster. "Let's find you something to eat and drink," suggested Gabriel, leading Anthony in the direction of the kitchen. "You're trembling. I daresay you've not had a bite to eat all day."

"Not since breakfast, Father," said Anthony honestly, wiping his nose on his sleeve in a manner that maddened Gabriel. "But that was ever such a long time ago, and I must have cycled a hundred miles!"

Gabriel suppressed a smile, thinking that poor Anthony Nicholson probably felt as though he really had cycled that far, going back and forth along that winding road no fewer than three times. "Well, it'll be nice and cool in the kitchen."

In fact, the kitchen was unpleasantly warm and bustling with members of the community washing and drying up the lunch things, so Gabriel gathered together a few bits and pieces for lunch—a beaker of milk, a round of bread, and some cheese—and took Anthony into the cool of the now virtually deserted refectory. He waited while Anthony glugged down the milk thirstily before asking, "What's happened, son? Why did you come back to the camp when you'd already been sent home?"

Anthony shook his head, talking with the beaker so close to his mouth that it acted as a miniature megaphone. "I had no choice, Father! My grandpa was so cross when I got home, he told me to go back immediately."

Gabriel sat facing Anthony, wondering what had really happened. "You didn't tell him why you'd come home, did you?"

Anthony looked positively offended. "I couldn't! He was so angry, he never let me get a word in edgeways! You don't know what he's like when he's cross."

"If he didn't know you'd been sent home, why was he cross?"

The child looked at Gabriel with the pitying condescension of a boy who is constantly struggling to manage the adults in his life. "He was cross because I wasn't where I was supposed to be. My father's ill, Grandpa didn't want me disturbing him, and when I came back he started telling me off for being a wet lettuce about spending a few nights under canvas!"

Gabriel was beginning to see Anthony Nicholson as something of a kindred spirit. He suspected that he would have risked the wrath of an authority figure rather than admit to his family that he had been thrown out of an event, and he shared Anthony's sense of injustice. No one likes to be called a coward, especially when it is not at all fair. "I'm sorry your father's unwell. Is it serious?"

"No, no, only a weak chest. He's had a cold, and now it's a nasty cough," said Anthony, repeating the expression he had heard adults use to describe the situation. "He was coughing and sneezing yesterday. Today he couldn't get out of bed. He has asthma; it happens sometimes. Grandpa was just cross because he thought I'd done a bunk." Anthony looked woundedly in Gabriel's direction. "Which I hadn't."

Gabriel sighed, wondering how best to remedy the situation. The child could not stay at the abbey. If Jack Harris was an implacable enough disciplinarian to send the boy home in the first place, he was unlikely to have a change of heart now and allow the boy to remain. However, the alternative was to send him home for the second time today, knowing that he was unwelcome there. "Do you live with your parents and your grandpa?" asked Gabriel, trying to gauge the situation a little better. "Is there anyone else at home?"

Anthony shook his head miserably. "My mother died during the war. It's just the three of us at home."

"Do you have any family living nearby? Aunts and uncles, cousins perhaps?"

Anthony shook his head again. "No. There's no one. We're only a small family. I think my mother came from a big family, but they'd all be living in France. She was French, you see," he added, in case Gabriel had failed to come to that understanding himself.

Gabriel stood up with great effort and went over to the window, noting to his dismay that a couple of boys had discovered Anthony's bicycle and alerted their scoutmaster like a perfect pair of sneaks. Jack Harris was now examining the bicycle in the manner of a country policeman. Gabriel could not make out the conversation but could see that Jack was engaged in an animated conversation with the sneaks, probably trying to work out where the miscreant had hidden himself. "Listen, Anthony, I think I had better take you home myself." He ignored Anthony's attempt at a protest. "It's all right, I'm not going to send you on your own to face your grandfather, but you can't stay here. Mr Harris won't allow it, and you'll only get yourself into more trouble if you try to force the situation. Why don't you help yourself to a little more milk while I explain things to Mr Harris? Then I'll go and find Brother Gerard to see if the car is available."

Anthony's face brightened momentarily at the thought of having a ride in a car, then fell again. "What about my bike, Father?"

Gabriel sighed. Dealing with children was a little like trying to solve one of those irritating puzzles one's parents would invent to keep the younger members of the family occupied on a rainy afternoon. *A farmer has a dog, a chicken, and a bag of grain. He has to take them all safely across the river, but he can take only one item at a time, leaving two on the riverbank at any one time. The dog will eat the chicken; the chicken will eat the grain . . .* As with the puzzle, there were too many movable parts to this situation. "I'll think of something," promised Gabriel, leaving the room to face Jack Harris with all the reluctance of a twelve-year-old Boy Scout.

"I don't care how angry his grandfather was!" declared Jack, which was exactly what Gabriel had expected him to say. "He's got a blasted cheek coming back a second time when he knew he had no business being here in the first place!"

"The boy said his grandfather never gave him the chance to explain," Gabriel said. "As soon as his grandfather saw him at the door, he began shouting at him for coming back when he knew his father was ill and needed some peace and quiet."

"I fail to see how this is my problem," answered Jack, entirely unmoved by the story. "The boy misbehaved, and he was forbidden to come to the camp. He knew he had no business turning up."

Gabriel raised his hands in a placatory gesture which might have been surrender in another context. "It's all right, Mr. Harris," said Gabriel, quickly moving the conversation in a safer direction. "I'll ask the abbot's permission to accompany young Master Nicholson home."

Jack Harris snorted. "Well, I suppose it might prevent the little boomerang flying back again for the third time." His shoulders sagged, and he gave Gabriel a sheepish smile as though remembering his manners. Whoever was to blame for Anthony Nicholson's irritating behaviour, it was certainly not Gabriel. "I'm very much obliged to you, Father. I have rather more to think about today than one errant Boy Scout who cannot take 'Go home' for an answer."

Gabriel nodded before going in search of Abbot Ambrose, whose steely manner suddenly held no fears for Gabriel. Abbot Ambrose was many things, but he could be relied upon to be scrupulously fair.

Some fifteen minutes later, Gabriel had changed into clerics and found himself speeding out of the village on his own unreliable metal steed, whilst his smaller, healthier companion churned up the path ahead of him, spraying clods of mud in all directions. Gabriel should, of course, have realised that the abbot's solution to the transport puzzle would be to tell Gabriel to get on the abbey's own bicycle, but he had not cycled with any regularity since he had been in a parish, and that had been mostly along the well-laid roads of a town.

A journey Gabriel would have quite enjoyed on foot flew past him in a blur of potholes, the screeching of inadequate brakes, and more falls into the adjacent grass verge than he cared to remember afterwards. The only benefit of the five-mile cycle to Dilton Wylye was that Gabriel's poor cycling skills cheered up Anthony no end; indeed, the child seemed to enjoy the spectacle of a middle-aged man struggling to keep up with him and finishing up cycling with blades of damp grass in his hair.

"Don't they teach you to ride a bike in the monastery?" asked Anthony innocently when he stopped to help Gabriel put the chain back on his bike after a particularly awkward tumble. The boy smeared his oil-stained fingers over his shorts, then waited with his hands on his hips whilst Gabriel plucked up the courage to get back on the bike again. "Are monks allowed to ride bikes?"

"I was riding a bicycle before you were even thought of!" Gabriel retorted, finding it harder and harder to hide his exhaustion. "I was a telegram boy during the first war, before I became a soldier."

"My father was too poorly to be a soldier, but my mother was a war hero," answered Anthony, destroying Gabriel's paper-thin confidence without apparently noticing. "None of my chums believe me. They say men fight and women stay at home, but it was the other way round. She was awarded a medal and everything. My father says I can have it for keeps one day, but I'll probably win some medals of my own when I grow up." Anthony's prattling came to a momentary halt as he looked Gabriel up and down, visibly unimpressed by the sight. "Do you have any medals?"

"Hadn't we better get going?" said Gabriel, secretly thinking he should have been given a medal after some of the flak he had taken as a telegram boy, giving the worst possible news to distraught women all around north London. "The lights on this thing are none too reliable, and I'd rather not end up cycling home in the dark."

Anthony shrugged and jumped on his own bike, speeding off and leaving Gabriel to catch up with him as best he could. Gabriel had felt great relief on many occasions, but nothing gave him greater relief that day than to see the small but cheerful sign at the side of the road welcoming him to Dilton Wylye.

The relief was short-lived. Gabriel did not know the village very well at all, nor did he know where the Nicholson family lived, but it soon became apparent that they lived quite close to the edge of the village, adding to the journey as they had to cycle through a series of narrow lanes, past a dilapidated cricket pavilion and the old abandoned lockup, before they finally reached the Nicholson home.

Gabriel saw Anthony ahead of him, jumping off his bike and running towards a large sprawling cottage, the like of which one might find on a picture postcard. It even had the requisite thatched roof and rose plants winding up the walls. The only incongruous detail was a smart motorcar parked in the lane at the front of the cottage, which Gabriel instantly recognised. Inspector Applegate was paying a visit, and that could mean only one thing. "Anthony, stay outside!" called Gabriel, but the boy was already at the gate. He had registered trouble shortly before Gabriel and was hurrying to the house to find out what was going on.

It was only at a much later hour that Gabriel fully appreciated the way Anthony had perceived the situation at the time. He was a boy in trouble, and the appearance of the long arm of the law at his home must have seemed to be his fault. Anthony had seen what Gabriel had not seen from a distance, the telltale sight of a policeman standing guard outside the door, blue helmet on his head, an immediately recognisable sign of danger.

Gabriel dumped his own bicycle in the grass verge and hurried over to the policeman, who was already engaged in conversation with Anthony. "You can't go in there, sonny," said the constable, placing a warning hand on the boy's shoulder. It was going to take more than that mild gesture to stop Anthony, who attempted to brush past him. The constable stepped in front of him. "I'm sorry, but no one's allowed in."

"It's my house!" shouted Anthony, his mounting panic causing his voice to come out in what was almost a shriek. He tried to duck past the impressive bulk of the policeman, but the constable was under strict orders, and nobody, least of all a persistent child, was going to pass him. He grabbed Anthony by the arms and moved him deftly back in the direction of the garden gate. "Don't! It's not fair!" the boy cried.

"For the last time . . ."

"Constable, this is his home," Gabriel explained, stepping forwards. "What's all this about?"

"I'm well aware that he lives here, Father," said the policeman, not unkindly. "I was told there was a child. But I can't let him in." He lowered his voice—pointlessly, as

Anthony could hear him perfectly. "It's best he don't go inside."

Gabriel had felt his heart hammering against his ribs the moment he saw the police presence at the house—there was never any good reason for the bobbies to pay a call to a private home—and the constable had confirmed his worst fears. Gabriel had been in this position before, standing helplessly outside a family home when disaster had struck, and he had arrived too late to prevent it.

There was no chance to ask for more information; Anthony had stopped struggling quietly and started screaming at the top of his voice. "Let me in! I want my father! I want my grandpa!" Anthony turned to Gabriel for support, perhaps imagining that he might be more important than a policeman in the grand scheme of things and would be able to help him. "Tell him to let me pass!"

"Antoine!"

The voice that called out from the house's doorway was penetrating enough to break through Anthony's shouts. The boy immediately went quiet, staring past the policeman at the grey-haired figure moving slowly towards him.

"Grandpa!" called Anthony. "The bobby won't let me in!"

The bobby in question stepped away from the boy without further argument, allowing him to run down the path into his grandfather's welcoming arms. Gabriel took in the old man's exhausted, shell-shocked expression and supressed a powerful stab of guilt. He knew that every human life was valuable, but his first thought at the sight of the grandfather was that the wrong man, the younger man, had come to grief. It was a vile thought, completely unworthy of him, to see the situation as worse than the alternative. The old man's life was as precious as his son's had been . . . and yet all Gabriel could think was that Anthony would suffer a great deal more now than he would otherwise have done.

Anthony was sobbing openly, and Gabriel saw that the grandfather had tears sliding down his face. Behind them, Inspector Applegate had made an appearance, drawn outside by the commotion. For once, Applegate had no jocular remark to make at the unwelcome sight of Gabriel, and he merely shook his head when Gabriel looked quizzically in his direction, silently beckoning for him to come inside.

"I hardly need ask what has happened if you're here," said Gabriel grimly, banging the front door shut when Applegate appeared unwilling to take him any farther into the house. "When I saw the policeman outside, I hoped there had just been an accident or something."

Applegate sighed. "I've only just arrived. Uniform got here first when the old man sounded the alarm. Got home from buying his morning paper to find his son on the floor with his head bashed in. The poor man was so hysterical it took a while to work out what had happened."

"What had happened?"

Applegate tugged at his ear in a nervous habit Gabriel had not noticed before. "Looks like a bungled burglary. There shouldn't have been anyone in the house by that time in the morning, but the victim was off work with a feverish cold, according to the old man. The study had been ransacked; the safe had been smashed open and emptied. It would have been the noise of the robbery that brought the victim down from his bed to investigate."

Applegate's train of thought was interrupted by what

sounded like an argument commencing on the other side of the door.

"That child can't come in here," said Gabriel. "Neither of them should come back in. It's horrible."

"Quite," agreed Applegate. "I hadn't expected the child to appear on the doorstep like that. His grandfather said he had gone off to a scout camp."

"He had," said Gabriel, "almost." He had no idea how to respond. This was not the time for lengthy explanations. "It's a long story, but yes, he was supposed to be at a scout camp. What about the grandfather? If they both need somewhere to stay, they could stay at the cottage in the abbey grounds, but it wouldn't be suitable for a boy on his own."

"Understandably, he's all over the place, but he will need to give me a statement when he's calmer."

Gabriel nodded, bracing himself for the raw emotions waiting for them outside, whilst Applegate turned the handle and led him back out through the front door.

The young police constable stationed outside looked up imploringly in Applegate's direction, apparently overwhelmed by the task of trying to calm two distraught males clamouring for his attention. The old man seemed to be remonstrating with the policeman. Anthony was lending his support by clinging to his grandfather's arm, protesting incoherently. "I'm sorry, sir," said the constable to Anthony's grandfather, "but I can't let you into the house. It's a crime scene, you see; we're gathering evidence."

"I'm well aware that it's a crime scene, my man—it's my son lying dead in there!"

Applegate took pity on the constable and placed a firm

hand on old Mr Nicholson's shoulder, gently turning him around. "Mr Nicholson, I am very sorry for what has happened, but we cannot allow either of you to enter the house until the team has finished. We want to find out who killed your son, and you have to let us do our work."

Mr Nicholson placed a protective arm around his grandson's trembling frame. Anthony had stopped crying now, but he was shaking uncontrollably and was showing the first signs of shock setting in. "You can't leave us out here for everyone to stare at," he said hoarsely. "It's not good for the boy. If we can't enter our own home, where are we supposed to go?"

Applegate nodded, indicating that he understood the man's concern. "It may be some days before you may return to the house, sir. You will need to accompany me to the station to make a statement if you feel able, but we should find you somewhere to stay for a few nights. Do you have any relatives or friends living nearby?"

Mr Nicholson shook his head without giving the problem much thought. "Not really, Inspector. We've no family hereabouts and no one we could impose upon like this. I am on friendly terms with the pub landlord, and he might be able to rent me a room for a few days, but it would not do for the boy."

"Yes, I understand," said Applegate calmly, though Gabriel guessed that he was frantically weighing up possibilities in his mind. The presence of a minor in the middle of a crime investigation was always a nightmare, especially when there was no network of extended family to step in and help. "Well, we'll think of something."

Gabriel touched Applegate's arm lightly. "Might I have a word with you?" he asked.

Applegate turned to the Nicholsons before answering Gabriel. "Sir, why don't you and the boy wait in the car for a moment? I shan't be long."

In the absence of any realistic alternative, the old man shepherded Anthony into the back of Applegate's car, where they could at least enjoy a modicum of comfort and privacy whilst uniformed strangers crawled all over their home. As Gabriel had discovered to his own cost years ago, the first thing to go in the aftermath of a serious crime was privacy, and the Nicholsons would have to resign themselves to the intrusive power of the law over the days and weeks to come. No stone would be left unturned, no article of clothing unexamined. Every detail of that family's daily lives would be picked over and scrutinised in the hope of building a picture of the victim's final minutes.

"What is it?" asked Applegate tersely.

"I appreciate that Mr Nicholson will have to stay near the crime scene to help with the investigation, but the child should be well out of it. Why not ask the Paiges if the boy could stay with them? They've got that lovely big house now, plenty of space for a child. It's conveniently away from this village but close enough for you to keep an eye on him."

Applegate looked distinctly uncomfortable, as he had every right to be. It was not so long ago that Applegate had locked up Dr Paige at the constabulary on a false murder charge, and Dr Paige had used words like "Gestapo" to describe Applegate's tactics. That the two men did not get along famously was the understatement of the decade. "I don't know," he said. "It would be an imposition, dumping a troubled boy on complete strangers."

"I don't think they would see it that way at all," Gabriel persisted. "The child needs a family at a time like this; he needs a mother. If you would rather not face Dr Paige . . ." Gabriel trailed off at the sight of Applegate glaring at him. As usual, his words had come out all wrong. "Well, you know, I thought—"

"I was merely doing my job at the time, as I'm sure the good doctor is aware," Applegate snapped, but he was visibly ruffled. "I was simply thinking that turning up at a young couple's house out of the blue might be taking liberties."

Gabriel shook his head confidently. "I'll take him myself, if you like. I know Mrs Paige, and I'm sure she would want to help."

Applegate gave a low growl before turning on his heel and hurrying in the direction of the car. Gabriel knew better than to follow; he was not sure why, but the plan had to look like Applegate's idea. He saw the inspector deep in conversation with Mr Nicholson; then the old man got out of the car and followed Applegate into the house, gesturing to Anthony to stay where he was.

Gabriel waited until the two men had disappeared from view before moving over to the car, where Anthony sat hunched in the backseat, looking to all intents and purposes as though he had been kidnapped. Gabriel's inner coward was tempted to tiptoe backwards away from the car and leave the child lost in his own thoughts. He had no idea what to say to a small boy who had waved good-bye to his father earlier that morning and come back to discover him dead. It would be no good Gabriel telling Anthony that he understood what loss felt like, since children experienced it so differently from adults. Gabriel had at least been blessed with a childhood in which death never encroached.

To Gabriel's dismay, Anthony looked up sharply as though sensing that he was being watched, and their eyes locked. Gabriel could not run away now; he tried to smile, but Anthony simply stared back at him, eyes red rimmed and unfocused—that shell-shocked face again, the sight of the boyish soldier in his trench, broken and confused by the carnage all around him. That face looked out at Gabriel from every recently bereaved relative, like an eternal reproach against the evil of the world.

Gabriel opened the car door, avoiding leaning in too far in case the child should find him intimidating. Anthony clearly did not and looked at Gabriel with a mixture of confusion and curiosity. "They won't let me back in the house," said Anthony, in the monotone voice of a child in shock. Despite his tears, the full import of what had happened had not entirely struck him yet. "My things are in the house. My bedroom is in the house. I shall have to sit in this car all day."

"They won't make you sit here much longer," promised Gabriel, though in reality he had no idea how long Anthony would be expected to wait. Children had a tendency to be forgotten about in moments of adult crisis, especially when they sat quietly and stopped making demands on the grown-ups around them. "In a little while, I'm going to take you somewhere safe to stay."

"I want to stay at home," said Anthony, his eyes continuing to stare unblinkingly at Gabriel. "Someone will have to look after Grandpa."

"Don't worry, he'll be found somewhere safe to stay as well. Just until—"

Until what? wondered Gabriel. He had no idea what the sequence of events was likely to be. Would Inspector Applegate allow grandfather and grandson back into the house as soon as the police had finished poring over the crime scene? Or would Applegate insist that the house be sealed until the end of the investigation? Would old Mr Nicholson—or Anthony, for that matter—want to live in that house after what had happened? Apart from his own situation, in which there had been no house to which Gabriel could have returned, Gabriel could think of only one occasion when a murder had taken place inside a private house, and the dwelling had been sold very soon afterwards. The only remaining inhabitant had been the elderly mother, and it had been determined that she should go into a nursing home in the absence of any family to care for her.

The sound of Anthony clambering out of the car jolted Gabriel back to the present and all its troubles. "I'm not leaving Grandpa," the boy said in an unexpectedly assertive voice, and he was planting his hands on his hips and looking fixedly up at Gabriel as though daring him to challenge the plan. "He's old and upset. What if he dies too?"

It was a reasonable enough fear; the old man was all little Anthony had left, and the boy was intelligent enough to appreciate the dangers facing an elderly person who had had a horrific shock. There was no further chance of conversation; the old man in question had emerged from the house with Inspector Applegate and walked towards them carrying a small suitcase. He was as haggard as he had been when Applegate had let him back into the house, but now he was making a brave attempt at nonchalance, giving his grandson a smile so false, Gabriel could not imagine that a toddler would have been fooled, let alone a bright boy of Anthony's age. Nevertheless, Gabriel appreciated the efforts the man was making to pull himself together.

"Antoine," Mr Nicholson began, handing him the case as though he were bestowing a generous gift upon him, "I think it might be a good idea if you go and stay with some nice people for a few days. It shouldn't be for too—"

"But I want to stay with you!" Anthony protested, pushing the suitcase away from him. "We can stay together! We can go and stay with the nice people together."

Gabriel turned to Applegate. "You know, the Paiges have plenty of space. I'm sure they wouldn't mind putting up both of them if necessary."

"No," answered Applegate in a tone that suggested he knew that he had made an enemy for life in Anthony by his refusal. "I think it best if we stick with the original plan. The fact is, Mr Nicholson here is going to have to help us with our enquiries, and it might be better if the lad is well out of harm's way."

Anthony glared at Applegate with the resentment any child feels when spoken about as though he were absent. "But I can help you! You'll need to talk to me too!"

Applegate shook his head, his patience already exhausted, and indicated that Gabriel should return to the car. Gabriel hesitated long enough to see old Mr Nicholson place an affectionate arm around Anthony's shoulders and promise him that it would not be long before they were together again. It was only as Gabriel was helping Anthony into his seat that he realised that Mr Nicholson had been speaking to his grandson in French.

3

The town was only ten miles away as the crow flies, but Gabriel doubted that Anthony had often strayed far from his village. The child sat with his face pressed against the side window for much of the journey. Of course, Gabriel could not be sure whether the boy was quite as fascinated by the scenery as he appeared to be or was just looking for a reason to avoid having to speak, but it gave Gabriel time to gather his own thoughts and plan what he was going to say to the Paiges when they arrived.

It also gave him a much-needed interval to brace himself for his return to a town that was still the stuff of some of his worst nightmares. The scriptural saying "A prophet is never welcome in his own country" certainly applied to Gabriel, if it had occurred to him to grant himself so lofty a title, but in Gabriel's case it was true to say that a sleuth was never welcome in any country in which a crime had been committed. He resolved to keep his head down and spend as little time as possible out in the open. Gabriel had a particular horror of meeting Bron Gladstone on his travels. Young Verity's appeal was due, and even if her death sentence were commuted, Gabriel doubted the Gladstone family would ever wish to speak with him again—nor could he entirely blame them.

A difficulty occurred to Gabriel as they entered the town.

Marie Paige's troubled history might possibly have left her nervous of the police, including plainclothes police inspectors, and he could not risk startling her when he needed to ask her to take on such a responsibility. He would have to risk a longer walk in the open rather than provoke a scene on Marie's doorstep. Gabriel leant forwards to address the driver. "Excuse me, I don't suppose you could park the car round the corner from the doctor's surgery? It might be easier if Mrs Paige . . . erm . . . well, she might prefer not to see Inspector Applegate or a man in a police uniform."

Applegate, comfortably ensconced in the passenger seat, turned around and glared at Gabriel. "I am not the Gestapo!" he exclaimed, ignoring the fact that his raised voice had caused Anthony to jump out of his skin. "You wore uniform for about five minutes, many moons ago."

"Yes, but I'm not wearing it now," answered Gabriel levelly, "and the Gestapo were a police force, not soldiers."

The remark could not have been more misplaced. "If you're making any comparison at all between His Majesty's police force and those torturing, murdering thugs," Applegate nearly shouted, "we have nothing more to say to one another!"

"I'm not making any comparison at all," answered Gabriel, still failing to appreciate the offence he had caused. "But Mrs Paige might. And after all, you did have to . . ." Gabriel had the delayed good sense to stop talking, Applegate's glare fixing itself unblinkingly on him.

Fortunately, Anthony seemed to find the spectacle of one grown man being told off by another grown man quite funny and gave a nervous giggle. The sound had the effect of bringing Applegate back down to earth, and he turned around to face the road.

"I think it's best if we park around the corner from the surgery," Applegate instructed the driver as though he had only just thought of the idea. "We'll let the priest here take our young charge to the house."

Gabriel squirmed in his seat, aware of young Anthony looking askance at him out of the corner of his eye. Gabriel did not have the nerve to meet his gaze. "I'm so glad I wasn't the one being told off for a change," remarked Anthony in the tone of a boy who has dodged a bullet for once and needs his fellow belligerent to know it. "Are you in trouble?"

Gabriel reassured himself that at least Anthony was talking and behaving a little more like an ordinary boy and less like a child who had just been orphaned. "No more than usual," said Gabriel. Anthony was in for a very long, hard journey during the months that followed, but Gabriel was sure he would recover in time with the help of good people like Marie and Dickie Paige. Gabriel allowed himself a sharp intake of breath as the car came to a halt at the curb.

Gabriel and Anthony exited the car onto a familiar street, familiar to Gabriel at least. It did not seem so very long since he had walked this way to Dr Whitehead's house, knowing he would receive a warm welcome in the family kitchen and a friendly chat over a slice of Mrs Whitehead's fruitcake. He knew he was likely to receive a warm welcome again at the hands of the new hostess, but he could not suppress a shiver as he walked up the garden path to the newly painted front door, thinking of all the people who had found refuge in this house in the past, until a hated woman's disappearance had scattered them around the world—Agnes, Douglas, Theresa, the old country doctor who had taken the law into his own hands, an unsuspecting wife kept ignorant of the whole sordid affair.

Forgive me, old friend, thought Gabriel, giving the doorbell a halfhearted tug. The doorbell was another new addition. *Forgive me for noticing all those telltale little signs, a chain of seemingly innocuous details that led me to a crime scene and all the little secrets that should by rights have been buried forever. Forgive me.*

The front door opened slowly, and Gabriel was greeted by a sight that immediately lifted his spirits. Marie Paige stood in the doorway, ready to welcome her husband's latest patient, and she could not have looked more different from the woman who had said good-bye to him at the abbey after her acquittal at the crown court.

"Father Gabriel, what a pleasant surprise!" exclaimed Marie, the professional smile of welcome changing subtly to one of genuine joy. "At least, I hope you're not ill?"

Gabriel shook her proffered hand and returned her smile. "Not at all, thank God, I'm perfectly well, but I'm afraid I do have need of some assistance." He stepped aside to reveal the saddest Boy Scout in the country, standing awkwardly several steps behind him; the brief moment of levity in the car was long forgotten. "I don't suppose we—" Gabriel did not need to say anything further. Marie stood aside and ushered them both indoors.

It dawned on Gabriel, as he stepped across a threshold that was both familiar and unfamiliar, that Marie probably imagined that the child had met with some minor mishap, grazed his knee or lost his packed lunch, and she was going to be asked to remedy the situation. The fact that Gabriel's plans were usually on a much larger scale than anyone else anticipated was something she had yet to appreciate.

"Perhaps young Master Nicholson could explore your lovely garden?" Gabriel suggested as Marie led them into the kitchen. He had a lot of explaining to do, and he would rather not have to talk in front of the child.

Marie took the hint immediately and opened the back door; she quickly pointed out to Anthony all the places in the garden that were most interesting, including the big oak tree right at the bottom of the garden that had the best climbing branches ever. Anthony hesitated, knowing he was about to be the topic of conversation; but it was a very fine oak tree out there, and he was a keen climber, as Marie had suspected. Seconds later, he was running down the path through the spacious garden, ready to leave the boring grown-ups to chat over a pot of tea.

"What are you up to this time, Father?" asked Marie, going mechanically over to the stove; she picked up the kettle. Marie was nothing if not astute, and it did not take a great sense of perception to appreciate that the child scrambling up a tree was reeling from some major crisis or other.

Gabriel watched Marie filling the kettle with water and putting it on to boil, noting deft, quick movements she would have found impossible once—the slipping on and off of the kettle lid, the striking of a match, the lighting of the gas. Marie had changed radically in the few months since she and Dickie had moved to this beautiful house, and only for the better. Her unhealthily thin figure was filling out, her face had lost its sunken, haunted look, and Gabriel fancied that she might even be wearing a little makeup. Marie still wore her hair short, but it was fashionably styled, and her skin had taken on the tawny glow Gabriel suspected she had had as a young girl before the concentration camp had bled the life out of her. The only jarring note was that her short-sleeved dress exposed the six-digit number tattooed on her arm, a perpetual reminder of the darkest circle of that earthly hell into which she had fallen once.

Marie noticed where Gabriel's gaze had fallen and gave him a knowing smile. "It's all right, Father, I'm not ashamed of it anymore. I have decided not to try to cover it up. It's part of who I am, part of my history."

"You have no need to be ashamed of it," said Gabriel, sitting gratefully at the kitchen table as soon as Marie gestured for him to pull up a chair. "You should wear it like a badge of honour. It's a reminder of the courage you showed when so many ran away."

Marie gave a self-deprecating smile, happily distracted by the sound of the kettle whistling. "I sometimes wonder if I would be so brave now. Courage belongs to the young."

"You're still young, Marie."

"The very young then." She glanced out the window as she prepared the teapot, frowning slightly at the sight of Anthony sitting nestled in the midst of the tree, some ten feet off the ground. It was as though he had begun climbing enthusiastically enough, then tired of the whole exercise and chose to sit and stare at the world unfolding beneath him. "That looks to me like a boy who needs to be brave," she said. "What's happened to him?"

Gabriel waited until Marie had sat down opposite him and poured the tea before summoning up the strength to answer. "I'm awfully sorry to intrude upon your home like this, Marie, but I couldn't think of anyone else I could turn to for help. If it's not convenient or you would rather not—for any reason—just tell me, and I'll take him away. You don't even have to give me a reason. It's just that I need somewhere for him to stay for a few days."

Marie leant forwards, either curious or trying to hide her alarm. "He's in trouble?"

"He's done nothing wrong," explained Gabriel quickly, "but yes, he is in terrible trouble. He was asked to leave a scout camp at our abbey earlier today, and he came home to find his father lying dead in the house." Gabriel hesitated as Marie sat back, a hand covering her mouth. Gabriel was reminded momentarily of how fragile she had been when he had first known her, but he could not think of an easy way to tell the rest of the story. "It looks as though the boy's father stumbled upon a burglar. No one was supposed to be in the house at that time of the morning. The child was meant to be at his camp, the grandfather out getting his morning paper, the father on his way to work. Unfortunately, Anthony's father was ill in bed."

"Murder," stated Marie coldly. She no longer appeared engaged in the conversation, looking fixedly down at her hands instead.

"Marie, I'm sorry. I should never have done this to you." Gabriel got up, horribly aware of his error of judgement. This was selfish. The poor woman had been through more than any human being should ever have to endure, including coming to the verge of being murdered herself. It had been an outrageous idea to visit this horror on her now, when she was only just beginning to recover. "I'm so sorry; please don't worry. I will find somewhere else for him to go. I should never have got you involved in this."

Marie stood up with considerable dignity and looked Gabriel directly in the eye. "No," she said calmly, "you were right to bring him here." If her previous jollity had vanished, so too had that moment of cold, quiet horror. She was looking at Gabriel in much the way she had regarded her judge as she had stood in the dock listening to the verdict. Marie was the sort of woman who would never lose her capacity for courage, whatever she imagined about herself. "He needs somewhere safe to stay, well away from the crime scene. That's why you brought him here, isn't it?"

Gabriel nodded. "Yes. His grandfather is going to take a room in the village, but somehow I felt it would be better if the boy was in a family home. His mother died during the war, and now he's lost his father."

Marie smiled, looking again out the window at the hunched figure sitting in the tree like a bewildered wood nymph. "Poor little soul. You leave him with us, Father. We'll look after him."

Gabriel stifled a sigh of relief. With Anthony and his grandfather taken care of, the process of piecing together what had happened could begin. It helped Gabriel's conscience that Marie seemed genuinely pleased by the idea of having a child in the house. Marie had not yet been blessed with a child of her own, and Gabriel wondered whether the years of ill treatment had deprived Marie of the possibility of ever becoming a mother. He hoped not, as he guessed that she had a natural affinity with children, especially the sort of children most people avoid—the troubled ones, the children forced to grow up too soon, the angry, frightened, isolated children whom life has let down. Marie had been only a child herself when she had been recruited into the Belgian resistance, and she knew what it was like to be dragged away from the innocence of childhood and thrown into the cruellest of adult worlds. She would be the perfect guardian for Anthony Nicholson.

"I think I had better call Anthony inside and discuss the arrangements," said Marie, intruding upon Gabriel's thoughts. "It will not be good for him to feel that we are planning things behind his back. He must be feeling very lost."

Gabriel moved towards the back door to call Anthony inside, but Marie got there first, gesturing to Gabriel to sit back down. She was the adult Anthony would have to answer to from now on, and it was important for her to step into that role immediately. "Anthony!" she called brightly, causing him to look up wearily from his sentry post in the tree. Gabriel noticed that the boy brightened at the sound of Marie's voice. She did not have to tell him to come in; he got the hint immediately and started climbing down the tree, swinging on the lowest branch and dropping down effortlessly onto the lawn. He did not move quickly towards the house, and Gabriel could almost feel the uneasiness settling over him. Marie felt it too and reached out a hand to Anthony when he neared the door, which he took instinctively.

Once he was seated at the table adjacent to Gabriel, Marie poured Anthony a glass of milk and brought out a tin of biscuits that looked as if they had been baked just that morning. It did the trick. After a moment's hesitation, Anthony began eating and drinking in earnest, allowing Marie some space to talk him through the plan. "I know that something very terrible has happened to you, my dear," she began, sitting opposite him so that she could be at his eye level. "Father Gabriel here has asked if you might stay here for a few days, and I'm very happy to have you if that's all right with you."

Anthony looked uneasily from Marie to Gabriel. "I want to be with Grandpa," he said quietly, as though suspecting that he was giving the wrong response. "We're always together."

"I know, and you'll be together again very soon," said Gabriel. "I promise. This is just until the police have finished their investigation." Gabriel did not want to tell Anthony that he was being got out of the way of the investigation, as he would understandably feel affronted. The word "police" immediately caused Anthony's face to darken with the recollection of what he had seen earlier that day. The boy was at a dangerous, uncertain age, not wholly a child but nowhere near adulthood. He inhabited that hinterland in which one moment he would be distracted by the excitement of tree climbing and another moment he would be overwhelmed with grief and shock.

"Anthony, how do you like to be called?" asked Marie, expertly changing the subject. "Do you go by a nickname at home?"

"My friends call me Tony," said Anthony, eyeing the biscuit tin. Marie pushed it gently towards him, watching as he slipped his hand into the tin and pulled out one of the larger biscuits. "At home, I'm Antoine."

"Yes, I'd noticed," said Gabriel. "Why is that?"

"My mother was French," Anthony reminded him. "She always called me Antoine. I liked it."

Gabriel was touched by the thought of an English father and grandfather making the effort to keep a dead mother's memory alive in such a way. "You speak French, Antoine. I heard you earlier."

Antoine nodded. "Yes, my father said every gentleman

should be able to speak French." His face fell again. Every way the conversation moved, this child kept hitting the brick wall of his father's violent death. He was suddenly angry, the biscuit forgotten in his hands. "It's not fair, Father! Why wouldn't the policeman speak to me? I want to help!"

Gabriel hesitated to answer, contemplating whether the risk was worth it. He decided it was, thinking guiltily that Marie would pick up the emotional pieces if it all went wrong. "Antoine, why don't you tell us what happened when you went home today? You said your father was ill. Is that right?"

Antoine nodded sullenly. "When I tried to go home, Grandpa was just putting his coat on so he could get his newspaper."

"Does he always go out to buy the paper?" asked Gabriel.

Antoine nodded again, more enthusiastically this time. He was enjoying telling the story. "Always. Every single morning after breakfast, Papa and Grandpa leave the house together, same time as I go to school. I get on my bike and go to school, Papa walks to the bus stop, and Grandpa goes to the shop to buy the paper."

"Every day, even Saturday?"

"Yes. Every day except for Sunday. I usually have Saturday school. We were off for the May Day weekend so we could go to scout camp. Papa works on Saturday morning." Antoine's face brightened further. "Sometimes I get on the bus after Saturday school and meet him at the pictures. If I'm good, we go to the chippy for fish and chips afterwards." The bright expression vanished as quickly as it had come. Antoine had been talking about his father in the present tense and had hit the brick wall again.

"Antoine," said Marie quickly, noting the tears welling up in the boy's eyes, "when did you last see your father? Was it when you came home from the scout camp?"

Antoine shook his head, gulping audibly with the effort of fighting back tears. "I said good-bye to him first thing. He was still in bed on account of his cold. When I came back, Grandpa said not to bother him. He said he was going out to get his paper and some tobacco, and he'd pop by the chemist to see if he could get Papa a tonic."

"So you didn't see him?" asked Gabriel, catching the thread of Marie's thinking.

"No, but I heard him upstairs," Antoine volunteered. He registered Gabriel's look of puzzlement. "He gets very wheezy when the blossom's out. Hay fever, you see. I can always hear where he is in the house. But it was much worse this time because he was ill." Antoine dropped his head into his hands. He had had enough, and Gabriel knew he had had enough. The boy's shoulders began to shake. Marie was at his side in a moment, folding the boy into her arms.

Gabriel got up to leave, glancing gratefully at the sight of Marie consoling the child who had been entrusted to her, who had given in to grief at last and was sobbing noisily on Marie's shoulder. Gabriel felt the tug of his own buried grief as he left the house, and he reassured himself that Antoine was in the kindest and safest of hands. He left the house as quietly as he could, walked around the corner and glanced vacantly at the empty street.

There was no car waiting for him. Applegate had understandably tired of waiting for him or, quite possibly, had never intended to hang about in the first place and was back at the crime scene by now. Not for the first time, Gabriel was stranded. He had no transport and no money to pay a bus fare. He contemplated returning to the Paiges' house, but his every instinct told him not to intrude any further for the time being.

These things happen for a reason, thought Gabriel as cheerfully as he could. Sometimes things happened because he was too away with the fairies to remember to tie up his own shoelaces, but today Gabriel fancied that there might be some purpose to this. He would walk over to the presbytery where he had so recently found shelter, have a cup of tea with Father Foley, and see whether he could purloin his priest friend's old bike from the shed. He would be back at the abbey by nightfall.

4

It was only when Gabriel had cycled about a mile away from Saint Patrick's Church that he realised he was in danger of scattering bicycles all over the Wiltshire countryside. He had left the abbey bicycle at the crime scene and had no idea how he was going to get two bikes back to the abbey. On the off chance that no one had made away with it yet—and he had some respect for the general honesty of people in this part of the world—he would have to ask one of the policemen whether he could take care of it for him.

It was to Dilton Wylye that Gabriel was cycling. It was only a small detour to pass through the village on his way back to the abbey anyway, and Gabriel wanted to talk to a few people just to get the lay of the land. He was grateful for the lingering spring daylight and that feeling of being pleasantly full, after tea and cake with Father Foley, and the comfort of conversation with an old mentor.

Gabriel was not sure why he had felt saddened by Father Foley's news that he was to retire at the end of the summer and make way for a young man better suited to the rigours of parish life. It was only reasonable that the diocese should be asking Father Foley to retire. He had recovered from the heart attack that had been the cause of Gabriel going to live with him in the first place, but age was creeping up on him. It was a natural process, yet another reminder of the passing of time, but Gabriel was not a man who appreciated change. He had loved the sense of stepping back into a corner of the town where he remained welcome. Father Foley had embraced him and welcomed him warmly into the cosy old presbytery kitchen, where Gabriel had once sat and puzzled his way through the mystery of a vanished woman and the death of a hated patriarch. It had felt a little like returning home.

"You should retire to the abbey," Gabriel had suggested over a second cup of tea; he had been only half joking. "We'll make a Benedictine out of you yet."

Father Foley had smiled, pouring his tea into his saucer to cool it. "I shall be retiring back to Cork, where I belong. My sister has kindly said that I can come and live with her. She has a pleasant little flat above her pastry shop, and she could do with the company since her dear husband died."

That was what he really had been playing at, thought Gabriel in bitter self-reproach, standing up on the pedals to urge the bicycle up a steep stretch of road. He knew that when Father Foley returned to Ireland he would never come back to England, and Gabriel would never see him again. If he had retired to the abbey, it would have suited Gabriel. He had never found it easy to part company with friends, and it was perhaps why he was better suited to religious life than the work of a secular priest. If he had remained a parish priest, Gabriel would have had to get used to being moved around every few years, to the sacrifice of having no permanent abode, no clear, inviolable network of friends and family around him. Yes, however hard monastic life was for him sometimes, Gabriel was sure he was in the right place.

Gabriel was surprised by how warm he felt as he cycled along the vast, exposed stretches of road that sliced through acres of farmland as far as the eye could see. The region was dotted with picturesque little villages, but in between the settlements the land seemed to roll on for an eternity with just a cluster of cottages or the odd barn to remind Gabriel that families and little communities lived here and worked the land. If Gabriel felt hot cycling at the end of April, he spared a thought for how the farm workers would feel, out in the fields at the height of summer with the sun beating down on them and no shelter anywhere.

He was relieved when he reached the outskirts of Dilton Wylye and found himself cycling through a tunnel of trees, the mottled shadows offering immediate relief. Gabriel's sense of direction had never been perfect, but he was able to orient himself well enough from his recollection of how quickly he and Anthony had reached the Nicholson house earlier, entering the village from the opposite direction.

Cutting through the village gave Gabriel the opportunity to get the measure of the place. Its layout was much like any other Wiltshire village, dominated by the parish church of All Saints, a small but lovingly constructed place of prayer built in the yellow-tinctured Bath stone of the region, not quite old enough to have been stolen from the Catholic Church during the Reformation.

The second most significant building was the pub, a Georgian tavern with a sign bearing the familiar image of an oak tree. The Royal Oak was a popular name for English pubs, a title coined—or so it was claimed—at the time of England's ill-fated Puritan republic, when a young Charles II hid in a hollow oak tree to escape the Roundheads. Thus, a humble oak tree had saved the monarchy, to be restored in happier times. Gabriel assumed that this was the pub where Old Man Nicholson intended to stay until he was permitted back to his house, a detail that would be useful to know if he should need to talk to the man again.

Gabriel knew he was approaching the correct house by the sound of a commotion wafting across the late afternoon breeze. This did not strike Gabriel as the sort of village where people habitually raised their voices—if someone was shouting, it could only have been provoked by a bloody crime. And this person really was shouting. Gabriel was aware of a female voice as harsh and guttural as that of a sergeant major in the heat of a particularly fierce battle. The woman's shouts were by no means the hysterics of a waif in distress; they were more the indignant commands of a matron who is used to having her every order attended to without demur from the inferior ranks.

Gabriel slowed down and jumped off the bicycle as quietly as he could, walking the last few yards to the house, where the young constable Gabriel had met earlier was facing up to the owner of the commanding female voice. The woman in question was a beefy individual, unusually tall and stocky in a manner that suggested a woman who had enjoyed a highly active outdoor life before middle age had slowed her down. She wore a wool coat that looked too warm for a spring day and a black hat that resembled an upside-down flowerpot. Whoever this woman was, Gabriel knew he had to introduce himself.

That, at least, was Gabriel's plan, but interrupting a matronly figure in full flow was easier said than done. "Now listen to me, my man," the woman was bawling at the constable, who had noticed Gabriel's angelic presence and looked suddenly hopeful of deliverance. "I am not some little slip of thing to be coddled and patronised by a spotty youth who thinks it his business to tell me mine. Out of my way!"

"Madam, I'm under orders!" pleaded the youth, who—for what it was worth—did not have any acne worth mentioning. "No one is allowed in the house, not even the residents! No one is permitted to touch the body."

"He's my brother!" roared the woman. "If what you say is true, I have a right to see him!"

Gabriel took his life in his hands and tapped the woman on the shoulder, causing her to spin around and scowl at him with the force of a hurricane. The constable took the much-needed opportunity to slink back. "Madam, I wonder if I may be of service?" asked Gabriel in a voice that sounded like a whisper amidst this storm. "I'm a—"

"Yes, I can see what you are, padre," interrupted the woman. "I'm a highly bred Anglican. I'm sure there are a few Eyeties living near the old barracks who might need your ministrations."

Gabriel gave a wry smile, thinking how much Giovanna would have loathed this woman. He was fairly sure that the Italian POWs, who had found themselves tilling the land during their captivity, had long returned to their homes—those that still had homes in the wasteland Mussolini and the Nazis had left behind. The few who had chosen to stay would have made their way to the cities and the promise of work on the many urban construction sites. "As far as I am aware, this is a Catholic home," Gabriel said. "The child is certainly Catholic."

Mention of the child had an immediate effect on the woman, whose look changed from casual contempt to concern. "Do you mean my nephew Antoine?" she demanded, looking at Gabriel as though she suspected him of kidnap. "Where is he? This ghastly little man informs me that he's been taken away, and won't say where!"

"It's for his own safety," said Gabriel, hoping he was not overdramatising the situation. "It's better for him to be well out of the way, Mrs—erm, Miss—"

"Miss Nicholson," said Miss Nicholson emphatically. "Miss Plantagenet Nicholson. Though I gather my nephew thinks it frightfully funny to call me Aunt Plant behind my back."

Gabriel did not dare laugh, but he could vividly imagine how such a larger-than-life woman, the primordial maiden aunt, would be a figure of fun to a little boy growing up without a female role model. "Antoine never said he had an aunt. I understood that there were no family hereabouts." The words were out of his mouth before he had considered the implications.

Plantagenet looked coldly at Gabriel in a manner that was impossible to read. She might have been angry, hurt, or resigned to having her existence denied by her own flesh and blood, but she was never going to reveal her feelings to a stranger. "Charles was my brother," she said finally, not looking away for an instant. "I received a garbled message on my telephone telling me Charles had been killed by a burglar. Naturally I did not believe a word of it, but the constable here informs me that it is true."

"Miss Nicholson, I am so sorry," Gabriel began. "I know this must be a terrible shock to you, but—"

"Of course it's a shock," interrupted Plantagenet, taking the tone of an impatient schoolmistress. "Men do not get bludgeoned to death in broad daylight in their own homes! This is Dilton Wylye! Nothing of any note has ever occurred in Dilton Wylye."

"Who gave you the message?" asked Gabriel. "Did he leave a name?"

"What does it matter? It was true."

"It might be important. Did the caller leave a name?"

"No name, I tell you, and it doesn't matter. What matters is that my brother is dead."

"I'm sorry for your loss, Miss Nicholson. Would you like me to walk you home? It's probably better to leave the police to do their job."

Plantagenet grunted but made no attempt to remonstrate further with the constable. Grief attacked people in complex ways, and Gabriel suspected that Miss Nicholson's strident behaviour was about to shift dramatically. "I daresay you are right," she said more softly. "And I should not mind some company for a little while, if you can spare the time."

Gabriel nodded, trying to conceal his relief that she was prepared to talk to him. "If you could wait a moment, I need to ask the constable to take care of the abbey bicycle. I arrived on a different machine earlier today, and I'll need to get it back to Sutton Westford."

Plantagenet looked quizzically at Gabriel as he went over to pick up Father Foley's bike, then indicated another to the constable. "Never mind the bobby, I'll take your bicycle," said Plantagenet, the imperious tone returning. "I'll ride it over first thing in the morning, if that suits. The exercise will do me good in my current state of mind, and I've not visited Sutton Westford in a good few years."

Gabriel could not shake the thought out of his head, as he walked alongside Plantagenet, that she might be offering to help him because she half suspected that Antoine was hiding out in the abbey. By making a lightning visit first thing in the morning, she might ambush him before he had time to hide. The thought was beneath him, but Gabriel could not get it out of his head once it had lodged there. "Antoine is not at the abbey," said Gabriel, but the statement sounded like a man protesting too much. *There is no money in my pockets. I didn't steal the sweeties.*

"I'm his next of kin; the boy should have come to stay with me," Plantagenet retorted, and Gabriel knew for certain now that she was hurt. "It's been such a long time since he's seen me, I daresay he's forgotten I exist. I send him a ten-shilling note every Christmas."

They were walking back through the village, past the church, and down a narrow road which cut between large, carefully manicured hedges intended to keep nosy neighbours away. Each hedge, Gabriel suspected, concealed an affluent house and probably a croquet lawn. A man in an elegantly tailored linen suit and Panama hat walked towards them, tipping his hat to Plantagenet as he passed. "Afternoon, Miss Nicholson."

"Good afternoon, Major."

Plantagenet sighed as they reached a red painted gate. "They'll all know my misfortune by the end of the day. I shall have to take my black clothes out of the ottoman box."

The comment was unnaturally cold, as though Charles

Nicholson's death was little more to Plantagenet than an inconvenience, the cause of an unfortunate alteration in her wardrobe for a few months. The lady was nothing if not a confusing customer. "How long has it been since you last saw your brother?" asked Gabriel, focusing his attention on wheeling his bicycle carefully down the garden path, judiciously avoiding the bloomless rosebushes. With a mistress like Plantagenet Nicholson, even the rosebushes had a combative air to them, as though she had planted them as thorny little sentries to tear at the ankles of any intruder rather than as the loveliest flower in an English garden.

Plantagenet did not look back to answer. "It has been well over a year," she said, climbing the three stone steps to her front door. Like the gate, the door was painted red, with brass fittings bright enough to show a visitor's reflection. For all her masculine appearance, Plantagenet either dedicated a considerable portion of her time to cleaning and tidying her home or—more likely, thought Gabriel—employed a hardworking housekeeper. Either way, she was fiercely house-proud.

Gabriel's musings were confirmed when a housekeeper opened the door and beamed in Plantagenet's direction. Such was the efficiency of Plantagenet Nicholson's house that the housekeeper had opened the door before Plantagenet had had the chance to knock, suggesting that the housekeeper was well attuned to listening for the sound of footsteps on the path and made sure to be at the door in time to open it.

"Afternoon, madam," said the housekeeper, stepping aside to let Plantagenet and her visitor inside. Gabriel smiled in the housekeeper's direction, calculating in his head how long this woman might have been in Plantagenet's service. She looked a similar age to her mistress but was so unlike her in every other respect that the pairing had shades of vaudeville about it. Unlike Plantagenet, the housekeeper was short and plump and moved with a brightness that was disarmingly girlish, returning Gabriel's polite smile with a Cheshire Cat grin and hands outstretched to take his coat.

The Cheshire Cat housekeeper had been part of the fixtures and fittings of this house for many years, Gabriel concluded. He watched as the two women moved around one another in perfect harmony, the housekeeper busying herself hanging up coats and hats on the stand in the hall whilst Plantagenet murmured her news under her breath, causing the housekeeper's smile to vanish in an instant. "No need for a lot of fuss, Mrs B," said Plantagenet in a steady voice. "Somehow I knew something was wrong when I woke up this morning. As you know, I am not superstitious, but I was not entirely surprised when I arrived at the house to find the police in residence."

"Well, you settle yourself down with your guest, madam," said Mrs B, "and I'll be through with the tea shortly."

Gabriel followed Plantagenet into a bright and airy sitting room, which benefited from its large south-facing windows. The room managed to be spotlessly clean and orderly but quite cosy at the same time. Gabriel wondered, with a flicker of unease, whether young Antoine would not have been better here with his own kin, however happy Gabriel imagined he would be with the Paiges.

"Miss Nicholson, I would like to apologise if I have behaved in any way out of turn," said Gabriel, seating himself in the comfortably cushioned armchair Plantagenet indicated to him. "I was not aware that Antoine had any relatives other than his grandfather. That was why I took him to stay with a family I know in the neighbouring town. I would never have interfered—"

"No need to sound so mortified, Father," Plantagenet broke in, with an air of impatience. She was clearly not a woman who had much time for social niceties. "You were not to know. I'm afraid I have been a rather neglectful relative over the years, and I daresay the child would find the company of his maiden aunt a little tiresome."

Gabriel watched as Plantagenet sat down opposite him, folding her hands in her lap as she had no doubt been taught at finishing school. "I assure you, Antoine will be very well looked after, and it's perhaps better that he is some distance away from . . . well, from . . ."

"From the place where his father was murdered," Plantagenet finished for him, putting Gabriel out of his misery. "Yes, I can see the sense behind such a move. I hope it will not be for too long. There cannot be many hiding places for a killer in a place like this."

"If your brother was killed by a burglar, I suppose the culprit might not be local," Gabriel ventured, studying Plantagenet's face for a response; she did not flicker. "If that is the case, he may be harder to find, but I trust that the police—"

"The police are barking up the wrong tree if they are looking for a burglar," said Plantagenet emphatically. Gabriel made a mental note to keep his responses as short as possible to avoid being constantly interrupted. "I cannot remember the last time there was a burglary in this village. No one locks his door; there is no need. Frankly, few people in the village have anything worth stealing, and it's just not done."

"But it seems plausible," said Gabriel. "If the robber believed that the house would be empty at that time, he would have been taken by surprise at the sight of the master of the house bearing down on him. He may have panicked. If it is any consolation, it is unlikely that the burglar intended to kill anyone. If he—"

"It is no consolation at all, Father, as it simply did not happen that way," Plantagenet retorted, pausing only because Mrs B had appeared in the room with the tea tray. Plantagenet paused whilst Mrs B set down the tray on the table before them, waiting in silence until she had poured the tea before speaking again. "Mrs B, when was the last time you remember a house being burgled in this village?"

Mrs B pressed her hands against her hips as though to ease an aching back. "I don't think I ever remember it, now that you ask. There was that time back in '32, when Colonel Wainwright's wife's maid run off with Mrs Wainwright's jewellery box, but she never made it as far as Salisbury before they caught her."

"Quite. In over fifteen years, there has been only one house robbed in this village, and that was by an insider." Plantagenet looked triumphantly at Gabriel. "Mrs Bramley has lived in this village all her life. She knows everything there is to know about life in Dilton Wylye, and she has never once felt the need to lock the door on her way out." Plantagenet held out the plate of custard creams to Gabriel as though offering him a consolation prize for failing a detection competition. "So no, I am not consoled by the thought that no one intended to kill my brother. Whoever entered my brother's house this morning did so with only one purpose, and it was not to empty the insubstantial contents of the safe."

Gabriel helped himself to one of the biscuits, using the opportunity to mull over what Plantagenet had said. He had to admit to himself that the idea of a bungled burglary had looked very convenient, and part of him had wanted to believe it had happened that way for the sake of moral expedience. A burglary gone wrong would mean that the killer might not have to bear the full legal and moral responsibility for taking a man's life. If a burglar had lashed out in fright, he had almost certainly not intended to kill anyone. He would still have killed, but it was not the same as the deliberate, cold-blooded tearing away of a human life.

"Who would have wanted your brother dead?" asked Gabriel, trying to suppress another more obvious question: *Why have you not entered your brother's house in nearly a year when you live in the same village?* Or the even more troubling question: *Why on earth are you so calm when you have just had the news broken to you that your brother has been killed?* Somehow, Plantagenet's icy behaviour did not feel like shock; she barely even appeared surprised by what had happened.

"Why should anyone have wanted him dead, Father?" demanded Plantagenet. "Why should anyone need a reason to kill?" The question was so blunt and so apparently illogical that Gabriel could think of no answer. "No need to look so appalled, padre. When Charles lost his wife, nobody asked why she was killed; she was just killed. One of millions to meet a violent end in violent times. And most of those deaths were entirely pointless, hers included."

Gabriel shook his head, trying to regain his bearings.

"That was wartime; it was different, surely? In time of peace, one tends to look for motives."

"Why?"

Gabriel was beginning to wonder whether Plantagenet's eccentricity might be something more serious. Was the woman really asking why motive was important in a murder investigation? "Well, most people don't get it into their heads to kill at random. There's usually some rationale behind battering a man to death."

"Really?" Plantagenet was all astonishment again. "When I was in France last year, I saw a man arrested for killing his friend during a fight outside a public house over whose turn it was to pay."

Plantagenet did not want to talk about her dead brother, Gabriel realised. It was bizarre behaviour, as the relatives of the recently dead were usually desperate to talk about the lost loved one in an attempt to give voice to their grief. For whatever reason—and there might be many—Plantagenet was making a colossal attempt at moving the subject to a person about whom she wished to speak. "Antoine told me his mother was French," said Gabriel gently. He noticed the slightest of changes in Plantagenet's demeanour, and he did not want her to notice that he had seen it. "That's why he likes to be called—"

"Antoine, yes, I know," came the response, but even the interruption was less forceful than it might have been. "Brigitte. A good girl, Brigitte. We were surprised by how fond we were of her."

Gabriel resisted the temptation to break the silence into which the room had descended, knowing that if he kept quiet, Plantagenet would have to say something else; he needed her to speak to him. Plantagenet inspected her nails methodically, picked up her teacup, remembered that it was empty, and put it back down again.

Gabriel glanced at her lowered head, trying to guess what was going through Plantagenet's mind. There was something quaintly predictable about the woman. Her dress, her physique, her manner left nothing to the imagination whatsoever. Gabriel could have guessed, just by looking at her, exactly what the interior of this house would look like, and he had not been wrong; he could have told her that she read the *Times* every morning and never left the house before she had finished the crossword; that she had voted for Churchill and was still bitterly disappointed to see the country lumbered with a Labour government.

Beyond these certainties, Gabriel could only guess that Plantagenet had lost a sweetheart in the trenches and had had neither the inclination towards nor the possibility of marriage. This last detail, the reason for Plantagenet's spinsterhood, was an educated guess. There were plenty of women of Plantagenet's generation who had chosen not to marry, but there was something about the sudden softening of Plantagenet's face when Brigitte was mentioned that made him think there had been a tender heart in that robust body once.

"Why were you surprised?" asked Gabriel finally, when it became clear that Plantagenet was not going to speak simply to render the situation more comfortable. "Was it because she was French?"

"Certainly not, Father!" Plantagenet retorted indignantly. "I'm an educated woman; what an idea! I could hardly hold her place of birth against her. If all her countrymen had been as brave as she was, the Germans would not have marched through the streets of Paris."

"I'm sorry if I presumed—"

"I hope you'll forgive me for being candid with you, Father," Plantagenet continued, apparently not hearing him, "but she was a Roman Catholic. Worse than that, she persuaded Charles to convert to Catholicism and demanded that their son be raised Catholic. The poor sop insisted upon keeping his promise to her even after she was dead."

"I see," said Gabriel. Plantagenet was an educated woman who regarded herself as sophisticated enough to accept a foreigner into the family, yet her horror at the idea of having a Papist as a sister-in-law was no cause for embarrassment.

"But she was such a fiery character," Plantagenet added. "We all came to admire her eventually."

Gabriel smiled, the picture forming in his mind of that quiet, unassuming family finding itself cordially invaded by a fiery, foreign Catholic who wore her heart on her sleeve. Brigitte and Plantagenet would have been polar opposites—ludicrously so—but it was not unheard of for sharply contrasting characters to become close friends. "I suppose she must have been very strong to go off to fight the Germans like that," Gabriel said.

Plantagenet gave a laugh as musical as a braying donkey. "She was a fighter before the war broke out, I assure you! One silly young man got a little too close to her once; he knew perfectly well she was married. I doubt he ever touched a woman again after that!"

Gabriel could sense Plantagenet warming to her subject and gently encouraged her. "Gave him a hearty slap in the face, did she?"

Plantagenet gave a knowing smile. Whatever Brigitte had done, Plantagenet had been cheering from the sidelines. "Oh no, an English girl would have slapped the lout's face, but not Brigitte. When the loathsome little tick came after her, her sharp little fingernails were all over his face. It really was like watching a lioness defending herself." Plantagenet's smile lingered a little longer at the memory. It was not unusual for a staid, serious woman to take pleasure in another woman's explosive act of passion, secretly wishing that she had thought to do such a thing herself; but a moment later, the present and all its troubles intruded, and Plantagenet's smile evaporated.

"You still miss her."

"She was a dear woman, Father, and Charles loved her. We all loved her." Plantagenet's eyes were shiny with tears now, and Gabriel knew she was desperate for him to leave. She would do what all women of her class did at such a moment: keep herself calm, get rid of her visitor, and weep behind a locked door where no one could witness the indignity. "She was perfectly safe here," the woman said. "Insisted upon returning to France to resist the Germans. Said it was her duty. While splendid heroes like de Gaulle were fleeing France, Brigitte was dashing back before the borders closed. We never saw her again."

"And now Antoine is an orphan," said Gabriel. "It's a terrible misfortune for a child to lose both parents."

"I assure you he is not alone," came the steely response, all sign of tears gone from Plantagenet's cold glance. "He has me, whether or not he likes it, and he has his grandfather. I assure you he will be well cared for."

5

Gabriel was alarmed by how late it felt when he left Plantagenet's house. The days were long at this time of year, but the sun was already beginning to dip, and without a wristwatch, Gabriel was unsure what time it was. His conversation with Plantagenet had left him disoriented, and even when he had picked up his bicycle and reassured himself that he would be home before long, he felt unsettled. This was an unknown village to him; had he been in a better frame of mind, Gabriel fancied that he would have been able to point himself in the right direction for home without too much trouble. But in his present state of confusion, Gabriel turned in the opposite direction to the Nicholson house, which would have given him a landmark to find his way back, and he found himself riding along a wide road with high banks of grass on either side.

He passed a red telephone box and considered trying to make a phone call to the abbey, then remembered that he had no change on him and abandoned the idea. In the little stone hut of the bus stop, a man sat reading the *Daily Mail*, the remains of a cigarette between his fingers. The man's face was almost completely concealed from view, and Gabriel did not risk stopping to ask for help. Whoever he was, Gabriel did not expect to be met with a friendly reception.

A little farther along, past a row of picturesque cottages, Gabriel saw the village shop and hesitated. He never liked to go into a shop penniless, but if anyone could give him directions, it would be the shopkeeper. He propped up his bicycle against some railings and made his way inside, hoping to meet with a friendly reception. Gabriel was barely indoors when a voice from behind the counter proclaimed, "I'm closing in ten minutes. You'd better make it speedy."

"I shan't be a minute," promised Gabriel, looking in the direction of the counter. The shop was a small, cluttered space, nowhere near the light, orderly emporium run by Reggie McClusker, but there were features of a village shop that were almost universal: a smell Gabriel could never describe, something between bread and fruit and carbolic soap; a menacing-looking till like a predatory animal, waiting to pounce and steal your every penny; and a meat slicer at the side of the counter that looked hardly used.

At the counter, a woman with a face heavily lined by years of anxiety and tobacco smoke stood serving a man in a long coat who did not so much as look back out of curiosity. The woman wore her hair tucked away beneath a cap—for hygiene purposes, Gabriel assumed—and wore a capacious housecoat that looked decades old, its material sporting a pattern of sad-looking daisies faded to a sickly lemon colour. Gabriel waited whilst she placed a large packet of cream crackers, a portion of cheese, and a number of apples into a series of paper bags. The shopkeeper looked up absently as she took her customer's money. "You're not from these parts either, are you?" she asked Gabriel. "Are you with this gentleman?"

"No, madam, he isn't," came the unmistakable voice of

Inspector Applegate. A second later, he turned round to face Gabriel, giving him an exasperated smile. "Mrs Paige thrown you out already, has she?" he asked before turning back to take his change. "Thank you, that'll do nicely."

Gabriel waited whilst Applegate picked up his paper bags. "Was old Mr Nicholson one of your customers?" Gabriel asked the shopkeeper. As usual, he had tried to think of a subtle way to open the conversation, had drawn a blank, and just asked the question.

The woman's eyes narrowed as though she expected a trap. "If you're not with the police, I'm not sure why you want to know."

"Because he's a nosy parker," Applegate chimed in helpfully. "Mostly harmless, though; you can tell him what he wants to know, or I can tell him."

Gabriel waited a few seconds longer than was strictly necessary to reach forwards and help Applegate with his parcels, which he was struggling to hold at the same time as carrying his hat. "I was just curious," said Gabriel defensively, quietly fuming. Applegate knew perfectly well why Gabriel was asking.

"Every morning, regular as clockwork," said the woman, "he bought his paper at the same time." She turned her back on the two men so that she could close the till tray she had left open. She shoved it closed with an abrasive clang of metal against metal. "He wouldn't hear of the paperboy delivering it," she added, turning back around. "He liked to have his morning exercise."

"Was he here this morning?"

"Yes," Applegate put in. "Same as ever."

"Did anything seem different?" asked Gabriel, aware that

he had phrased the question in such a way as to sound desperate for the shopkeeper to answer in the affirmative.

"Course not," answered the woman, disappearing under the counter and emerging with a cloth. It was tidy-up time at the end of a long day that would have started before dawn. She was giving every possible indication that she wanted them to leave so that she could clean up, lock up, and relax for the rest of the day. "He said good morning as usual, and I handed him his paper before he had to ask. The only thing he did say was that his son had taken poorly, and he didn't want to be out too long. I suggested milk and honey. Always works for me."

Gabriel nodded, but he could sense Applegate looking frustratedly in his direction and felt the overwhelming need to leave.

"Wasn't there something you wanted?" asked Applegate, moving towards the door. "You must have come in for something other than a chat."

"I . . . well, I was going to ask for directions, as it happens. I really need to get home."

"I assumed you'd get a lift," said Applegate, moving towards the door. He pushed the door handle down with his elbow and nudged the door open with his foot. It was such an impressive show to watch that Gabriel quite forgot to offer to open the door for him.

"It's a long story, Inspector, something to do with bicycles, and I need to cycle home now."

Out on the pavement, Gabriel placed the paper bag he was carrying for Applegate into the bicycle basket and wheeled it along, in what he assumed was the direction of the Nicholsons' home. "I was just buying some food for the boys," Applegate explained. "It will be some hours before they can go home, and we'll have to start again early tomorrow. We have to make a thorough search of the house, not just the room where the deceased was found. I'm aware that this is somebody's home; I don't want the old man and his grandson to have to stay away too long."

"That's awfully decent of you," said a preoccupied Gabriel; a thought had lodged itself in his head, and he could not work out the best way to ask his question. There was no easy way, same as usual. "I don't suppose I could take a little look at the house myself?" asked Gabriel, as casually as he could manage.

"I doubt there'll be much to see," answered Applegate. "I do not anticipate discovering much beyond what we already know."

"And what's that?"

"At the moment, nothing much other than that our burglar was a professional. Left no fingerprints. If you want to go snooping about, I'd look elsewhere."

"I want to look only once you people have found what you need. I don't want to get in the way or anything." Gabriel could almost anticipate Applegate's snort of contempt. "Come on now, Inspector, you know I prefer to cooperate with the police if I can."

Applegate stopped in his tracks and looked askance at Gabriel. "The first time you cooperate, Father, they'll be nailing down the lid! What are you looking for anyway? We'll find anything of interest if there's anything to find."

"I'm not going to start going round looking for fingerprints and things," Gabriel promised. "I'm more interested in the details of the people who lived in the house. I've just had the most absurd conversation with Antoine's aunt."

Applegate's face went from bewildered to glacial. "I had

rather intended to question the lady myself. Now that you've gone and rubbed her up the wrong way, I don't imagine she'll be very cooperative."

"Who says I rubbed her up the wrong way?" protested Gabriel. He hated that expression, but this was not the moment to say so. "I just said it was an absurd conversation. I'm not sure if she's a bit touched or at least determined to make me think she is. It left my head spinning."

"Now you know how the rest of us feel talking to you," snapped Applegate, quickening his pace the way he always did to make life a little more difficult for Gabriel. Applegate was taller and in considerably better physical shape. When the distance between them began to look awkward, Gabriel stood on one pedal of the bike and scooted along to keep up. "You won't want to hang around the house too much longer, Father," said Applegate, slowing down his pace as though realising he was being infantile. "I doubt that bicycle light is dependable; you do not want to be cycling around the countryside in the darkness. If you're quick and you keep your hands to yourself, you can have a look around."

Gabriel jumped off the pedal and walked contentedly beside Applegate, round the corner to the house, where the whole building and garden had been cordoned off and a group of curious children were loitering with intent. The constable who had had such a hard time on the receiving end of Plantagenet's temper was trying to shoo the children away, with no success. "Clear off!" barked Applegate, marching in the direction of the children. "There's nothing to see here. Away home with you!"

The children—three boys and a younger girl who looked like the little sister of one of them—took one look at Applegate's forbidding countenance and scarpered down the road. "They're bound to be curious," said Gabriel. "I don't imagine much of any interest happens around here."

"They're a damned nuisance," Applegate retorted, "touching everything with their grubby paws, spreading rumours."

"They were only looking." Gabriel glanced in the direction of the small retreating figures, already almost out of sight. "I suppose it should be discouraged. They might go to the same school as Antoine."

"You gone all Frog on me?" asked Applegate, leading Gabriel indoors. "His name is Anthony."

"He said he prefers to be called Antoine. His French mother used to call him that."

Applegate shrugged as though the whole idea were too silly to contemplate. "I'll call him Jemima Snooks if he likes, as long as he's kept safely out of the way until all this is over."

Gabriel was relieved to discover that the body had been removed when he glanced into the sitting room. He could not bring himself to step inside the room in case he disturbed anything, but he could see streaks of blood on the rug where the man had fallen. "Did you say the victim was struck across the back of the head?" asked Gabriel, closing his eyes so that he could conjure up the exact position Charles Nicholson had been lying in when he was found by his father.

"Yes, that was likely to have been the fatal blow at least," said Applegate. "There may have been others, but we'll have to wait for the postmortem to get all the details."

"It feels so cowardly to attack a man from behind."

Applegate snorted. "Burglars aren't heroes, Father G."

"Yes, but if Nicholson had confronted a burglar, wouldn't

he have been struck in the face?" Gabriel stood in front of Applegate to demonstrate the point. "If the burglar had been taken by surprise, surely he wouldn't have dashed behind the man and biffed him from behind?"

"He may have knocked him down and then dealt the fatal blow to his skull," suggested Applegate, "or the burglar may have seen Nicholson walking around and sneaked up on him from behind." Applegate sounded impatient already, and Gabriel had not even started searching the place. "Was there something in particular you were looking for?"

"I suppose I'd like to learn a little more about what was wrong with this family," mused Gabriel, casting his eyes around the hallway. It was a narrow, claustrophobic hall like those in so many cottages in these parts. The oak panels that lined the walls would keep the place warm and snug in winter but made the room feel dark and oppressive. Directly opposite the front door, a steep wooden staircase led up to a closed door, and to the left were two open doors, one leading to the sitting room where Charles Nicholson had met his end, and the other, Gabriel presumed, leading to the kitchen. "Neither old Mr Nicholson nor Antoine mentioned the existence of a relative living just a short distance away, and Plantagenet Nicholson's behaviour was so peculiar, I hardly know where to begin."

"She was always peculiar," came a voice from the front door that made Gabriel flinch. Despite the official nature of the conversation, Gabriel was sensitive to the dangers of gossip and felt an instinctive shame at being caught talking about another person in her absence. Old Man Nicholson stepped into the hallway, glancing morosely from Applegate to Gabriel. "I was told I might return to pick up a thing or two. It seems you've been talking to Aunt Plant."

"I'm sorry, sir," said Gabriel, feeling his face growing hot. He knew he was blushing with embarrassment, and there was little point in trying to conceal it. "I happened to meet with the lady after I'd settled your grandson. She had come to the house."

"Yes, I can well imagine what that must have been like," answered Mr Nicholson, and for the first time, something resembling a smile flickered at the corners of his mouth. "I daresay she came marching over to the house like Genghis Khan, making demands at the top of her voice. Kind of her to show an interest in her little brother as soon as he was dead."

"Mr Nicholson, are you all right?" asked Applegate. The old man was looking distinctly unsteady.

Mr Nicholson leant back against the oak panelling, trembling visibly. "I'm sorry, Inspector, I cannot stay in this house another second. I keep seeing my son dead on the floor."

Applegate and Gabriel helped him outside, Gabriel praying that there were no prying eyes to watch the poor man stumbling out of his own home, tears trickling down his face. This time the day before, three generations of the Nicholson family had gathered under this roof to settle down for the evening, as they had done for many hundreds of nights before. All of a sudden, that world of gentle rituals and quiet, predictable days had come to a halt for no obvious reason. Plantagenet was wrong—deaths like this were never motiveless. The motive might turn out to be insultingly petty, but there was always a reason why a person took it into his head to commit such an act of violence.

"Mr Nicholson, I can arrange for an overnight case to be brought to you, if you prefer," stated Applegate when

Mr Nicholson had seated himself on the low wall at the perimeter of the garden. The man nodded wearily, taking a large white handkerchief out of his pocket to dab at his eyes. "I'll need to talk further with you in the morning, but it might be better if you rest for now."

"Thank you, Inspector," said Nicholson weakly. "I'm not sure I'd be much use to anyone today." He looked beseechingly at Gabriel, as though expecting him to be the more sympathetic of the two men. "I've seen death before, but it belongs on the battlefield. It should have been . . . *he* should have been safe . . ." Nicholson gulped and gasped with the effort to remain calm, but Gabriel knew that, in his mind, he was walking unsuspectingly into his home and finding his son lying dead at his feet. He would replay that moment repeatedly until he drove himself out of his mind with the torment or simply became too numb to feel the pain any longer.

Gabriel placed a hand on Nicholson's shoulder. "Why don't I walk you to your rooms?" suggested Gabriel. "I know it's not far, but it might be easier if you have some company."

Nicholson forced himself to his feet by way of an answer. "It's most decent of you, Father. The pub is just around the corner." He looked fixedly at the house as though taking in its every detail for the last time. "I'm not sure I shall ever be able to face returning here, but I suppose I shall have to in time. It's Antoine's home too."

Gabriel tried hard not to think of how low the sun was in the sky. The day was waning fast, and he was growing weary. As a Benedictine, Gabriel was used to rising while the world still slept and retiring for the night before darkness fell. He felt the anxiety of being far from home even though he was only in the next valley, a feeling not helped by the gnawing hunger that was assailing him. "I hope they are looking after you," said Gabriel, determined to put such selfish thoughts away from him. His need for supper and bed could wait; he was walking in the presence of a man who was no doubt experiencing the worst day of his life.

"It's comfortable enough in there," answered Nicholson, though Gabriel was sure that the old man was slowing his pace with every step they took towards the pub. "I suspect it will be a little noisy, but I have never liked silence."

Gabriel felt suddenly aware of how unkind it had been to separate old Mr Nicholson from his grandson at such a moment. However practical it was for him to stay in the vicinity of the crime whilst the boy was kept safely away from it all, it felt harsh to isolate a man who was already struggling to come to terms with the loss of his only son. "You know, Mr Nicholson, if you'd rather be with Antoine, I could always ask if you might join him. It seems unfair—"

"No, no, Father," Nicholson cut in quickly, "it was enough to ask strangers to care for my grandson. I couldn't possibly impose on these good people as well. And the inspector is right, of course. I need to be nearby in case they need anything from me. Keys to open doors and cabinets, that sort of thing."

The pub was a welcoming sight in the gloaming. Unlike the other buildings round about, it had painted white walls and leaded windows that winked at them as the landlord put on the interior lights one by one to fend off the encroaching darkness. Above the door, a lamp swung, guiding them inside and away from the sinister forces prowling a village overshadowed by death. "I suppose you're right," said Gabriel, removing his hat. The interior of the pub was a fug of cigarette smoke, the only odour more powerful than the yeasty mist of hops that assailed Gabriel's nostrils, making him sneeze.

"Are you allowed in pubs?" asked Nicholson solicitously, mistaking Gabriel's sneeze for inexperience in such a venue. "You can leave me here if you prefer, though I should like to buy you a pint if I may."

"It's permitted," said Gabriel, but he realised a more pressing problem a moment before Nicholson had stepped sideways in the direction of the snug beside the bar. The pub was not too busy yet, and the few faces Gabriel could see had turned to stare at the two of them as they had entered. More to the point, they were looking pityingly at Nicholson, a reaction Gabriel remembered all too well. Nicholson was the tragic victim of a murderous attack on his family. In a small village community, everyone would know by now what had happened, and Nicholson would never live it down. However genuine the sympathies of his neighbours might be, it would soon become a curse to be perpetually identified as the sad man who had lost his son. He would be assailed by concerned looks and whispers everywhere he went until the village became unbearable to live in.

Tucked away in the snug, a small, private room containing a table and two benches, Nicholson was safe from prying eyes. "Perhaps when this is over, you should consider going away for a little while," Gabriel suggested. "Not permanently, of course, but a little trip away might do you and Antoine the world of good."

Nicholson nodded. In the peace and quiet of the snug, the taut muscles of his face were beginning to relax. "I shall certainly need some breathing space. I've often wondered about taking Antoine back to France to see his mother's people. It might be good for him now that there's . . . well, there's not much on his father's side left for him. Only me. He has many relatives in France he does not yet know."

Before Gabriel could answer that he thought this was an excellent idea, a young man in an apron stepped into the snug carrying two glass tankards of beer. "Here you are, Uncle Roland," said the young man, putting down the beers on the table. "A pint of your usual, and I took the liberty of getting the same for your friend."

"That's very kind of you, Terry," answered Nicholson. "Don't forget to put it on my tab."

"Those are on the house, Uncle," said Terry, "and Ma's got our best room all ready for you. Now, can I tempt you to something to eat? I've got some lovely cheese and onion pies just out of the oven if you'd like."

Nicholson nodded gratefully. "I've not eaten a thing since this morning. I think I could eat a bite of supper now."

Terry patted the old man's shoulder affectionately and stepped out of the snug. "Your nephew?" asked Gabriel, but he was certain he knew the answer. It was quite common for young people to call their elders "Uncle" or "Auntie" if their families were on friendly terms.

"He's the landlord's younger son," Nicholson explained. "I've known him and his brother, Clive, since they were babies. That's why he calls me Uncle Roland." He took a long draw from his beer. Gabriel thought guiltily that the man must be desperately thirsty as well as hungry. No one had been looking after him today. "They lost Clive at El Alamein."

Loss. Every conversation always seemed to come back

to loss. Every family, even in this sheltered corner of the world, had its own story of grief. Virtually none had been spared a death, and some had lost so much—all their children, all their grandchildren, sometimes entire families had been erased from the world, reduced to a pathetic list of names on a war memorial somewhere. And here was Roland Nicholson, who had lost his daughter-in-law in war and his son in peace. "I sometimes wonder how the world can ever recover from so much death," Gabriel said.

"It will recover," said Roland without missing a beat. "When Brigitte went away, that was almost what she said. 'If I die at the hands of the Germans, I will still be Brigitte. I will never stop being the person God meant me to be. And the world will renew itself, and there will be another tomorrow.' "

"That's very eloquent."

"She was eloquent," agreed Roland, "and she left us each a letter—me, Charles, Plantagenet, and little Antoine, though he was not to open his letter until his eighteenth birthday. She knew she was not coming back."

Gabriel watched as Roland stared down at his beer, slipping into a protracted silence. He was curious about the choice of family names, all with a regal flavour to them—Plantagenet, like the dynasty doomed by the Wars of the Roses; Charles, a popular enough name, but evocative of two English kings and one doomed Scottish prince; and Roland, the knight of medieval myth who fought under Charlemagne with his mighty sword. The Nicholson family had style in an eccentric sort of way.

The silence was becoming uncomfortable, but Gabriel knew better than to interrupt whatever train of thought it was that had lured Roland away from his present miseries. Gabriel remembered becoming lost in thought for hours at a time after Giovanna and Nicoletta had died, resisting any well-intentioned attempts at snapping him back to the unbearable present. He waited patiently for Roland to emerge, allowing himself to be distracted by the lazy ticking of the clock on the wall and the murmur of voices on the other side of the thin wooden partition as men arrived at the pub after a long day, ready for a few hours of relaxation away from their wives. It was a strange sensation, being so isolated and yet so close to people enjoying the company of friends.

"Look here, old man," said Roland quietly, "you're no fool. I've heard that you're a bit of a Sherlock Holmes." Aware of Gabriel squirming before him, he added, "No need to be modest, Father. Reputations are made very quickly in this part of the world."

"I see," said Gabriel, though he had no idea how to take the backhanded compliment.

"I know you will have puzzled out a few awkward details by now, especially if you have had the misfortune to speak to my daughter."

"It was no misfortune, I assure you." Not a misfortunate, just bonkers, but Gabriel suspected that Roland knew exactly how his daughter must come across to strangers. "She's in shock, evidently."

"Plantagenet has been in shock, as you put it, since Brigitte went away." Roland paused at the sound of the door to the snug being nudged open. Terry walked sideways into the room with a tray and set it down on the table. There was a disquieting moment when Terry straightened up and looked from one patron to the next, apparently wondering whether to say something. Another second passed before Terry understood that the two men were deep in conversation and wished to be left alone, and removed himself from their presence as quickly as he could. Roland hesitated again, apparently blown off course by the interruption. "Look, all I wanted to say was that it's probably best that I be entirely honest with you. From what I've heard, you'll get to the truth sooner or later, and it's better that you hear it from me."

"If you know anything that may help bring your son's killer to justice," Gabriel began, but stopped when he saw Roland shaking his head. "If you wish to unburden yourself, perhaps . . ."

"Unburden is the better word to call it, Father," said Roland, his fingers playing absently with the crust of the pie before him. He was making no effort to make eye contact with Gabriel, and Gabriel thought it for the best. It was not for nothing that confessionals hid the priest's face from the penitent. It was always easier to be honest that way. "I know you must think my family very strange, Father. My son is dead, and here I am talking about his long-dead wife. My daughter was estranged from her own brother, even though they are close neighbours."

Gabriel was unsure how best to answer and gave a nod of encouragement, which he immediately worried might look as though he were wholeheartedly agreeing that the Nicholson family were a grape short of the bunch.

Roland cleared his throat. "You need to know that Plantagenet is not very well. When Brigitte did not return home from the war and we were told she had been killed, Plantagenet made it her business to go to France to try to find out what had happened to her. Charles begged her not to go. I think he knew that something truly terrible must have happened to her, and he preferred to be ignorant of the details. It's like that sometimes. When one truly loves a person, one can prefer to lie to oneself that perhaps nothing so very awful happened to him or her after all. Without knowing precisely how Brigitte had died, Charles could tell himself it must have been quick or perhaps that it had never happened at all."

"Did you want Plantagenet to go?" asked Gabriel, crossing himself before picking up his knife and fork. He was ravenously hungry, and Gabriel told himself it would make it easier for Roland to talk if his companion was occupied with eating. And he wanted Roland to talk about himself. For once, he wanted the person to whom he was talking to be a little self-obsessed. "I mean, did you encourage her to make the journey?" It was not that he did not want Roland to tell him about Plantagenet's journey; but he was always a little suspicious of what people had to say about others, and he wanted to know what Roland's place was in this sad little family drama.

"I didn't want her to go; no sane man would want his daughter venturing alone into such a country." He looked at Gabriel as though he expected affirmation. "You must understand, I'm not old-fashioned. It's not that I did not wish her to travel and to find out what she could about poor Brigitte. It was terribly dangerous; France was a smouldering ruin. One heard terrible stories of shootings and reprisals, young girls having their heads shaved. I understand how angry everyone was, of course, but I could hardly encourage my daughter to travel into such a lawless place."

"Did you not consider accompanying her if you were fearful for her safety?" asked Gabriel, hoping the question did not sound accusatory.

Roland gave a low chuckle, which sounded more like a groan of despair. Gabriel noticed that Roland had finished the beer but had not touched the food. The alcohol had already loosened Roland's tongue, and the full effects of it had not yet made themselves felt. "Plantagenet is a grown woman. She would not have taken kindly to her papa insisting upon holding her hand. Poor Charles was in no state to go anywhere. He had Antoine to think of." Roland pushed his plate away and nursed his temples as though he had a headache coming on. "That was when it all went wrong. I still have very little idea of what Plantagenet discovered, but I believe she blamed Charles for what had happened. There was a blazing argument. Plantagenet was shouting the most terrible things, that it was all Charles' fault. That Charles had betrayed Brigitte. To this day, I have never known what she meant, but they never spoke again."

There it was. The brooding horror behind any violent death. Blame. Guilt. Gabriel remembered how he had avoided his in-laws in the months and then the long years after Giovanna's death, tormenting himself constantly with the thought that they blamed him for failing to protect Giovanna and Nicoletta. He had imagined them, over and over again, standing in judgement over him, whispering to him that those two precious lives would never have been lost if he had stayed in the house that evening. If only he had not gone back to his school for a work engagement, if only he had sensed that something was wrong, if only he had got back in time to save them from the fire. If only, if only, if only . . . but even deaths in wartime never completely avoided the temptation for friends and relatives to blame one another: it was your idea for him to enlist in the navy, you sent him to a watery grave; you should have persuaded her to leave London while there was still time; you should have got her out of that factory, you knew how dangerous it was . . .

"Mr Nicholson, why don't you eat something?" suggested Gabriel, nudging Roland's very full plate back towards him. The pie would be cold by now, but still very edible, and Roland desperately needed some sustenance. Gabriel knew how hellish the days ahead would be for the man, once the initial shock had worn off and the long, empty days stretched ahead of him. "You need your strength."

Roland looked steadily at Gabriel, and the priest could see that the old man's eyes were wet and swollen with tears he was holding back with the utmost effort of will. "What Plantagenet saw in France turned her head. Charles played no part in Brigitte's death," he whispered. "He did everything he could to protect her. He begged Brigitte, begged her and begged her not to leave, made her think about their son and what would happen to him if she did not return. He would have done anything to keep her safe."

Perhaps he would, thought Gabriel miserably, watching as Roland sat back and closed his eyes. *But in the end, Charles Nicholson could not even keep himself safe.*

6

Gabriel's habitual sense of uneasiness crept over him the moment he left the snug and made his way out of the now crowded pub. He had never been entirely comfortable in the company of strangers, and he could not shake off the feeling that he was being watched as he stepped outside into the darkness. Gabriel had left Roland dozing in his chair, with Terry promising to help get him safely to his room. Gabriel had no idea what time it was and wondered, as he wheeled his bicycle back onto the road, whether he should have asked Terry to ring the abbey to let them know that he was on his way.

There would probably have been no point, Gabriel told himself, setting off with the enthusiasm of a swimmer leaping into freezing-cold water. He doubted anyone would have heard the telephone ringing, and in any case, if he kept up a good pace, he would be back within the hour. Contrary to his expectations, the bicycle's light glowed as he pedalled along, casting a reassuring, if weak, beam across the narrow road. The darkness in the countryside was almost absolute. Apart from a few lights from the windows of farmhouses dotted along the route, the night covered everything, obliterating hills and hedgerows that would usually have guided a traveller as he ventured between villages.

Gabriel may not have been fond of crowds, but he was

not meant for the life of a hermit either, and the silent emptiness around him was stifling. He knew it was only a mile until the next village and picked up his speed, willing the lights of Little Danvers to appear on the horizon. To calm himself, Gabriel began to sing, hoping that if there was any wayfarer on the road to hear him, he would not be mistaken for a drunkard.

Magnificat anima mea Dominum,
Et exultavit spiritus meus in Deo salutari meo.

There was light on the road, but it was coming from behind, not up ahead as Gabriel had hoped. He could hear the purr of an engine gaining on him and instinctively speeded up. It was strange, though not unreasonable, for a person to be driving along this road after dark, but Gabriel suspected that the driver would not anticipate the presence of a cyclist ahead of him and might not spot him in time to swerve. The lights were getting closer, bright lights that suggested something large, perhaps even a tractor. Gabriel considered swerving into the verge to avoid whatever was coming; but with the road lighting up, Gabriel could see that there were deep ditches on either side, and he risked seriously injuring himself if he rode into either of them.

The vehicle was directly behind Gabriel. He did not dare look back in case he was thrown off balance, but he felt certain that the driver saw him and was deliberately bearing down on him. He pedalled as though his life depended upon it even though he knew he could never outrun a petrol engine.

Gabriel could feel a stabbing pain in his side as the exertion began to make itself felt. He looked around wildly for any way out; he saw a five-bar gate up ahead, just a few yards away, promising a way off the road and into the adjacent field. He made one last effort . . . and a powerful force struck the bicycle, crumpling the metal frame beneath him. He was thrown clear and felt himself falling into the void, falling, falling . . . then something hard and sharp struck him in the small of the back, tearing cloth and skin as he skidded ever further downwards. The few remaining lights in the world had gone out; Gabriel was lost.

Gabriel had always hoped to avoid purgatory, but he knew that he had failed in that endeavour the moment he opened his eyes. His whole body felt as though he had been caught up in a singularly violent dust-up with a gang of Dantesque angels, intent upon purging him of his earthly sins. Gabriel's every breath caused a series of crippling pains to erupt across his torso, and he did not dare move after his first abortive attempt to sit up.

There was a presence in the room. An angelic presence, sitting in a chair and watching over Gabriel, had probably been watching for hours as Gabriel had lain unconscious in this bed. Gabriel's eyes fixed on the black, hazy figure near him but could not make out what kindly creature was guarding him. The figure stood up slowly. "Morning, you numpty!" came the chirpy Lancashire tones of Brother Gerard. Gabriel's eyes snapped into focus, and he saw the short, dark figure of his old friend grinning down at him. "Glad you could join us."

Gabriel sat bolt upright, letting out a roar of agony. He felt Gerard's hands on his shoulders pushing him gently back into the bed. "What in heaven—" he blurted before pain squeezed the breath from his lungs and he lay back on the pillows, gasping through the pain as it ebbed away. "How did I get home?"

"You didn't, Gabbers," said Gerard seriously. "You very nearly went to your Eternal Home. Someone's looking after you, that's for sure."

"But—" Gabriel looked around the room, searching for clues as to his location. He thought momentarily that he must be in a hospital, but this was too cosy and cheerful a room to be part of a hospital ward. The bedroom he occupied felt deliciously warm and seemed to be fragranced with lilac. It was simply but cheerfully furnished, most likely by a woman with a keen eye for detail—a Christian woman, as there was a wooden crucifix hanging on the opposite wall next to an image of the Holy Family. A foreign woman too, if Gabriel's instincts about the image were correct; the artwork was not at all in the English style and resembled more the sort of religious object Giovanna would have prized. "I don't suppose you could tell me where I am?" asked Gabriel, his head beginning to cloud again.

Gerard sat down in his armchair and leant forwards to nudge Gabriel awake. "Don't nod off on me again, mate, I'm not sure it's good for you. You got a bump on the head."

Gabriel suspected he had bumps everywhere; he could almost feel the bruises forming. "Gerry, do me a favour and tell me where on earth I am."

"Gabriel, you were found unconscious in a deep ditch. It's little short of a miracle that you were found. I meant it when I said someone's looking after you. A passerby happened to see the accident and ran for help when he realised you were knocked out. As it was, it was nearly an hour before he was able to get help to you. He ran to the nearest house to sound the alarm. The old couple living there had a telephone and called their doctor."

"Oughtn't they to have called an ambulance?" asked Gabriel. He was still confused as to why he was in a stranger's bedroom rather than a hospital. Last time he had come to grief in the street, he had woken up to find himself in a friend's home because there had been a fear that Gabriel's life might be in some danger; a hospital was too public a place for a man who had got himself caught up in London's criminal underworld. This time, he had merely been the unfortunate victim of a hit-and-run accident.

Gerard looked searchingly at Gabriel, trying to gauge how much he should say, but Gerard had never had any sense of discretion whatsoever and did what he usually did—told Gabriel everything and hoped for the best. "The young lad who came to your rescue told the couple that he had seen you being deliberately forced off the road. He said that when he tried to get a word of sense out of you, you were rambling about calling Dr Paige because someone was trying to kill you. The lad thought you were probably delirious, but since he'd seen the crime himself, he did what you asked."

Gabriel closed his eyes, irritated by Gerard grabbing his arm and shaking him awake again. He felt exhausted beyond measure, and he had no recollection of saying anything. "I'm sorry, but I can't remember a thing after I started falling. I can't remember saying anything to anyone!"

"Do you remember the accident? Try to remember, Gabriel; it may be important. You'll have to tell Applegate. The boy won't report it to the police; he was too scared witless to tell the couple his name."

Gabriel had started shivering. He may not have remembered his confused ramblings in that ditch, but he remembered his panic as he had tried to evade the assailant who was deliberately trying to run into him; he could feel the jolt of his bicycle being crushed beneath him and the horrific sensation of helplessness as he had fallen through the air into the ditch, crashing and bumping along the stony embankment. No, he did not remember an accident. He remembered that someone had tried to kill him. "This is Dr Paige's house then?"

Gerard nodded. "As soon as the doctor was sure it was safe to move you, he put you in his car and drove you to his house. Poor Mrs Paige sat up most of the night watching over you while Dr Paige drove over to the abbey to let us know what had happened."

"I'm sorry," murmured Gabriel, trying very hard not to think of the havoc he had caused. "What a mess."

"We were worried sick, Gabriel," said Gerard. "Father Abbot says you're not to go wandering off on your own from now on. You're the sort of bloke who needs a minder."

Gabriel opened his mouth to protest, but he heard the door creaking open slowly and swallowed the retort—which was probably for the best. Marie stood at the end of the bed with a breakfast tray, smiling bravely though Gabriel could not miss how anxious she looked. Marie had made her usual effort with her appearance; she was smartly dressed, and her hair was brushed and pinned away from her face; but there were the telltale smudges under her eyes that spoke of lack of sleep. "Good morning, Father," said Marie with forced brightness. "It's good to see you back with us."

Gerard got up and took the tray from her. Gabriel noticed that it contained two plates of scrambled egg on toast and two cups of tea. Gabriel not only had handed over an orphan to the Paiges to care for, out of the blue, but now had burdened them with taking care of two more visitors, one apparently an invalid. "I'm awfully sorry about this, Marie," Gabriel began. "I didn't mean to—"

"I'm sure you didn't mean to get knocked off your bike, Father," answered Marie with an exasperated laugh. "Don't you even think of apologising."

"Is Antoine all right?"

Marie nodded. "Don't you worry about him. He slept through all the drama in the night, and he's snuggled up in my front room reading comics. He'll probably be quite diverted by all the activity."

Gabriel drew in a deep breath. It could be a great deal worse. He was alive, he was in one of the safest places he could be outside of the abbey, and these lovely people would recover from the inconvenience to which he had inadvertently put them. Gabriel heard footsteps on the stairs, and Dr Paige knocked rhythmically on the door before entering, carrying a medical bag casually in one hand. "Good morning, Father," said Dr Paige brightly, and in his case, his high spirits seemed perfectly natural. He looked as fresh as a daisy, quite unlike a man who had been called out to a roadside accident in the middle of the night. "And how are you feeling?"

"A little as though I've been hit by a steamroller, Doctor."

Dr Paige nodded. "That's only to be expected. Don't worry; you've got off pretty lightly under the circumstances."

Gerard vacated the armchair, anticipating that Dr Paige

would want to sit down at his patient's bedside, but Dr Paige gestured for Gerard to remain where he was and took up his position at the other side of the bed, standing over Gabriel in a manner that looked protective rather than intimidating. Gabriel had to hand it to Dr Paige—he had an excellent bedside manner, his every movement deft but calm. He had learnt the art of putting nervous patients at ease during the trial by fire that had been his war duty. It was hard to imagine, as he took Gabriel's pulse and checked the dressings he had applied while Gabriel was still out for the count, that he had once treated the survivors of Hitler's murderous regime.

"Shall I live to fight another day?" asked Gabriel, feigning nonchalance, which he never did well.

The professional smile again. "I should like to see you eat something, Father," said Dr Paige. He reached forwards to help Gabriel sit up, placing a pillow behind Gabriel's back to protect him from the cold brass bedstead. "Take it nice and slowly."

Gabriel waited while the tray was set down gingerly on his lap before attempting a stiff sign of the cross. The food looked most inviting, but the simple act of picking up a teacup was almost too much for him. Gabriel's co-ordination felt out of kilter, and his hands trembled as he brought the cup to his lips, causing a few drops of tea to spill down his front. "What's wrong with me?" demanded Gabriel, looking up to Dr Paige for an explanation.

"You'll feel better when you've eaten," promised Dr Paige. "You'll be a little hypoglycaemic by now, and it won't help your concussion. You got a nasty bump on the head when you were thrown into that ditch. You were rambling your head off by the time I reached you."

"Whatever I said, I apologise," said Gabriel, stuffing his mouth with scrambled egg to avoid the need to say anything else. He detested the thought that he had talked nonsense in his confusion. At the tender age of eleven, he had been given laughing gas by a dentist and emerged from a blissful tunnel of fluffy clouds to the sound of the nurse giggling inanely. Apparently, Gabriel had sworn his undying love for her, and he was never to be allowed to hear the last of it.

"It's all right, Father. I've heard a great deal worse," said Dr Paige, "but the fact is, you've had a very close shave. I have already informed the inspector, and he will want to talk to you about this."

"It was an accident," said Gabriel lamely. He had known from the moment he had sensed the vehicle on the road behind him that it meant him harm, but sitting up in a comfortable bed, surrounded by kindly friends, Gabriel did not wish to believe in any person's evil intentions. "It was dark; my light was weak . . ." He sank into silence, wincing as Dr Paige sat at the end of the bed, that slight pressure causing his aches and pains to erupt again.

"Father Gabriel, if the person who knocked you down had not intended to hit you, he would have stopped," said Dr Paige gravely. "This is not London. I've never come across a hit-and-run on these roads before. No one drives away and leaves an injured person in the middle of nowhere. Whoever struck you meant you to die out there. You may thank a kind stranger and your guardian angel that you got off with a bumped head and a few broken ribs."

"He's right, Gabriel," said Gerard before Gabriel could find some way to contradict what he knew to be the truth. "You were found on the most isolated stretch of road hereabouts. Whoever hit you knew you were unlikely to be found before morning. They knew that you'd be thrown down a rocky ditch."

Gabriel stared down at the patchwork quilt draped over him, trying to relive those final moments before the crash. He cursed himself for not looking back, for not taking the risk of turning his head long enough to get a glimpse of whoever was seated behind the wheel. If he had not recognised the driver, he would at least have got some kind of a description of the car in question. But then it had been dark, and he might not even have been able to make out the colour. Gabriel became aware of the singsong voice of the one female in the room and looked up gratefully at Marie, as though he expected that she would change the subject. "Father, can you think of anyone who would have done this? Anyone you spoke to yesterday? Perhaps someone who saw you near the house while the police were there?"

Gabriel shook his head. "There's no reason for anyone to do such a thing. I'd only just started asking questions. The fact is, though, a pub full of people saw me talking to Roland Nicholson. Anyone might have followed me out. You know what it's like in a pub—it was crowded, it was noisy, and there was smoke everywhere. I didn't know any of the people in that room in any case. I wouldn't recognise their faces if I saw them again."

Marie took the empty tray from Gabriel. "I think we should leave you to rest a little longer," she said sweetly, motioning for her husband to leave the room with her. "You've had a nasty shock."

"I need to get on," said Gabriel before the Paiges could leave. "I need to speak to the inspector."

Dr Paige stood at the end of the bed and shook his head

slowly, the smile never leaving his face. "I'm awfully sorry, Father, but I insist that you stay in bed today. You're in no condition to go racing round the countryside. I will let your abbot know that you will be spending at least another night here. We'll see how you feel in the morning."

Gabriel threw back the bedclothes and attempted to swing his legs round to the side of the bed. It was the first time he was aware that he was wearing what must be a pair of Dr Paige's pyjamas; with embarrassment he realised that someone had undressed him in the middle of the night. Then the pain hit him again like a punch in the stomach, and Gerard helped him back into bed. "No!" Gabriel wheezed, fighting back the beginning of panic. "I can't rest now; there's a murderer on the loose! It wasn't a robbery!"

Marie and Dr Paige looked blankly at him. "I can telephone the inspector if you like," said Marie. "Then you can stay in bed, and Inspector Applegate can come and speak to you."

"Please," pleaded Gabriel as he was struggling to breathe. "It wasn't . . . it wasn't a robbery. If someone is trying to kill me for asking questions, it means . . . can't you see?"

Dr Paige put a hand on Gabriel's shoulder. "You need to rest, old man. I'm just going to prepare you a little something to help with the pain; then I have to go to Mass. Haven't been yet. Brother Gerard here is under strict instructions to watch over you."

When Dr Paige appeared again at his side with a syringe full of something that was meant to make him comfortable, Gabriel was too ashamed to admit that he could not stand needles. He could almost hear Gerard's suppressed giggles as he screwed his eyes tight shut, gasping at the sudden sharp pain, shortly before a pleasantly warm feeling crept over his battered body. The other fact that Gabriel would never admit to anyone, especially Brother Gerard, was that there was something reassuring about dozing off to sleep with a friendly presence watching over him. It was like being back in the nursery again with his nanny sitting in the corner with her sewing; though this time, Gabriel's guardian sat praying the rosary or his breviary. Nevertheless, for those few short hours, Gabriel felt safe, and he delighted in the sense of being cared for.

7

It was sometime in the early afternoon that Gabriel awoke again, feeling a little more comfortable than when he had last opened his eyes. The chair beside him was empty, and the creak of several sets of feet on the landing outside cleared up the mystery of Gerard's miraculous disappearance. Gerard had inevitably become bored out of his tiny mind with his prolonged sentry duty and gone walkabout but was now returning with company. Gabriel inched his way up into a sitting position, careful not to make any sudden moves. He could still feel his ribs aching every time he drew breath, but Dr Paige's medicine had worked wonders in taking the edge off the pain.

Applegate entered the room, trilby hat in hand, giving Gabriel the most unsympathetic smirk imaginable. "What are you doing in that bed, you old fraud?" he teased, sauntering over to the chair, no doubt to claim it before Gerard could. To Gabriel's surprise, Gerard did not follow Applegate into the room. It was Marie who appeared, her hands clasped around what looked like a pious object of some kind.

"Thank you for coming to visit me, Inspector," answered Gabriel dryly. "I hope you've brought some grapes." Gabriel glanced uneasily at Marie, aware of Applegate's bad manners in sitting down without offering the chair to the lady in the room. "Marie, I do hope we're not rushing you off your feet. You must be exhausted after last night's little drama."

Marie giggled. "I've had more peaceful nights." She was abruptly serious. "I'm sorry to trouble you with this, Father—I feel like a frightful sneak—but I thought you ought to see it." She reached forwards and handed Gabriel a medal. No ordinary medal, it was the George Cross, the highest award for bravery that could be given to a civilian. In the centre of the silver cross, there was a circle containing an image of Saint George on horseback, slaying the dragon, surrounded by the words *For Gallantry*. Unlike most medals, which are kept on display or stored safely away, this one had been much handled; Gabriel could see traces of little greasy fingerprints all over it, as if it had been passed from one hand to another by a nervous child. "I found it under Antoine's pillow when I went to air his room this morning," Marie explained. "I shall have to replace it before the poor boy goes looking for it. I don't want him to think he can't trust me."

"Antoine told me his mother had been awarded a medal," said Gabriel, weighing the George Cross in his hand one last time before handing it back to Marie. "I assumed he had meant a French honour, but she wasn't fighting for France; she was fighting for Britain in France."

Applegate raised an eyebrow. "Am I allowed to know what you are talking about?"

"Antoine's late mother returned to France at the start of the war," Marie explained. "She wanted to fight the Germans."

"I should have enquired further when Antoine said she had been given a medal," said Gabriel, "but it did not seem important then. Brigitte was not a lone fighter; she was working for Britain."

Applegate sat back in his chair, considering the information. "I'm not sure it always works like that," he said finally, "but in this case it would make sense. Someone had to know what she was doing; someone had to know how she died. If she went out alone, off her own bat, I doubt anyone would have known to nominate her for an award. The Germans killed so many brave people. Most of them vanished without trace."

Marie winced, but Applegate did not appear to notice. "I should put this back straightaway," she said, making directly for the door. "Why don't I let you gentlemen get on?"

"How is Antoine?" asked Gabriel, keen to prevent Marie from leaving on such an uneasy note. He doubted that she resented her own lack of medals, but he thought that Applegate's mention of people who had vanished without trace—friends, family—must surely rankle. "How is he coping?"

"Very tearful today," said Marie, easily distracted by another person's unhappiness, "but it's only to be expected. Dickie says it would be worse if he didn't cry. Brother Gerard has taken him to the park to cheer him up. I found an old kite in the loft. I think they're going to try to get it airborne."

Gabriel opened his mouth to respond, but Marie gave a little nod and left the room, closing the door softly behind her. "Who ran into you?" demanded Applegate as soon as the coast was clear. He had never been fond of prolonged interrogations, but this was abrupt even for him. "I'll have him up for attempted murder."

"I couldn't see a thing."

"Nothing at all?"

"No. Couldn't see the driver. Couldn't see what he was driving for that matter."

Applegate's look of frustration made Gabriel feel like the class dunce being handed back a particularly abysmal maths exercise. "Did it not occur to you to glance over your shoulder for ten seconds and *look* at who was chasing you?"

"I had rather a lot on my mind, Inspector, like not getting killed!" answered Gabriel, feeling his temper beginning to flare. Anyone would think the whole incident were his fault. "In any case, it was pitch-dark, and the headlamps lit up only the road. Whoever it was did not intend to be identified."

"Only because you weren't supposed to live to identify him!" retorted Applegate. "He must have thought you'd snuffed it, or he would have come back to make absolutely sure, mark my words. You shouldn't be here today, Father."

Gabriel sat back and closed his eyes. The metal edge of the bedstead pressed uncomfortably against the back of his head, forcing him to shift position. He could hear the roar of the engine ringing in his ears like a devouring dragon; he felt that unearthly force knocking the breath out of his body, throwing him into oblivion. He wanted so much to believe it had been a moment of carelessness on the part of some hapless driver, when every detail of his memory shrieked the truth at him like an air-raid siren. "The last time I experienced anything like that was when I got myself blown into the middle of next week in the trenches," said Gabriel to the world in general. "One never knows if one will survive the landing."

"Gabriel," said Applegate cautiously, leaning forwards and giving Gabriel's arm a gentle shake to stop him from dozing off. "So, you didn't see anything useful on the road. Did you talk to anyone yesterday? Who knows that you're asking questions about the murder?"

Gabriel half-opened his eyes. "Roland Nicholson, his sister Plantagenet, the pub landlord's son. Plantagenet Nicholson's housekeeper, the shopkeeper at the village shop, half the menfolk of the village as they drank their evening ale . . ." Gabriel swivelled round to look at Applegate, aware of the enormity of the task he had given the inspector. "I haven't been very discreet, have I? Most of the village must have seen me with one or other Nicholson by the end of the day."

Applegate grimaced. "Let's face it, Catholic priests are always conspicuous in these parts. Walking around like something out of *The Cabinet of Dr Caligari*."

Gabriel ignored the pointless anticlerical jibe, as he always did, focusing on the matter in hand. "I suppose we at least know for certain that Charles Nicholson was not killed in a burglary gone wrong. I'd warrant the contents of the safe have been hidden away somewhere. If we could find out where, it would probably lead us to the killer. Another thing . . ." Gabriel shifted position. He could feel pins and needles shooting up his left leg, and it was starting to annoy him. "The killer is evidently terrified and clueless, if last night's antics are anything to go by."

"I think we can rule out the burglary theory right enough," Applegate admitted. "None of it felt right from the start. I can count on one hand the number of burglaries that've have been committed in broad daylight in this neck of the woods. Most folk don't even trouble to lock their doors."

"Do robberies happen at all in the countryside?" Gabriel

enquired, thinking of the tedious frequency with which petty crimes had been committed on the streets of London—pickpocketing, bag snatching, shoplifting . . . He became aware of the silence all around him and noticed Applegate staring at him. He had no idea whether he had spoken his thoughts out loud as his mind wandered or whether Applegate had asked him a question and was wondering why Gabriel was refusing to furnish him with an answer. "Yes, yes, I quite agree," Gabriel ventured, working on the assumption that agreeing with the inspector was the safest policy.

"You must not have heard me when I said that robberies do happen around here," Applegate said with some annoyance, "but they usually involve some light-fingered scamp trying to filch sweeties from the counter of the village shop. Most thieving never gets as far as the police anyway. People find ways of dealing with it themselves."

"Rough justice?" A thought was pestering Gabriel through the muddle of bruises and exhaustion. The thought had wormed its way into Gabriel's thoughts the moment Roland had told him about the vicious family row that had ended in Plantagenet and Charles becoming estranged. "Rough justice, Inspector," said Gabriel with more certainty. "I knew that there was something I had to tell you. Plantagenet Nicholson made the most awful suggestion when I spoke with her yesterday."

Applegate finally looked interested. "Go on."

"Frankly, she's a very odd woman, but she seemed to think that someone had betrayed Charles Nicholson's wife when she had worked for the resistance in France."

Applegate looked nonplussed. "I daresay most of the poor

sods who ended up in the hands of the Gestapo were betrayed by someone."

"But it's worse than that, Inspector," Gabriel persisted, trying to remember precisely what Plantagenet and Roland had said to him. "There seemed to be some suggestion that Charles had done something to betray his wife. Plantagenet appeared to blame him."

Applegate rolled his eyes. He had a healthy hostility to the upper classes at the best of times, but Gabriel could hardly imagine Applegate getting along swimmingly with a woman who would probably remind him of the schoolroom. "Plantagenet! Bloody silly name."

"Antoine calls her Aunt Plant."

Applegate's sneer erupted into a guffaw of laughter. "Now there's a lad with a sense of humour." He shook his head, remembering himself. "Look, I'm under strict instructions from the good doctor not to worry you today, so if you've nothing much to tell me, I'll tell you a thing or two." Applegate got up, as though giving notice that he was shortly to depart. "My boys found nothing of much interest in the house. It was exactly the sort of place you might expect three males of different generations to live in. There was just one item I thought you might like to see."

Gabriel's heart soared. Applegate was sharing evidence with him. The inspector pushed a browned, faded newspaper cutting into his hand.

"What's this all about?" Gabriel asked.

"Take a look. The study was ransacked, papers scattered all over the place. One of my constables found this and thought it might be important."

Gabriel opened up the flimsy paper to reveal a grainy

photograph cut inexpertly from the middle of a page. There was no headline, and it looked as though a large part of the surrounding news report had been damaged by damp; the words were virtually indecipherable. Fragments of sentences jumped out at Gabriel: "Later that afternoon . . .", "Nichols was accused of . . .", "reports of a disturbance . . ."

"A strange memento to keep," said Gabriel, giving up on trying to read the rest of the spoiled print. The damaged text hardly mattered. The photograph was of poor quality, taken from some distance away, but it needed no explanation.

"The reporter wrote Nichols instead of Nicholson," Applegate explained in case Gabriel had failed to notice the error, "but reporters aren't known for checking little details like a person's name."

Gabriel wondered how many times Inspector Applegate had been misquoted in the press but decided against asking. The photograph captured an altercation between an older and a younger man in the middle of a street. As far as it was possible to read their expressions, the older man appeared calm but serious whilst the younger man was in a towering rage, his mouth partially open as though he were about to shout. In the periphery of the picture, there were other blurred figures, some who appeared to be waving banners, though it was impossible to see what messages were displayed there. At least two of the blurred heads wore the distinctive tall helmets of the police. "The older man is obviously Roland," Gabriel said. "I assume that the younger man is Charles?"

"Correct. Looks like young Mr Nicholson was a bit of a tearaway during his student days."

"He looks very young," observed Gabriel. "One wonders why a family would even keep an article like this. Neither man would wish to be reminded of such a moment." Gabriel looked back at the picture and the sight of the approaching policemen. If the photograph had been taken at a political rally or demonstration of some kind, the police presence might be quite innocent, a few bobbies sent along to ensure that there was no trouble, but "disturbance" was one of the few words Gabriel had been able to make out. "Inspector, was Charles arrested? It looks as though he's about to be."

Applegate took back the picture. "There is no evidence of Charles Nicholson ever being charged or convicted of so much as a breach of the peace."

"Which newspaper is that?"

Applegate shook his head. "Doesn't say. All it really tells us is that Charles Nicholson was possibly a bit of a hothead years ago. Hardly damning, if I'm honest."

"Maybe not damning, but it helps to build a picture of the victim." Gabriel stifled a yawn to avoid aggravating his bruised ribs, but he did not want Applegate to realise how tired he felt either. "When I'm out of this bed, I don't suppose I could take a little look at the house?"

"I thought you'd ask me that," Applegate said with a smirk. "I meant it when I said that there's really not much to see. The only thing you might like to take a look at is the summerhouse, just to satisfy your curiosity about the dead wife. Very unusual."

This was definitely Gabriel's idea of something of interest. "Was it her summerhouse?"

"It might have been. Looks more like a shrine to her

memory in my opinion. Take a look yourself." Applegate walked to the door, but stopped in his tracks, weighing up an idea in his mind. "Father, there is something that really does trouble me about all this. You know the way you thought it strange that a burglar should have struck from behind if he were being confronted? Well, I'm not sure about the dead man's injuries either." Applegate turned back to Gabriel, indicating the places on his own head where the fatal blows had fallen. "There were multiple injuries. The pathologist may tell us more, but it looked to me as though none of the injuries alone would have been enough to kill the man outright. If he were ill, and it looks that way, he would have been no match for a determined killer unless the killer was very weak and had to strike multiple times."

"Or lost his nerve," suggested Gabriel. "Or hers, of course."

Applegate nodded, acknowledging the possibilities. "Get well soon, Father, and mind your back. You mightn't be so lucky next time."

Gabriel watched as Applegate left the room and pulled the door shut. He had never believed in luck, but he knew he had been spared to do something of use to someone. Slowly but determinedly, Gabriel swivelled round and inched his way forwards until his bare feet touched the wooden floorboards. He might not be able to get back to the abbey today, but he was not staying in bed a moment longer.

Gabriel found it easier to get out of bed than he had expected. Walking was not very difficult either, so long as he was upright. It was bending and stretching that he was going to have trouble with for some considerable time, he realised as he dressed. Walking down the stairs he smelled the aroma of roast chicken and roast vegetables emanating from the kitchen—the smell of Sunday lunch—and Gabriel registered for the first time that it was, of course, a Sunday. Sunday, and he had been too unwell to say Mass.

The thought depressed him in the way a missed invitation to a friend's wedding might distress a person, but Gabriel resigned himself to making a spiritual communion and thanking God for his deliverance. It had been good of Applegate to visit him on a Sunday, now that Gabriel thought about it, taking himself away from his family on his day of rest—that is, if he had a family.

Applegate had always struck Gabriel as the sort of man who had no personal life whatsoever, living and breathing crime as a substitute for all worldly pleasures. A kind of monk, in a way, who worshipped Law and Order. *Poor Applegate if that's the case*, thought Gabriel. *Poor Applegate*.

The grandfather clock at the bottom of the stairs read ten past five, and Gabriel was aware of subdued chatter from the dining room. The delectable aroma of food drew Gabriel's attention to how ravenously hungry he was. He suspected that Marie had not wanted to bring him anything to eat while the inspector was there. She was an excellent hostess, but serving food to Gabriel would have meant providing a further meal for Applegate, and her stock of meat was probably already stretched with the sudden appearance of three visitors. Gabriel tapped gently on the door and stepped diffidently inside.

Marie, Gerard, and Antoine were seated around a dining table that was draped in a pristine white cloth and positively heaved with food, but not the food Gabriel had been expecting. It was, of course, long past lunchtime, and they were tucking into a hearty high tea. There was a teapot neatly covered in a yellow tea cosy, surrounded by plates of bread and jam, scones, Victoria sponge, fairy cakes, and what Gabriel took to be Eccles cakes, a treat of which Gerard was especially fond. There was one place at the table conspicuously empty.

"It's so good to see you up and about!" trilled Marie, leaping to her feet to greet her visitor. "Please sit down. I'm afraid Dickie has been called out, but I'm sure he'll be back soon. You must be ravenous."

Gabriel sat down gingerly, feeling the now-familiar ache of his body protesting. "Thank you," he said warmly as Marie poured milk and tea into his cup, sensing with the eye of a doctor's wife that Gabriel might struggle to stretch across the table.

"Would you prefer some hot food?" asked Marie, remembering herself. "I did save you a portion of lunch, but you were sleeping so peacefully I didn't like to disturb you; then you were busy with the inspector. I can bring it out for you now if you like."

Gabriel hesitated, but only for a minute. The roast chicken would be a good meal for Marie served cold the next day, and she still looked a little pale. "High tea would be wonderful, thank you," he assured her, helping himself to the plate of bread and jam closest to him. "This is a marvellous spread." Gabriel suspected that Marie was in the habit of doing as his own mother had done long ago—baking all her cakes and buns for the week on the Saturday, to save time and fuel. It assured a sumptuous high tea for Sunday and plenty of leftover treats to last the next five days.

Five minutes later, Marie had heaped Gabriel's plate with

all manner of mouth-watering delicacies and sat down again next to Gerard. Gabriel signalled to Gerard to distract Marie, waiting to see whether Gerard had understood what he needed to do. Without acknowledging the hidden message, Gerard began engaging Marie in a hilarious story about one of his many childhood mishaps. Gabriel waited until Marie was laughing, before turning to the silent Antoine. "Why did you tell me that you have no relatives?" whispered Gabriel. "You have an aunt."

Antoine looked up balefully at his interlocutor. The boy was dry-eyed; the last thing Gabriel wanted to do was to set him off again, but he needed an explanation. Everyone lied during a murder investigation—big lies to hide guilt, little white lies to conceal the sordid details that inevitably emerged with the police poring over the minute details of a victim's life. Gabriel was attuned to the signals people unconsciously gave off when they were lying, but he had not questioned Antoine's claim because there had been no obvious reason for the child to lie. If Antoine had a tendency towards dishonesty, Gabriel needed to know.

Antoine, however, was in no mood to cooperate, shaking his head slowly by way of an answer.

"Antoine, you're not in any trouble," whispered Gabriel, "but you need to tell me what's going on or I won't be able to help you. You must have known I'd find out about your aunt before too long."

"She's not my aunt!" Antoine blurted out with unexpected force, causing Gerard and Marie to stop talking immediately. "She said my father was a murderer! She said Mama would still be alive if it hadn't been for him! Papa was so cut up about it, he didn't speak for days!"

"All right, son, it's all right," reassured Gabriel, placing a steadying hand on Antoine's shoulder as the boy looked ready to make a bolt for it. "It was a horrible thing to happen. Your father must have been so upset."

"Everyone loved her, Father!" cried Antoine, tears pattering a well-travelled course down his face. "Papa and Grandpa turned the summerhouse into a shrine to her. Papa used to sit in there for hours, touching all her things. Grandpa said Aunt Plant wasn't a member of our family anymore; she was dead to us."

Marie got up from the table and went over to Antoine, kneeling by his side so that he would not have to look up at her. "I'm sure your mama and papa loved one another very much," she said, and it took a moment before Gabriel realised that Marie was talking to Antoine in French. "They're together again now; just think of that!"

Antoine looked blearily into Marie's thin, Madonna-like face, his mouth opening and closing with the effort of trying to speak. Then he gave up the struggle and threw himself in Marie's arms, sobbing into her shoulder as though he had always belonged in Marie's welcoming embrace and this was the most natural action in the world.

Gabriel smiled, certain now that he had been right to bring Antoine here. Like most women who have been broken by suffering and slowly recovered through the care and love of another, Marie had a huge capacity to love and care for others. Antoine would be safe here. He would be safe, and he would heal. It was Gabriel's turn now to leave the sanctuary of this house and find out what horror had provoked such a rift in a close family and who besides Plantagenet had been caught up in it.

8

"Out of the question, Father," said Dr Paige firmly. "You shouldn't even be dressed and out of bed yet."

Dr Paige had come home from a visit to an old lady who had taken a tumble, convinced herself that she had broken her neck, then got up, walked over to the telephone and rung for help. Dr Paige had prescribed hot water bottles, plenty of cups of tea and some rest before he had hurried home, tired and hungry.

"I can't lie in bed forever; there's a killer out there!" protested Gabriel. As soon as the words were out of his mouth, Gabriel realised how pretentious he sounded. A detective inspector and a full team of highly trained British bobbies were searching for the killer around the Wiltshire countryside; it was unlikely that they really needed his assistance in the matter. "It's not fair to you and Marie," said Gabriel, trying a different, more considerate tack. "This isn't a hospital, and you've got your work cut out looking after Antoine. I've caused you enough trouble as it is!"

Dr Paige chuckled, but his face clouded over, and Gabriel had a few seconds to wonder what he had said wrong before receiving the answer. "I don't want to stop you finding a killer, Father. We wouldn't want Applegate pinning the crime on the wrong man again now, would we? One more night, and you can go home tomorrow. Does that sound like a plan?"

Gabriel nodded nervously, aware that he had been walking on eggshells and had smashed a few in the process. "He was very embarrassed about that mistake if it helps," he said, then abandoned the effort. Dr Paige bore the look of a man who had struggled between his Christian duty to forgive Inspector Applegate and the insatiable urge to make him suffer for his mistake for the rest of his life.

"He was only doing his job," answered Dr Paige, in the blank tone of a child repeating a Latin exercise he has been forced to learn by rote. "He didn't have to enjoy the process quite so much, though, and that's what I found hardest to forgive."

At least you forgave, thought Gabriel, or rather, hoped. Dr Paige was a fine man, but Gabriel suspected that he had a tendency to bear a grudge, especially when it involved a man in some sort of authority. He would have learnt that unfortunate attitude whilst serving in the army, and Applegate had given Dr Paige little reason to revise his instinctive contempt for anyone in a position of command.

Ten minutes later, the five of them were seated comfortably in the sitting room, having what Gabriel's mother would have called "a cosy time of it". Gabriel sat in an armchair, propped up by crocheted cushions, enjoying the mug of cocoa Marie had poured for him from a vast ceramic pot, the like of which Gabriel had never seen before. It was no doubt one of Marie's continental additions to this most English of homes, along with the plate of iced pastries he could not name. Gerard and Antoine sat on the rug playing a game of draughts, which Gerard was losing, accidentally or by design.

Gabriel could not help thinking that they were looking like quite a family together, but just two days ago, Antoine had been a member of a very different family, perhaps playing draughts with his own father. Murderers did not just kill individual men and women, they killed families, shattering the bonds that held generations together and scattering the survivors. Gabriel wondered whether his daughter might have found a husband by now. He might have been sitting in a room just like this, with a grandchild crawling around the hearth rug . . . *No*. Gabriel commanded himself to stay away from that dark train of thought. He was where he was meant to be, in the home of hospitable friends and a child who had a right to justice.

Gabriel woke up on the third of May warm and rested after a rare night of uninterrupted sleep. May Day was a bank holiday, a national holiday celebrated joyfully in this part of England, yet the local festivities were far from Gabriel's mind as he dressed. He felt a quiver of regret knowing he would soon be leaving the sanctuary of the Paiges' welcoming home. He washed and shaved his face, swallowing his discomfort at using another man's shaving brushes, soap and razor, which Dr Paige had insisted he borrow. "When a man has had a shock, it's important to act as normally as possible," he had said. "You are used to shaving every morning; therefore, you should shave."

Gabriel was not at all used to being treated to a plateful of fried bread and eggs first thing in the morning and could hardly contain his excitement as he sat at the kitchen table, where Gerard and Antoine were already demolishing what looked like second helpings. "Brother Gerard and I gathered up the eggs from the henhouse this morning," Antoine declared with obvious pride. "Mrs Paige says the hens like me."

It was the first time Gabriel had seen Antoine grin, and he returned the smile. "I'll have to introduce you to my bees one day," he said. "You can help me rescue all the lovely honey."

"I do wish you didn't have to go," said Antoine, looking across at Gerard as the brother finished his tea with a flourish and stood up to help with the clearing up. "Can't your boss let you stay?"

"You can come and see us at the abbey any time you like," promised Gerard, "and there won't be no scoutmaster sending you packing. Father Gabriel here can teach you beekeeping if you like, but they're not so friendly as chickens. I won't go near the things."

Antoine looked back at Gabriel, who had evidently gone up in the child's estimation. "Do you really keep bees? In proper hives? Isn't it frightfully dangerous?"

Gabriel shook his head, getting up to join Gerard at the kitchen sink. "Not at all, once you've made friends with the bees. And the honey is wonderful."

"Will you see Grandpa today?" asked Antoine, throwing Gabriel off balance. Gabriel had observed that children had a tendency to jump from one subject to another without any transitional conversation, which was either refreshingly straightforward or bewildering. "Can you tell him to come and visit me?"

"I might not see him today, but I'll certainly send a message to him through the inspector," promised Gabriel. "He's a reliable messenger, most of the time."

Antoine's smile looked a little fixed, and Gabriel knew he was wondering why his grandfather had not come to live in the same house with him. Marie picked up on the boy's uncertainty at the same time. "Don't worry, Antoine," said Marie. "I'm going to invite your grandpa to come and stay with us as soon as he's finished helping the inspector. How does that sound?"

Antoine virtually jumped for joy. "Can you do that?"

"Absolutely! I know he doesn't want to make trouble for anyone, but visitors are never trouble. Once he's given a statement to the inspector and answered all the questions the inspector has about your father, he can come and stay here."

"Doesn't it seem a bit odd to you that a man is staying away from his grandson when he most needs him?" asked Gerard when they were back on the road to the abbey. The car had needed some assistance to get started after a few days' idleness, but the engine roared along happily enough now. "Wouldn't you want to be close to your loved ones at a time like this?"

"Of course," said Gabriel, "but I think he is desperate to protect the child from the police investigation. Roland wants to go home, but home is where he found his son brutally murdered. He might be able to return to the house before long, but he might not want poor little Antoine forced to live with all the memories. They will probably have to move away eventually."

"It would give me the heebie-jeebies, living in a house where someone got killed like that," said Gerard. "I'd be looking out for ghosts whispering around the chimney pots. If I were them, I'd sell up as soon as ever I could and move as far away as I could."

"That sounds like superstition," commented Gabriel, but before he could say anything further on the subject of Gerard's spooky feelings, Gerard steered the car around a blind corner a little too fast as always. Gabriel saw the plump, feathery mass of a pheasant flapping wildly before them; there was the screeching of brakes, the slipping, sliding motion of the car failing to stop, the filling of the windscreen with brown fuzz, then finally the nauseating thud of the car striking the doomed bird. The ex-pheasant fell lifelessly onto the verge.

Gerard scrambled out of the car, as white as a sheet. "Terrific!" he almost wailed. "Now I'm the Wiltshire pheasant murderer!"

Gabriel went over to the carcass and picked it up by the scrawny neck, examining it for any signs of life. It was very clearly dead, but Gabriel was preoccupied by how deliciously heavy it was. There was rather more meat on a pheasant than he had imagined, and he could not help thinking what a wonderful dinner it would make. Gabriel had not grown up in the country and most certainly did not belong to the class of men who went game shooting on country estates in season, so he had never eaten pheasant before. In these times of austerity, this was a meal sent from heaven. He placed it gently across the backseat of the car.

"It's only a pheasant," said Gabriel, but to his astonishment, Gerard got back into the driver's seat and sat with his hands trembling violently against the steering wheel. A rough, tough, straight-talking Lancashire man had been reduced to a gibbering wreck by a pheasant slamming against his windscreen. "Gerry, you've never killed anything before, have you?"

Gerard shook his head meekly. "I'm a city lad, Gabbers. The only time I ever saw meat, it were drowning in me ma's stew. That bird were flying about perfectly chipper five minutes ago." He glanced back at the pheasant lying in state across the backseat, beak in the air, and shuddered. "You're not really going to take that back to the abbey to eat, are you?"

"No point in leaving it for the rats," said Gabriel. "They're fat enough already."

Gerard placed a cigarette between his lips and attempted to light it, but he was too clumsy to strike a match. In the end, Gabriel had to take the matches off him and strike a light himself. The role reversal did not please Gabriel at all. Normally it was Gerard being direct, chirpy and practical whilst Gabriel needlessly overreacted, but Gabriel wondered whether his dealings in human killing was hardening him somehow. As a boy he would have bawled his eyes out if he had seen a bird die like that, but Gabriel the boy had not been to the trenches, had not seen his home engulfed by flames, had not witnessed a woman being hanged, had not been at multiple crime scenes. "Let's go home before anything else happens," said Gabriel quietly.

"You really shouldn't have brought the pheasant here," said Dominic anxiously, when he had got over his shock. He had heard the sound of the car pulling in through the driveway and lumbered over to greet his two friends. His first thought had been to lead Gabriel to the infirmary, so that he could check that his injuries were healing well, but he had been greeted instead by Gerard retching uncontrollably by the side of the car and Gabriel standing with a dead pheasant under one arm. "Gabriel, you do realise that's technically poaching, don't you?"

"I didn't shoot it," protested Gabriel. "It flew in front of the car. You'd best attend to poor old Gerard. He's taken quite a turn."

"If you accidentally kill a game bird, you're supposed to leave it," Dominic explained, because unlike Gabriel, he was more than familiar with the rules of rearing and dispatching the various delicious birds bred for sport. "If you take it away with you, it's poaching."

"We'd better eat the evidence for dinner then, before their lordships notice the loss," remarked Gabriel, nodding his head towards Gerard, who was leaning forwards against the body of the car, sweating profusely with the effort of stopping himself vomiting. As soon as he knew that Gerard was safely in Dominic's hands, Gabriel hurried in the direction of the kitchen with the pheasant, to dispose of the stolen goods. He felt furious with himself for his bitter tone: *Before their lordships notice the loss*. He had no idea where his disdain for the upper classes had come from; he never remembered feeling that way in the past, and he knew it was a failing. They were no better or worse than he was, but there was a certain inverse snobbery that could easily creep up on an educated middle-class man who has had just enough contact with the aristocracy to make him feel pointlessly inadequate.

It's only a pheasant, thought Gabriel, striding along the corridor to the kitchen with undue haste. *It doesn't take much to give me an existential crisis.* Fortunately for Gabriel, he did not have to go as far as the kitchen, as Brother Boniface came bounding out just in time to intercept him. Boniface had entered the abbey while Gabriel was away assisting Father Foley at Saint Patrick's; he was the most junior member of the community and the one Gabriel knew least well. It was unfortunate for Gabriel's troubled conscience that Boniface was from a highborn family and could allegedly trace his ancestry back to Saint Thomas More—though plenty of old English Catholic families made such claims—and he spoke as though he had just left the service of His Majesty the king. Despite his privileged background, Boniface had adapted quickly to the austere life of the abbey and become quite a favourite within the community.

"I say, a pheasant!" chirped Boniface, reaching out to take it as though he were embracing a cuddly toy. "Did the scoutmaster give it to you? It's a frightfully nice way to say thank you."

"Not exactly," answered Gabriel, reddening. He knew Boniface would think it most unsporting of him to have retrieved the bird from the grass verge after it had been knocked out of this life by Gerard's dodgy driving. "I . . . er . . . I picked it up on my way home."

"Splendid!" exclaimed Boniface, and Gabriel wished earnestly that the boy would stop stroking its little head with one hand as though he expected it to wake up and make a scene any moment. "I'll get plucking."

"You know how to do that?" asked Gabriel dubiously.

"Of course! I was never very much good with a gun, but

I always had a knack for preparing the birds. I'll make sure I get the shot out before I roast it."

Gabriel cringed. It was no good; he was going to have to admit what had happened, or Boniface would spend a fruitless hour searching through the flesh for any stray bit of lead. "No need, I'm afraid we ran it over."

Boniface looked mortified for a moment, then burst out laughing. "Oh, how frightful! The police will be after you for poaching!"

Gabriel grimaced and left Boniface to the happy task of plucking and dressing the pheasant for dinner. At least he had not come back to the abbey empty-handed. As he moved back outside, he noticed the scouts packing up to leave and realised that he had been absent during one of the busiest weekends of the year, when his assistance had been badly needed.

Jack Harris was certainly a formidable scoutmaster. The boys moved with the efficiency of a regiment of soldiers, systematically taking down tents, dealing with metal pegs, ropes, and the billowing swathes of canvas as though they had spent months marching through the desert and were thoroughly hardened to the outdoor life and all its privations. It felt odd, almost wrong, that these children had been innocently enjoying campfires and expeditions in this place whilst one of their number had gone through a horror no child should have to endure.

"Father Gabriel!" came a shout from the other end of the lawn. Jack Harris, who had been surveying his troop with the confident authority of Lord Kitchener, was waving to Gabriel, windmill style. The shout was friendly rather than urgent, and Gabriel walked slowly across the lawn, acknowledging the smiles and greetings of the scouts he passed. Many of them attended his catechism class, and he had known some of them, particularly those with older siblings, for years.

"Had a good camp?" asked Gabriel when he was comfortably within earshot. "You've certainly had good weather for it."

"It's gone swimmingly, Father," said Jack, "despite the obvious."

Gabriel looked round at the boys and noted their infectious cheerfulness. "Mr Harris, have you broken the news to them yet?"

Jack frowned, judiciously avoiding Gabriel's glance. "I haven't, as it happens. It seemed wrong to ruin an enjoyable weekend, and some of the boys will be very distressed when they find out. Anthony is a popular boy, and most of the scouts know him and his family well." Jack placed his hands behind his back, in what Gabriel suspected was a nervous habit. "I almost wish they didn't need to be told. How does one explain to a child that another boy's father was battered to death by a burglar? And in his own home? That's what will frighten them. Children should feel safe at home, but now they never will."

Gabriel understood the dilemma. It would be far easier to send the children home happy and excited, leaving their parents to shatter their little worlds for them, but somehow it seemed cowardly. "It's a pity Antoine had to go home and face that."

Jack gave Gabriel a sidelong glance. "Now, you know that was not my fault. How was I to know what was waiting for him at home?" He turned to Gabriel, angling his head so as to cast his face into shadow. His voice, when he found it, was low and conspiratorial. "Look here, I know you're up to your neck in all this—you always are, from what I've heard. I've also heard a little rumour that Charles Nicholson's death had nothing to do with a burglary."

"I believe that's one possibility," answered Gabriel cautiously. There was unlikely to be a nefarious reason why Jack Harris wanted to know the juicy details—gossip and rumour were part of the fabric of village life—but he had learnt to be careful with whom he chose to confide. He added, "The police will have to consider everything, I suppose."

Jack bent his head closer to Gabriel to emphasise his superior height. "That was no accidental killing, Father," he whispered. "Little Charlie Nicholson was no saint, and we all knew it."

Gabriel could not resist the urge to move away, feeling suddenly trapped and rather repulsed by the man who seemed to be taking an uncalled-for delight in the whole ghastly affair. A minute ago, Jack Harris had been an affable middle-aged man whose only fault might be that he was too much of a stickler for rules and protocol. Now Gabriel was almost wondering whether he were talking to the same person. People sometimes reveal unpleasant character traits out of the blue but usually in the heat of temper, not with this sudden, chilly lapse into . . . Gabriel was not even sure what to call Jack's tone. "That's a nasty scar you've got there," Gabriel blurted out, partly because he had never stood close enough to Jack Harris before to notice the jagged white mark on the man's cheek. He was desperate to change the subject in any way possible, even at the risk of being rude.

Jack's hand slapped lightly at the scar as though he could swipe it away; then he gave a hearty laugh and was all charm again. "Cut myself shaving many years ago. I never had a very steady hand as a young man, I'm afraid."

A boy aged around ten came bouncing up to the two men, calling, "Skipper! Skip!" It provided a welcome distraction for Gabriel, who slipped away inside before he could be tempted to continue the conversation. The low level of rumbling pain from his broken ribs had left Gabriel feeling constantly out of breath, and he used the excuse to return to the kitchen, where he could be away from the heat of the sun and the noise of overexcited children.

The incident with the pheasant had left Gabriel wondering whether he was being melodramatic about his accident. The fact was that accidents happened on the roads all the time, for no more sinister reason than a momentary lapse of concentration or a young driver showing off. The consequences could be horrific, but there was seldom a deliberate intent to cause harm. Gerard had not meant to kill a blameless bird as it went about its business, but if he had been driving more carefully, the pheasant would still be contentedly pecking in the dust now. Likewise, when Gabriel had been cycling along that road, his light had been weak, and his black clothes would have given the driver no clue that there was anyone there at all. Larger vehicles were slower than cars but notoriously unwieldy. Gabriel had investigated murders before that had turned out not to be murders at all. It was so easy to see a malevolent force behind what was merely a blunder: an inattentive driver knocking a cyclist into a ditch, an ugly scar made by a clumsy adolescent attempt at a shave, a man killed by a panicked burglar. It was so easy to give the victim's death a significance it did not have.

"Boniface?" asked Gabriel when he entered the kitchen and found the brother systematically relieving the pheasant of its feathers. The very sight made Gabriel want to sneeze, and that would never do in his current predicament. Laughing, crying, and sneezing were strictly off-limits until his ribs healed. "Boniface, may I ask you a question?"

Boniface looked up at Gabriel, giving his customary cherubic smile. "Ask away! I hope I shall be able to answer it."

Gabriel went over to the sink and poured himself a glass of water. He filled a second tumbler for Boniface and placed it on the table before him. "You're a country boy, aren't you? You grew up on an estate."

Boniface's plump face reddened lightly. "Oh, nothing quite that grand, Dom Gabriel. It was quite a modest pile compared to some. We farmed most of the land ourselves, stabled horses, that sort of thing. Why do you ask?"

"Were you ever robbed, as far as you remember?"

Boniface tilted his head to one side, the half-naked pheasant forgotten. "My mother had her bag snatched once when she went up to town to do her Christmas shopping. She was frightfully upset about it afterwards, said the lout who took it half dragged her into the road."

"But at home, I mean," Gabriel persisted. "Was your house ever burgled? If it was secluded, it would have been easy enough for thieves to get in."

Boniface shook his head. "When we had evacuees living with us, a couple of the boys were a little light-fingered to begin with, but Father soon put a stop to that. That was the only time I remember anyone trying to steal anything from the house. It was quite a rambling building; it would have been easy for a thief to get in, but I never remember it happening."

Gabriel leant forwards, meaning to rest his arms against the tabletop, but pain forced him to sit up straight. "That's what I'm finding so strange. My every instinct tells me that Charles Nicholson's murder had nothing to do with a bungled burglary. No one else seems to think so either; in fact, anyone I talk to seems quite keen to tell me it was not a burglary. But what if it was? In London, burglaries happen all the time, and nobody is surprised."

Boniface sat down opposite Gabriel, and Gabriel tried very hard not to notice the bird laid out between them as though they were about to take part in some dodgy Druid ritual. Boniface noted Gabriel's discomfort, chuckled and pushed the pheasant away to the edge of the table. "Why don't you tell me what happened?" asked Boniface. "Nobody ever tells me anything."

Gabriel smiled at his companion. Boniface really did look as though he ought still to be at school. It was not unusual among the English Benedictines for boys from their schools to enter the religious life immediately after finishing at eighteen. Boniface must have been at least twenty, but he had such a beatific face that he looked as though age would never touch him. Various ghastly murders aside, there had to be something to be said for raising a child among the rivers and green hills of Wiltshire.

"There's not much to tell, but I suppose it will help me to get things clear in my own head if I go over it again," said Gabriel. "Listen carefully. Three generations live in the same house: the grandfather, Roland Nicholson; the father, Charles Nicholson; and the child, Anthony Nicholson, mostly known as Antoine. Six days a week, including Saturday, the three members of the family leave the house at more or less the same time. Charles goes to catch his bus to work; Roland goes to the village shop to buy his newspaper and, once a week, some tobacco. Little Antoine cycles to school."

"On a Saturday?" Boniface chipped in. "He has Saturday school?"

"Yes, his school has lessons on Saturday morning. All except this past Saturday, when lessons had been cancelled in honour of the May Day bank holiday, during which a number of the boys were going on a scout camp—this scout camp here at the abbey. It's a popular gathering, and the boys talk about it for months before. The point is, the house was supposed to be empty. That's why I think that even if the crime had started as a burglary, it must have been someone who knows the household because a robber from outside the village is unlikely to have known the comings and goings of the family."

Boniface nodded. "Isn't it true that most victims know their killers, or is that something I've read somewhere?"

"Generally speaking, that is correct. A person is more likely to be murdered by someone he knows than by a complete stranger, horrible thought though it is." Gabriel paused to take a long drink of water, fighting back the thought that always entered his head at such a moment. If this was the case, Giovanna must have known her killer. *There are plenty of exceptions to the rule*, Gabriel tried to remind himself, forcing himself back to the case in hand. "The fact is, two things went wrong that morning. Charles was ill in bed so never left the house, and Antoine was in disgrace. Antoine had been banned from going to the scout camp as a punishment for bad behaviour earlier that week. The thing is that he had been too ashamed to tell anyone and had gone along to the scout camp anyway, hoping that the scoutmaster might relent and let him stay. The scoutmaster didn't, which is why poor Antoine arrived home in time to see the police swarming all over the house. The safe was open and empty; the scene bore all the hallmarks of a bungled burglary. It did look very much as though someone had entered the house, only to be confronted by Charles Nicholson."

"Was there any sign of a break-in?" asked Boniface. "A forced door, a broken window?"

"No, nothing of the sort. But of course there was no need for forced entry; the door—"

"The door was not locked. Of course." Boniface hesitated, and Gabriel could not work out whether the man's habit of placing a finger to his lips was an affectation to assure Gabriel that he was thinking very hard or an old habit. Whatever it was, he did look very contemplative as he pondered over the details, which did not seem so very substantial now that Gabriel had spoken them out loud. "What makes you think that it wasn't a burglary, other than the fact that it's unlikely anyone would rob a house in broad daylight in a small village?" asked Boniface sensibly.

"Isn't that reason enough?"

"Possibly," admitted Boniface, sitting back in his chair. "Quite possibly."

"I suppose there's just too much about all this that doesn't add up," said Gabriel with an air of frustration. "For a start, his family seem far more interested in a woman who died years before than the poor man who died in his own home less than forty-eight hours ago. That never happens; people *always* want to talk about the victim." Gabriel noted Boniface's blank expression. "The dead man's wife died during the war. A heroine by all accounts and purposes."

"I see. Poor child. The little boy, I mean."

"Indeed. But there's something else that feels wrong. When a victim's family talk to me, they are usually keen to give humanity the benefit of the doubt. Nobody wants to believe that his loved one was murdered; it's too horrible." Gabriel noticed that Boniface's intent expression had changed to something unbearably like pity, and he focused his attention on the whitewashed wall behind Boniface's head. "One wants to believe that it was a terrible accident. Even a moment of mad, blind rage, quickly regretted, is preferable to the thought of cold-blooded, premeditated murder."

"Yes, I can understand that," said Boniface in the small voice of a young man who knows perfectly well that he can understand no such thing.

"But in this case, those closest to Charles Nicholson seem very keen to have me believe that he was deliberately killed. Even the scoutmaster has said as much, and why should he want me to believe such a thing?"

To Gabriel's astonishment, Boniface gave him a mischievous grin. "That scoutmaster is the worst skipper I have ever seen!" he exclaimed, barely controlling a laugh. "He's been distracted all weekend. I had to step in to help twice when he wandered off."

Gabriel stood up decisively, causing Boniface to draw

back, momentarily alarmed that he had spoken out of turn. "He wandered off?"

"Well, yes," answered Boniface, with an air of apology. "At least, no one could find him. A fight would break out, or a scout would take a tumble or something, and the boys would come running to us for help. No one had a clue where Mr Harris was."

"The really clever ones always hide in plain sight, don't they?" remarked Gabriel before making for the door. He remembered his manners in the nick of time. "Thank you, Boniface."

Gabriel hurried back in the direction of the temporary camping ground. He should had known better than to walk away from Jack Harris when he was just warming to his subject. It was problematic having scruples about gossip and gossips when it came to sleuthing, as most valuable clues were almost invariably revealed that way. Gabriel should have asked more questions, probed a lot deeper into the reasons why a respectable scoutmaster should feel the need to blacken the name of a man not yet in his grave. It had been a costly error of judgement on Gabriel's part.

The camp had virtually disappeared from the grass, the last of the tents collapsed and folded away, and the scouts who had not yet left were walking the grounds in pairs, collecting any bits of rubbish that had blown about during the course of the weekend. The abbey grounds would be as clean and tidy within an hour as they had been before the scouts had arrived. Gabriel scanned the area for Jack Harris but could not immediately locate him. The man could not have gone home before the last of the scouts had left, but Gabriel's tendency to overthink matters made him wonder whether Jack Harris was now trying to give him the slip. Nonsense, of course; he was standing near a clump of trees, pointing up at the branches and talking to one of the scouts.

Gabriel drew nearer, sensing trouble, and noticed that there was a child in the tree, climbing towards a paper bag that had blown into the branches and lodged itself there. The scout in the tree was climbing perilously high in pursuit of the thing, and Gabriel's immediate thought was how irresponsible it was for an adult to send him up there in the first place. "That's really not necessary!" called Gabriel, hurrying towards Jack Harris. "It's only a paper bag. It'll blow down on its own, or the next shower of rain will see it off. Please tell that boy to get down!"

Jack laughed in a way that jarred Gabriel. Gabriel stood as close to the tree as he could, wondering whether he could catch the child or at least break his fall if he tumbled the twelve feet or so between the branch he was kneeling on and the ground. In fairness to Jack, the boy in question was clearly an experienced tree climber and clambered up through the branches with the litheness of an acrobat. Gabriel suspected that it had been the child's idea to go up there in the first place. "He's perfectly all right," Jack reassured Gabriel, with only the slightest hint of condescension. "He's like a monkey, always swinging from tree to tree."

Gabriel winced, noting the boy's caramel-coloured skin, which spoke of Gypsy ancestry. He hoped the monkey reference had been accidental but doubted it. "Mr Harris," Gabriel began, not daring to move his eyes from the boy in the tree, who, as Jack had stated so confidently, swung up onto a higher branch and snatched at the paper bag, to the cheers of the boys on the ground. "I wonder if I might ask you—"

"Scrunch it up and drop it to me," commanded Jack, apparently unaware that Gabriel had been talking to him. "There's a good lad."

"Here!" called the boy, scrunching the bag into a ball and dropping it as instructed.

It was Gabriel who caught it. "Well done!" he called without enthusiasm. "Mr Harris, you said—"

"Easy now, Ernie. It's harder coming down than going up."

"Mr Harris, why did you tell me . . ."

Gabriel's voice trailed off as Jack turned his back and moved away from the tree, ostensibly to give the climbing child space to descend without kicking anyone in the process but appearing as though he did not want to be drawn into another conversation with the priest. Gabriel sighed and made a discreet retreat. He had enough to go on for now, and he obeyed the chiming of the bell calling him to prayer.

9

Gabriel remembered in choir that he had meant to seek out Abbot Ambrose's counsel about Brigitte's war history. The thought pestered him as he struggled to focus his attention on the psalms they were chanting:

> Glory be to the Father,
> and to the Son,
> and to the Holy Ghost.
> As it was in the beginning,
> is now, and ever shall be,
> world without end . . .

Gabriel's questions would have to wait. They would go straight from Sext to the refectory for lunch, and Gabriel would have to rush to find the abbot before dashing off to tend to the monastic beehives. As the congregation sang a joyful hymn, Gabriel's thoughts turned from the question of Brigitte's George Cross to the awful thought that the bees might have been neglected in his absence. Had anyone kept an eye on them? Had anyone even remembered they were there? Gabriel comforted himself that bees were pretty good at making their collective presence felt if necessary, then rebuked himself for letting his mind wander.

> In all his words most wonderful,
> most sure in all his ways!

Gabriel calculated that Jack Harris was around Charles Nicholson's age, give or take a few years, but the two were certainly the same generation. If they had grown up in the same village, they would have known one another since they were children. As Gabriel had already had the misfortune to learn, childhood rivalries could become poisonous in adult life, and he had seen one such rivalry end in a murder, a poisoning, and an execution by hanging.

Charles Nicholson was no saint . . . but how many men truly were? How many men and women could be sure beyond reasonable doubt that they had not one enemy in the whole world? If the safe had been forced open and emptied as a decoy, Gabriel suspected that everything would become clear if he could only find the place where the Nicholson family's money and valuables had been hidden.

Gabriel was still meandering through the various lines of enquiry as he ate the last morsels of a lunch he had barely tasted. He did not notice the figure approaching him from behind and jumped out of his skin when a hand gently touched his shoulder, the violent shock causing him to give an unmanly whimper of pain. "Steady on, old man," said Dominic softly, "no need to go through the ceiling. You've a visitor waiting for you in the parlour."

Gabriel was not sure whether the police worked on bank holidays but assumed that Applegate never rested with a killer stalking the county. He would no doubt be waiting in the parlour with a cup of tea (and a biscuit if he was fortunate), ready to give Gabriel the latest information about the case. When Gabriel stepped into the parlour and saw Plantagenet sitting imperiously before him, it was as much as his life was worth to stifle his disappointment.

"Miss Nicholson, how nice to see you," Gabriel managed

by way of greeting. He noted on closer inspection that Plantagenet was red in the face and breathing a little laboriously as though she had been running, which seemed unlikely. A lightbulb lit up in Gabriel's head. "Miss Nicholson, have you travelled here by bicycle?"

"Your bicycle," she answered with an air of pride. "I'm sorry I was not able to return it as quickly as promised, but I gather that you have been somewhat indisposed yourself."

That's one way of putting it, thought Gabriel, casting aside the memory of a rumbling engine bearing down on him and the ghastly crunch of Father Foley's bike crumpling beneath him. "Indeed. I have only just returned to the abbey."

"I trust that you are well recovered?"

Gabriel ignored the mild throbbing across his torso. "Very much so, thank you. I'm grateful for the return of the bicycle. I am in need of one just at the moment."

Plantagenet smiled good-naturedly before rising to her feet. "Well, I should not keep you. I suppose you have a lot of praying to do."

Gabriel, who had never been well versed in the art of the delaying tactic, stood between Plantagenet and the door, smiling awkwardly as an idea came to mind. "Oh, Miss Nicholson, you must at least allow me to get you a cup of tea. You've cycled ever such a long way."

"It's not such a long way, really," Plantagenet assured Gabriel, stepping sideways, only to find that Gabriel was still in the way. "I'm as fit as a fiddle."

"How are you going to get home?"

"I shall catch a bus home," said Plantagenet, "or I may walk. It's a pleasant enough day, and the exercise will help me to clear my head."

Gabriel gave up trying to stall for time and opened the

door for Plantagenet before he could be accused of kidnap. "Let me ask for the car. I can't bear to think of you walking all that way after doing me such a kindness."

Before Plantagenet could protest, Gabriel had glanced down the corridor to see whether there was anyone he could press-gang into helping. He was in luck and began waving frantically at Dominic, who strolled over to him without demur. "What are you doing, Gabriel?" he asked amiably. "Would you like me to fetch some tea?"

"No, no, Miss Nicholson needs to get home, and I need to ask Father Abbot for use of the car. Do you suppose you might . . ."

Dominic gave a wry smile. "Why don't you show your visitor the broad beans, and I'll sort everything out."

Dominic was either just the right or just the wrong person to send on such an errand, thought Gabriel as he watched him limping back along the corridor until he disappeared up the stairs. He would be ages wending his way to Abbot Ambrose's study and another age finding Gerard to tell him to bring the car round. If Plantagenet proved to be talkative, the time would be well used; if she did not feel cooperative, he was in for an unbearably uncomfortable walk around the garden.

Fortunately, Plantagenet was amenable to a little stroll in the monastic gardens and walked alongside Gabriel without protest. "I must say, it is very peaceful," she remarked, surveying the scene with evident satisfaction. "I imagine that one could be quite content in such a place. One has solitude and companionship at the same time."

"Do you enjoy solitude?" asked Gabriel, immediately wondering whether he was going to regret the direct approach.

Plantagenet shrugged, as though the question was an irrelevance. "No man is an island, as Donne informs us," she said glibly, "but a woman may be an island if she so chooses. And I chose to be." Plantagenet glanced sidelong at Gabriel. "Oh, I know what you're thinking. There are plenty of old maids my age and all that, but I never felt the slightest desire to place myself under the thumb of some snivelling male."

"I see," said Gabriel as diplomatically as he could manage. He adjusted his initial image of a heartbroken girl at a railway station, waving off a dashing young officer in khaki as he left for the trenches. He was now seeing a small, green-scaled dragon roaring flames of female indignation whilst every male within a radius of five miles ran for cover. "You are very independent."

"I was blessed to have the choice," responded Plantagenet. "My father made his money out in Malaya, had a rubber plantation. I came of age with a large legacy, an education, and a penchant for my own company."

Plantagenet walked several steps ahead of Gabriel, as though she had walked around this garden hundreds of times and was perfectly at home. There was something about her aristocratic manner that made Gabriel think of the Duchess from *Alice in Wonderland*: *"He only does it to annoy, because he knows it teases . . ."* "Miss Nicholson, why did you not tell me that you had travelled to France to find out what had happened to your sister-in-law?"

Plantagenet stopped abruptly and snapped round to face Gabriel like a sergeant major inspecting his unsatisfactory troops. "Because it was none of your business, Father, if you'll forgive me. You are not the police. I was not obliged to tell you anything. What can it matter that I travelled to France? It was a natural enough thing to do."

"Of course it was," said Gabriel quickly. "Your beloved sister-in-law died in France. It was absolutely right that you should have wanted to find out what had happened to her."

Plantagenet turned away, clasping her hands neatly behind her back. "She died, Father. That much we knew. And we knew it could not have been an easy death either. It might have been best if I had let sleeping dogs lie. There was nothing my travels could have told me that I did not already know."

"It was laudable of you to try to find out what had happened," said Gabriel, following Plantagenet as she walked in the direction of the orchard. She seemed to be deliberately trying to move as far away from the abbey building as possible. "You owed it to her memory to discover the truth."

Plantagenet looked back at Gabriel, and he could not be sure whether she was disgusted with him or with herself. "Father, Brigitte did not return to France under her own steam. She was trained by the Special Operations Executive. That was one thing I found out."

"Does it make any difference?" asked Gabriel.

"Only in that the Germans knew she was coming," said Plantagenet. "They were watching her from the moment she landed. She did not last long at all before they captured her. They knew she was a spy; they knew she was working for the British. Someone told them she was coming."

Gabriel shuddered. He remembered Dr Paige talking about the day Marie had been betrayed to the Gestapo by her best friend. Betrayal was the sin reserved for the deepest circle of Dante's hell; it was the kiss of Judas Iscariot echoing across time. "I suppose everyone who was captured must have been betrayed by someone."

Plantagenet leant forwards, placing her face a little too close to Gabriel's for comfort. "Don't you understand, Father? If Brigitte was in the SOE, she would have been forbidden to speak of it. The only other person who knew she was going was her husband. SOE personnel were not permitted to tell anyone other than their spouses—not their parents, not their children, not their closest friends. That was why I knew Charles had betrayed her, even though I found it hard to believe. He was the only person who could have done it."

Gabriel took a moment to process the information. In a discussion about the "dirty war" he once had with a murder suspect, he had learned that the SOE's work was so dangerous that it was kept strictly confidential. It was unlikely that Brigitte had told her husband about the details of her work. Gabriel decided to take a risk and say as much. "She may not even have told Charles," said Gabriel. "If she really was working for the SOE, it's likely that only her minders, or whatever they're called, would have known where she was going. And it's unlikely you'll ever find out who they were."

"She told Charles everything!" Plantagenet persisted, but she was already speaking with a hint of uncertainty. "They were inseparable, Father. She never made any decision without discussing it with him first." Her expression clouded at her own unfortunate choice of words. "Well, I suppose they weren't so inseparable, because she went away from him." Plantagenet shook her head violently. "No one else knew! None of us knew. It came as a complete shock to everyone. We all thought—me, my father, all our friends, even little Antoine—that Brigitte's journey had been a personal crusade against the Germans. It's the sort of thing she would have done. Brigitte *contra mundum*!" Plantagenet brought a hand up to her mouth, but she was unable to suppress the choking sound in time and turned away. "We used to call her Joan of Arc, she was so determined . . . so French, I suppose."

"If she returned to her people in France, any one of them might have given her away by accident. It must have been easy enough to do. A careless word here or there."

But Plantagenet was still shaking her head. "You don't understand, Father. My decision to trace her family was a mistake. She never went anywhere near them when she returned to France. They knew about her work only when the Germans murdered her in the middle of her hometown, *pour encourager les autres*. She must have been terrified of incriminating them; she must have known it might raise questions if she suddenly appeared in the neighbourhood she'd left years before."

They were standing near a cherry tree, and Gabriel watched as Plantagenet picked out the leaves and blossoms at the end of a low-hanging branch, working with a strange thoroughness as though she had been tasked with the job of stripping the branch bare. "You know, Father, part of me was almost glad that Brigitte had not lived to see what happened to her country when the Germans were finally driven out. It was a wasteland. Most of her family were dead. They had . . ." More tiny leaves and blossoms were torn from their life source and fluttered to the ground. Gabriel knew that Plantagenet was crying but did not attempt to approach her, knowing it would only infuriate the woman. "Her sister, her brother-in-law, and all their children were killed trying to flee the city. They said the Luftwaffe bombed the refugee columns. So many dreadful things happened during the war, but I cannot imagine how a pilot could do that. Brigitte's aunt told me that she saw the planes flying low over the heads of all those people—women pushing perambulators, old ladies walking along the road with their grandchildren—and they opened fire as though they were playing a game. What did any of those innocents do to deserve to be slaughtered like that?"

It was the same question that was being asked by so many people around the world, but Gabriel knew that there was no easy answer. Every question about the war was really the same question phrased a little differently, depending upon the experience of the questioner: Why were women and children gunned down in those refugee columns? Why were Jews forced onto trains to die in the gas chambers? Why did people burn in the Coventry blitz? Why were millions of blameless people starved, tortured, bombed, shot, gassed, burnt, obliterated? *Why?*

"That was the evil Brigitte went back to France to fight," said Gabriel. "Perhaps it helps you to understand why she did it. Gave up everything, I mean."

Plantagenet nodded wearily. "Oh yes, I can understand why she wanted to fight. I hope I might have done the same if England had been invaded." She stamped her foot into the soil in an almost petulant gesture. "But she was never given the chance to fight! Not really. They came for her! And since the organisation that sent her out there is so secretive, I'm not supposed to know it exists. I can never find out who it was who betrayed her. If it was not Charles, it was one of the men who sent her to France. The SOE may well have had double agents in their midst."

Gabriel fought against the sense that he was walking into a brick wall again. Plantagenet had a point, of course. The trouble with spies is that they are by definition unreliable. It is the role of the undercover agent to deceive, and Brigitte would have had no reason to doubt her own comrades, her mentors, the shadowy team—both men and women—who trained people like her in the art of cloak-and-dagger warfare. "Brother Gerard should have the car ready for us by now," said Gabriel. "Why don't we get you home."

Gabriel noticed, with some relief, that Gerard drove a good deal more carefully with Plantagenet in the car, either because she was a lady or because she was an outsider; he felt the need to behave in much the same way that a man might put on his Sunday manners for a stranger and then immediately play an outrageous prank on his own family.

It was the only pleasant reflection Gabriel could make about the whole sorry journey, apart from its brevity. Plantagenet spent much of the journey lost in thought, gazing out the window as though she was still thinking about the stories she had been told in France, or perhaps she was still weighing up the question of who had betrayed her sister-in-law. It occurred to Gabriel that she might be feeling the first pangs of guilt that she had accused her own brother of such a heinous crime and allowed herself to become estranged from him. There might be an opportunity to discuss that with her one day, but this was clearly not the time.

Plantagenet came to life only as they neared the village and she was obliged to give Gerard directions to her house. The landmarks of Dilton Wylye were already becoming familiar to Gabriel, and he recognised Terry, the landlord's son, standing a little furtively outside the pub, the stub of a cigarette in one hand. Gabriel was not sure why Terry should be so nervous about his parents seeing him smoking, as Gabriel was sure he had seen Terry's father lighting up a pipe when he had accompanied Roland Nicholson to the pub the other night. Then again, men could be inconsistent when it came to their children's behaviour.

"Gerry, can you stop a minute?" asked Gabriel suddenly. "Could you drop me off here?"

Gerard slammed on the brakes. "Here?"

"Yes, just here, please," Gabriel confirmed, opening the door and jumping out before he could change his mind. "Take Miss Nicholson home."

"What about you?" demanded Gerard. "I can't tell Father Abbot I've mislaid you again!"

"I'll find my own way home; don't worry," promised Gabriel, dashing in Terry's direction before either Gerard or Plantagenet could demand an explanation. Terry's look of panic when he saw Gabriel hurrying towards him was enough to confirm to Gabriel that he had not been mistaken. "Terry!" he called as the boy made a mad rush for a blue-painted van.

Gabriel had anticipated Terry's escape attempt and cut across his path, reaching the driver's door before the young man could clamber in. "Get outta me way!" shouted Terry, trying to push past Gabriel, but Gabriel was as immovable as a tree trunk. "I got me deliveries to make."

"It looks as though your van could do with some attention before you go driving around the countryside," Gabriel retorted, planting a hand against Terry's chest and pushing him lightly but firmly in the direction of the front of the van. "The bodywork looks a little the worse for wear."

Terry glanced in the direction of Gabriel's accusing finger as Gabriel trembled at the memory of this very vehicle bearing down on him. In broad daylight and perfect safety, the van did not look nearly as large and ominous as it had on that dark, lonely road, but Gabriel would have known by sensory memory alone that this was the van that had driven him into a ditch. Not that he needed his memory. The van was lovingly cared for, the paintwork in pristine condition, except for a deep dent in the metalwork between the headlights and an ugly smudge where black lines and tiny flecks of black paint had become embedded in the blue coating. The black of Gabriel's wrecked bicycle. If he had placed the twisted remains of his bike in the dent, Gabriel was certain they would have fitted perfectly.

"I hit a lamppost late last night," Terry ventured, his eyes fixed on the damage to the van. Gabriel could see where Terry had attempted to cover up the scratches on the paintwork by covering them with mud, but in the warm weather the mud had dried and crumbled off, leaving only a faint residue. "Look, don't tell me dad—or the bobbies. I'd had a skinful. I wasn't likely looking where I were going."

Gabriel leant forwards and touched the dented bodywork. "That was never a lamppost," he said, a great deal more confidently than he felt. "The dent is too narrow for a collision with a lamppost, and the way it tapers suggests that you hit a moving object, not a stationary one."

Terry took one mortified look at Gabriel and made another attempt at getting back into the van, presumably to drive off somewhere and hide, but Gabriel grabbed him by the arm and frog-marched him into the pub, in a manner that would have been comical if the boy were not facing an attempted murder charge. The fact was, Gabriel had no idea whether the dent in the van was indeed too narrow to have been made by a collision with a lamppost, and he had made an educated guess about the rest; but Terry had made no attempt to stand by his story. More than that, Terry was too shocked to put up much resistance, which was fortunate for Gabriel, who was not used to using brute force in any situation. In any event, he was wincing in pain himself as his recent injuries began shouting at him to stop moving.

"Will you get off of me!" pleaded Terry in a whining tone, shaking himself free of Gabriel's grasp as soon as they were in the pub. "I can explain everything! Please, please don't tell me dad about this."

"If you end up in the nick, he's going to have to know about it," answered Gabriel, signalling to Terry to step into the snug so that they could speak undisturbed and unobserved. "Listen, son, I'm not about to go running to the police to get you locked up. I survived, and I don't think you'll ever try anything quite that stupid again. But I need you to be completely honest with me about why you tried to hit me the other night."

Terry sat down at the table, nodding frantically. "I can tell you everything. It's not so bad as it sounds. There's not even very much to tell."

Gabriel sat opposite Terry and leant back in his chair in the hope that it might help Terry to relax. It appeared to have the opposite effect, as Terry shrank back from Gabriel as though he were facing an outwardly calm interrogator who might pounce on him at any moment. "Just tell me why you did it, Terry. I think I have a right to know why you tried to kill me."

"I weren't exactly trying to kill you," Terry wheedled, "just trying to get you out the way."

"You ran into me, knocked me into a stone-lined ditch and left me for dead."

Terry was swirling his long fringe around his fingers, a habit that only made Gabriel want to tell him to get his hair cut. "I just wanted to give you a scare."

"You did. Why?"

Terry was many things, Gabriel suspected, but "as cunning as a fox" was not a simile with which he would ever be burdened. It took an inordinately long time for him to answer. "Old Man Nicholson's a good sort; the three of 'em were decent sorts. They never hurt no one, just looked after one another. We used to call them the Three Musketeers. Now one of them's dead, and Old Man Nicholson's all alone. Everyone's so upset about it. They didn't deserve this."

So far so good, thought Gabriel, *but you haven't even tried to answer my question*. "I can only imagine how distressed everyone is. No one deserves that family's fate. Why did you knock me off my bike, Terry?"

Terry was rocking back and forth now, his chair making a maddening creaking noise with every movement. "I overheard you asking the poor man questions. He were upset; you needed to leave him alone, and you wouldn't. I just wanted to get you out of his hair. Folk like you always turn up, poking your noses in when something bad happens. It ain't right. You're not the police. You should've left him alone."

Gabriel nodded, taking in the information. "I quite understand your feelings, Terry," he said finally. "Now who told you to run me off the road?"

Terry looked up at Gabriel, his eyes darting to the door as though he expected someone to come in and rescue him. The door remained sullenly closed. "No one. I don't know what you can mean. Why would anyone ask me to do that?"

"You tell me. You can tell me, or you can tell that nice Inspector Applegate." Gabriel hated threatening the boy with the police; it felt a bit too much like a prefect threatening a miscreant with the headmaster. "But unlike the inspector, I can't arrest you."

"You can have me arrested, though," Terry pointed out, reasonably enough. "You will, won't you?"

"It doesn't have to come to that," said Gabriel calmly. "I'm not the police, but I need you to tell me the truth."

Terry squirmed in his chair. There was a battle going on inside him with which Gabriel could not interfere, and his answer when it came was so quiet, Gabriel had to lean forwards to hear him. "He's not a nice man to cross," whispered Terry. "He knows everyone hereabouts. He could get us turned out of the pub tomorrow; we could lose everything. As it is, I might be in trouble because I didn't finish you off proper."

"Terry, who is this man?" Gabriel felt his heart fluttering. This was the moment when the beam over their heads ought to come crashing down, crushing Terry and silencing him forever. "Terry, his name? I can't help you if you don't tell me."

Terry moved forwards so that their heads were virtually touching before whispering in Gabriel's ear, "Jack Harris."

Gabriel jolted back as though he had received an electric shock. He was really not sure which name he had expected to come from Terry's mouth, but Jack Harris had not been at the top of the list. "The scoutmaster? But he's been camping at the abbey all weekend!" *He has not*, Gabriel suddenly thought, remembering his conversation with Boniface. *He was missing repeatedly, if Boniface is to be trusted, and I have no reason to doubt his word*.

Terry shook his head miserably. "Nobody's supposed to know. Harris likes his drink; he's been like that since the war. He don't come in the pub; he comes round the back to buy his booze. He don't want to lose his position, see."

Of course Gabriel could see. If Jack Harris were known to be an alcoholic, he would hardly be seen as a good role model for young boys. Gabriel remembered his first encounter with the tanned, confident scoutmaster. *Peppermints, and I had thought he was hiding his choice of tobacco*. He looked at Terry. "But how could he have found his way here? It's five miles away from the campsite!"

"He came on his motorbike," said Terry. "He said he were only popping back 'cause some kid had been taken ill, but could he have a quickie since his nerves were shot. Then . . ." Terry had stopped rocking back and forth and was picking viciously at a scab on the back of his hand, which Gabriel found unbearable to watch. The next words came out in a rush of panic and embarrassment. "He said there was some idiot monk who thought he was Sherlock Holmes who needed knocking off his perch."

Gabriel told himself that the insult was irrelevant, but the thought of Jack Harris' charming conversation rankled.

Rudeness was unfortunate; hypocrisy was unconscionable. "You didn't have to do it."

Terry was sweating profusely. The scab on his hand had detached itself, and a large bead of blood had taken its place. "I did have to do it, Father. I told you, he'd have ruined us."

"Terry, he was the one with the secret. Surely it was the other way round? Oh Terry . . ." The man did not need to explain anything else; it was glaringly obvious what he had done. "The alcohol you supply to Mr Harris is black market. Black market or worse."

Terry nodded. "Ay. Father, me parents don't know about it. I've a mate who supplies me. I said to Mr Harris that I'd tell the police that he were buying the stuff, but he said they'd not believe me, but they'd believe him if he pointed the finger at me."

"It was you who rescued me, wasn't it? You lost your nerve."

Terry brought his hand to his face, but it was too late; a sob escaped him, then another and another. "It didn't seem so bad until I were out there on the road! But after I'd drove off, I kept hearing your screams as you fell."

How embarrassing; I don't remember screaming like a girl, thought Gabriel, blushing, but Terry's distress was overwhelming. "It's all right, son. Here's what you need to—"

"I couldn't leave you out there to die! I just couldn't!" wailed Terry. "I drove home and walked all the way out so's it would look as if I'd found you by accident. I made sure you was safe and scarpered before anyone could recognise me. I'm . . . I'm sorry!"

"Terry, listen to me," said Gabriel, a little more sharply than he had intended, but he needed Terry's cooperation as a matter of urgency. "Terry, you have to pull yourself together; this is very important." He handed Terry a handkerchief, which he accepted gratefully, blowing his nose with such enthusiasm that Gabriel was determined never to touch the piece of fabric again. "You need to do a little spring cleaning. Understand?" Terry nodded. "I know you regret what happened out on that road, and I don't want to see you get into any trouble; but I need to talk to Jack Harris, and there's no way I will be able to keep the police away from you. You and Jack are too entangled with one another's business for that. Spring-clean your room, get your affairs in order, then make an excuse to your parents and clear off for a few days."

Terry blew his nose again, with all the delicacy of an elephant in its death throes. "Where am I supposed to go?"

Gabriel got to his feet. "Use your imagination! Tell your parents whatever you think they'll believe and live in a ditch for a week if you have to. Anything will be more comfortable than the nick."

10

Gabriel had no idea how many crimes or—more important—sins he had just committed. He would have to seek the good counsel of Abbot Ambrose before the day was out, but his first concern was to alert Applegate to the new developments without implicating Terry if it could be avoided. Gabriel had no sympathy for black marketers who had profited and continued to profit from the country's hardship, but he had meant it when he had said that he had no desire to see a young man go to prison with hard labour either.

There was no particular malice in a boy like Terry. Like so many young men finding their way in the adult world, he must have grown up in the shadow of a father who had fought in the trenches and come home broken and unsuited to a quiet family life. Terry might have developed a weak character and become susceptible to the threats and enticements of more serious criminals, but Gabriel doubted that a brush with the police would do much to help him. Gabriel hoped that the shock of being found out would be enough to start the lad on the right path, but he endeavoured to keep an eye on Terry in future, to see whether there was anything he could do to help him.

Gabriel set out on the long road to the abbey, stopping as soon as he came to a red telephone box. At least this time he had had the presence of mind to come out with a handful of coins in case of an emergency, just enough to put a quick call through to the constabulary. He stepped inside with a sense of relief, picking up the receiver with a quiet prayer that Applegate would be in the building when he rang. However long it took Gabriel to get back to the abbey, Applegate could get there much faster in his car.

The phone seemed to ring for an inordinate amount of time without an answer, and Gabriel found himself staring through the glass panels of the box, hoping that no one was going past. Telephone boxes were designed to give the impression of privacy, but he knew he could be seen from all angles by anyone walking or riding past. There was a click and a voice reciting the telephone number of the constabulary. "I need to speak to Inspector Applegate urgently," said Gabriel quickly. "It's—"

"Oh hello, Father Gabriel," came the friendly, lilting tones of PC Stevens. "'Fraid he's not here. Can I—"

"Tell him he must come to the abbey immediately. He needs to talk to Jack Harris."

"Sorry, did you say the abbey? Why would Jack Harris be at the abbey?" Gabriel could hear the pips sounding already, warning him that he was about to run out of money. He did not want to put another coin in the slot if he could avoid it, but telephone calls were always more expensive than he expected them to be. "Yes, he's at the scout camp packing up, but the inspector must go straightaway. If he's not quick, he may be too late."

The pips sounded again. Gabriel made a quick judgement, told himself that Stevens had understood what he meant and hung up the phone. He left the stuffy interior of the telephone box and carried on his way along the wide, winding road back to Sutton Westford. At least it was a bright, warm day. The walk would have been a pleasant one if Gabriel had not been in so much of a hurry. He walked past a farm that had had a busy lambing season this year, as Gabriel could hear a chorus of bleating before he had turned the corner to see the little white figures dotted about the long grass.

Gabriel felt guilty for being such a sentimental Londoner, but part of him quailed at the thought of those adorable fluffy lambs turning into tomorrow's mutton stew. A few farm labourers attended Mass at the abbey, and he had made the mistake of expressing his misgivings on the subject on one occasion. "You wouldna think 'em so sweet if you'd got kicked a few times," one old shepherd had said with a laugh. "They can be awfully stubborn when they want to be. The shepherd in the scriptures wouldna need to lead the lost sheep home; he'd a dragged the little blighter every step of the way."

It had been that shepherd who had told Gabriel that Jesus was rightly called a lamb because sheep have an instinct to remain passively silent, even when they are being slaughtered. It made it easier for the farmers that they did not squeal like pigs under the butcher's knife or run around squawking like chickens. According to this shepherd, anyone who wanted to understand the scriptures at all should spend a week on his farm, not three years at some poncy university.

Gabriel flinched at the sound of an engine roaring and stuttering behind him. *It's only a car!* he thought, drawing a long, deep breath to steady his nerves, but he moved back from the road until he was pressed against the hedgerow, just in case. There was nothing to worry about. Speeding along the road came a man on an old army motorbike, his face partially concealed by helmet and goggles.

As soon as the rider glanced in Gabriel's direction, he began to slow down, coming to a halt as soon as he was level with Gabriel. "You going to the abbey?" shouted the man over the rumble of the idling engine. "You've a fair way to walk. Hop on!"

It had been difficult to see who the young man was, but Gabriel remembered where he had seen the motorbike before and recognised the owner as the son of Sutton Westford's most morose landlady. Gabriel was too embarrassed to admit that he was terrified of getting on the back of such a machine, but he told himself that it could not be much harder than sitting aboard a bicycle. "Are you sure?" he asked, clambering behind the rider and placing his arms awkwardly around the man's waist. It might even be easier than a bicycle since he did not actually have to do anything.

"Hold on to your hat, Friar Tuck!" called the rider. "Here we go!"

The engine revved, and they were racing along, tilting left and right as the expert rider negotiated the winding road. Gabriel felt beyond terrified, shaken to the core . . . then strangely exhilarated. He had no idea how fast they were going. It was a long time since he had experienced such a glorious sense of speed, and he gasped as the rush of cold air struck his face and head. The last time he had ridden on a machine like this had been shortly after his arrival in Flanders, and the ride had not been pleasant. He and his fellow soldiers had bounced and skidded across the shell-pocked terrain in the direction of the Front, through a man-made wasteland of burnt trees and barren, mud-clogged roads. His current excursion was motorbiking as it was meant to happen.

"This is wonderful!" shouted Gabriel, the last of his fears dissolving as the two men thundered down a long, straight stretch of road, looping past a bus as it crept round the villages in a long, lazy circuit. He wondered whether he could ever persuade Abbot Ambrose to invest in such a contraption. Gabriel was sure there must be plenty of redundant army motorbikes kicking around, just looking for a new owner . . .

All too soon, they were slowing down as they entered Sutton Westford, trundling along the high street, past Reggie's shop and on to the boarding house where the rider lived. It was only as they were slowing down to stop that Gabriel became aware of the disapproving glares of passersby, and he realised that a monk on a motorbike was beyond the pale for the inhabitants of this Wiltshire village. The purchase of a monastic motorbike would have to wait for now.

To his dismay, Gabriel could barely stand once he had alighted the motorbike. There were sharp cramps creeping along his feet and up his legs, and the sensation of jolting along a rough road had set off his other aches and pains. Gabriel managed to stand up straight long enough to shake hands with the rider. "Thank you, young man," he said breathlessly, "that was awfully decent of you."

The young man took off his headgear and grinned back at Gabriel. "No problem at all, it would have taken you ages to walk all that way. She's a fine motor, isn't she? American."

"It's a very fine beast," Gabriel agreed, pretending to inspect the wheels. Gerard would have been in his element.

"Sorry I didn't take you all the way home. I'm getting a bit short of juice."

Gabriel assured the young man that it was no trouble, pressing his feet firmly into the ground as he walked away to dispel the pins and needles that had started to plague him. Gabriel was not awfully sure how Abbot Ambrose would have felt if the silence of the monastic gardens had been wrecked by the infernal roar of a Harley Davidson. It was probably for the best that he had been dropped off some distance away from the abbey and could walk innocently across the fields and up the hill without anyone noticing.

The abbey grounds were as clean as a whistle by the time Gabriel arrived home, with not a hint of a sweetie wrapper or tent peg in sight. The pervading quiet made it clear that the scouts had all left for their homes, hot baths, and dinners, but Gabriel scanned the grounds in the vague hope that Jack Harris might not yet have left.

Better still, he hoped that Applegate had found his way to the abbey as the advanced party, and Gabriel entered the abbey grounds from the wrong direction to see whether there was a car parked at the entrance. Sneaking inside through a side door inevitably took Gabriel back to his schooldays, but it always felt like the safer option when he had been detained outside longer than he had intended. It was pretty futile to hope that no one had noticed his absence, all things considered, but Gabriel was a master in the art of wishful thinking.

"Where have you been?" demanded a voice that hailed from rainy Lancashire, making Gabriel jump. Gerard was striding down the corridor towards him, looking fit to be tied. "Have you any idea what Father Abbot had to say to me when I arrived home without you?"

"You could hardly have glued me to the seat," said Gabriel. "It was my fault, not yours."

"Tell that to Father Abbot!" cried Gerard indignantly. "I told him how you'd jumped out of the car and done a little walk into the sunset, but he told me to stop making excuses." Gerard gave an unmanly sigh and made a halfhearted attempt at a smile. "Anyway, you can face him later. Your mate Inspector Appleface is in the parlour with the scoutmaster. He said to tell you to join them as soon as I found you."

Gabriel gave a little skip of relief and hurried in the direction of the parlour, smoothing over his windswept hair as he went. For some reason, he suspected that Applegate would find his motorcycle adventure absolutely hilarious, and he had no intention of drawing attention to it. The door to the parlour was closed, and Gabriel could hear no sounds of raised voices within, which he took as a bad sign. Now that he was standing outside the door, Gabriel began to wonder whether the apparent peace in the room, and Applegate's failure to take Jack Harris directly to the constabulary, might be a sign that Applegate was unconvinced by Gabriel's suspicions. It was too late to worry about that now. Gabriel knocked three times before opening the door.

The scene inside looked like a disastrous attempt to bring the diplomats of two warring countries to the table. Both men wore thunderous expressions, neither of them moving when Gabriel stepped into the room. Jack's face had flushed so deeply that the shaving scar on his face almost glowed white on his skin. If Terry really was correct about Jack's drinking problems, the scoutmaster would be in a state of severe stress by now, in desperate need of Terry's black-market whisky to see him through the rest of the interview.

"I'm just having a little chat with your friend Mr Harris," said Applegate, without turning to look at Gabriel, "not that he seems very sociable today. Must be the exhaustion of the scout camp."

Jack swung round to glare at Gabriel. "If you've gone and told this idiot that I killed Charles Nicholson, I'll have you up on a charge of slander. I was nowhere near the scene of the murder. I was here, in your abbey grounds, surrounded by dozens of witnesses."

"I didn't tell the inspector that you were the killer. I merely said that he needed to speak to you," said Gabriel gently. "But your alibi is not as watertight as you seem to think it is. In a busy environment, it is easy to slip away, especially if your little witnesses imagined that you were elsewhere in the grounds when they went off on their expeditions. And I have just been given a ride on a motorcycle that proved to me how quickly a man can travel from one village to the next on two motorised wheels." Jack started, but Gabriel ignored his look of silent fury. "You could quite easily have travelled between the camp and Dilton Wylye in that time, and in your helmet and goggles, it is unlikely that anyone could have identified you."

Jack lurched to his feet. He managed to control himself almost immediately, but the sudden upward movement had given away his unsteadiness. Applegate got up a moment later, positioning himself strategically between Jack and Gabriel. "Why should I have wanted to kill Charles Nicholson?" demanded Jack, sounding as though the thought disgusted him, not so much because there was something morally wrong with killing a man in cold blood but because it was ill-mannered. "I might as well say I didn't like the man. I'll admit it before you go weaseling it out of people, but no one bashes a man over the head because he gets on his nerves!"

"I never said he was bashed over the head," said Gabriel slowly.

"It's common knowledge by now; everyone's talking about it!" blustered Jack, but he had realised his mistake. "Look, news travels fast in these parts."

"You've been tucked away at the abbey all this time; how could you have heard the details?" asked Applegate, causing Jack to turn to Gabriel as the apparently less threatening interrogator.

"I'm sure I heard one of the boys say something—" Jack was cornered, and it had not even been difficult. "I didn't do it! I was here all weekend. You can ask any of the boys, and they'll tell you!"

"As I've said, I'm sure they will be good boys and tell me that you were here, because not one of them has reason to suspect that you would have gone anywhere else," Gabriel responded. "Why did you tell Terry to run me off the road, Mr Harris?"

Gabriel was not sure afterwards which man looked the more astonished, the sweating, panic-stricken Jack or the characteristically confused Applegate. The last observation was unfair; Gabriel was pretty sure that Applegate only ever looked so bewildered in his presence. "Gabriel, where did you get that from?" asked Applegate, his focus on Jack's strangled reaction. "Mr Harris, is there something you need to tell me?"

Jack was gasping horribly with what sounded like rage. "The man's a bloody liar if he told you that! He's a liar, he's a thief, he's nothing better than a common spiv!"

"I found the evidence on the front of his delivery van," said Gabriel, "which spoke to me eloquently enough, even with poor Terry having tried to hide the marks. Why did you do it?"

Jack collapsed back into his chair. "I didn't. I told you. The man's a damned buffoon, filling his pockets with food and booze while the country goes hungry."

"You're the one filling his pockets, Mr Harris."

"Just a moment, are you saying that this individual is selling alcohol on the black market?" demanded Applegate, his hackles rising. No policeman liked to discover that there was dirty dealing going on under his nose, though it could hardly have been much of a surprise. Farmers eked out a poor living, even from land as fertile as that of the Wiltshire countryside, and the lure of the easy money offered by spivs must have been overwhelming for some. But black-market alcohol was more serious than a few pounds of sausages slipped under the table. If it were home brew, it threatened madness, blindness, even death. "Mr Harris, what precisely is your part in all this?"

"Inspector, I'm an alcoholic!" thundered Jack. "Do I have to spell it out to you? I am an alcoholic; but I am not a murderer, and that's all there is to it." He turned to Gabriel, the scar drawing an incriminating line on his cheek. "I told Terry to give you a scare, to put you off. I didn't tell him to do you any harm, I swear. I just knew that if you asked enough questions, you'd find out about the secret I was hiding." Jack looked down at his hands, which were raw and blistered from a weekend of putting up tents and taking part in tug-of-war contests. Scouting was his life, and if he were arrested, it would spell the end of everything; he would never be trusted with the welfare of children again. "That's the truth, Father. Take it or leave it."

Gabriel pulled up a chair and sat next to Jack. "I'll leave it, if it's all the same to you." Gabriel deliberately looked at the opposite wall to avoid making direct eye contact with Jack, but he could see the man glaring at him, willing him to say nothing further. "You have a far greater secret than your furtive trips to Terry. You and Charles Nicholson are around the same age, and you grew up in the same village. Yet not only did you show no distress whatsoever when you found out that he had been murdered, but you thought it acceptable to speak ill of the dead man before he was even in his grave."

Jack made an undignified dash for the door but was deftly intercepted by Applegate, who manoeuvred him back into his seat. "I will not be held here against my will!" roared Jack, struggling ludicrously whilst Applegate leant on him, trapping him in his seat. "I want to speak to my solicitor!"

"I'm more than happy to read you your rights, put the cuffs on and march you out of here under arrest if that's what you prefer, Mr. Harris," said Applegate testily, "but it might be a little less humiliating for you to talk about this over a cup of tea. It's entirely up to you."

"You can't arrest me! I didn't do it!"

"Mr. Harris, I have enough evidence to arrest you for your involvement in the black market and for your part in the attempted murder of a Catholic priest. As to a possible murder charge for the death of Charles Nicholson, you will have to do a little better in court than stamp your foot and shout 'I didn't do it.'"

Jack turned back to regard them both, and Gabriel knew he was weighing up the relative risks of staying to talk to them or making a run for it. In the end, common sense won out, and he sank back, showing all the grace of a defeated schoolboy. "I'm sorry about your accident," he said tersely, "but when amateur detectives start poking their noses into everything, all sorts of secrets come out. My bad habits had nothing to do with the case."

"Your past bad habits might," answered Gabriel, matching Jack's tone. "That scar on your face was not caused by a slip of the razor. It's too jagged to have been caused by anything as sharp as a razor blade, and it looks a little too high up on your face."

Jack touched his scar reflexively. "It's an old scar, and it's none of your business how I came by it," he said emphatically.

"It certainly is an old scar, as the woman who inflicted it is long dead. Charles Nicholson may have forgiven you for assaulting his wife, but you never forgave him for being Brigitte's husband."

Jack threw his hands up as though expecting to have to defend himself. "I barely touched her!" he protested. "She . . . she gave every impression of wanting my attention!"

"Men always say that," Applegate chimed in, with the bitter experience of dealing with years of rape cases. "She was a married woman."

"She was French," Jack spat back. "They do things differently, all right? All she need have said was 'Go away,' and I would have left her alone. Instead, the claws came out."

Gabriel winced, then prayed that no one had noticed. He imagined that Brigitte had been quite like Giovanna in temperament, and Gabriel was certain that Giovanna must have fought off her attacker when it came to it, much good though it had done her. But it was equally possible that he tended to see Giovanna in every woman who had found herself a target of male aggression or lust. A much darker thought was impinging upon Gabriel's troubled mind, and he looked over at Applegate, wondering whether he had had the same idea. Applegate was giving nothing away, looking stonily at Jack as he squirmed in his chair. "Might I have a word in private, Inspector?"

Applegate got up without acknowledging the request, picked up his hat and followed Gabriel to the door, stopping only to address Jack briefly. "Don't do anything stupid," he instructed the man, who was sitting very still now, exuding an unsavoury combination of fear and self-pity. If he had any plans, it was not to make a dash for freedom.

A moment later, Applegate and Gabriel were standing in the echoing corridor, Applegate glaring at Gabriel, and Gabriel wondering what on earth he had done on this occasion to earn such a look. "How did you know about Jack Harris messing around with our murder victim's missus?" demanded Applegate in a stage whisper. "That scar could have been caused by anything—walking into low-hanging brambles, an awkward fall. What do you know?"

Gabriel realised his error. He had held back information from Applegate without intending to, but the inspector would never believe that such important information had just slipped Gabriel's mind. "Plantagenet Nicholson was telling me all about her dead sister-in-law, Brigitte, and what a gutsy character she was. She mentioned that a man had made a pass at her once, and instead of giving him a slap in the face, she'd gouged him with her fingernails. As soon as she said that, I knew exactly where that scar had come from. Jack Harris is a similar age to Charles: they would have grown up together in this village; he would have been a young man when Charles first brought his French bride home." Gabriel hesitated, wondering whether Applegate would be particularly interested in his speculations. He threw caution to the wind and continued. "Jack Harris strikes me as a rather egotistical gentleman. There's something about the way he carries himself—"

"Gabriel . . ." came the warning, always delivered with a mixture of annoyance and faint curiosity.

"I know, I know, it doesn't prove anything in itself, but I think you had better arrest him."

Applegate raised an eyebrow. "For murder?"

"No, for something you know he's already done. I need him locked up and out of the way for at least twenty-four hours." Gabriel glanced back towards the outdoors and the wide-open green space where the scouts had so innocently camped for two nights. "If you are discreet about it, no one need see. He deserves to hang on to his dignity for the moment."

"I'm loath to nick a pillar of the community, but there's plenty I can arrest him for," admitted Applegate. "I'll be as careful as possible, make it look as though he's just doing his civic duty by helping the police."

Gabriel gave a wry smile and walked away, leaving Applegate to make the arrest. Gabriel could not avoid the thought that, if Jack Harris had had a lowlier social status, Applegate would have done nothing to spare him the public humiliation of being frog-marched to the local nick in handcuffs. But Jack Harris was a pillar of the community. Jack Harris held a position of authority, and his reputation was too valuable to be harmed by his dalliances into the criminal underworld.

The bell began to chime, calling Gabriel to chapel. He had barely taken a step when he remembered that he had forgotten to ask Applegate a favour that could not wait. He cringed, watching as the other monks began to file into chapel, knowing that he could not possibly wait until after prayers to catch Applegate before he left.

Worse, he was going to have to face Jack Harris' anger when Gabriel's inner coward would have done virtually anything to avoid going near the man again—especially after Applegate had informed him of the various charges against him and his right to remain silent. Gabriel took his courage in both hands and hurried back in the direction of the parlour, stopping dead at the sight of Jack Harris walking side by side with Inspector Applegate. Applegate had been as good as his word. Jack was not handcuffed, and the two men gave every impression that they were engaged in conversation together whilst taking a walk, even if the conversation was on an unpleasant and possibly contentious subject.

It was only when Jack's eyes locked with Gabriel's that the stern expression turned into one of open hostility. Gabriel turned his attention to Applegate. "Inspector, would it be possible for me to enter the Nicholson house? Has Roland Nicholson been allowed home yet?"

Applegate made a low noise that sounded unfortunately like a growl. "Dare I ask why? If there were anything useful there, my men would have found it," said Applegate. "And yes, Mr Nicholson has been allowed back, but he has chosen to stay away for a few more days."

"So, it would be all right for me to go then?" asked Gabriel, ignoring the obvious subtext. Gabriel was wasting his time; worse, Gabriel was presuming that he had a better eye for a clue than trained police officers. Gabriel did not greatly care. "You did mention that there was one room I should look at. I'll be very careful."

Applegate shrugged as though he were giving in to a troublesome child. "I did, didn't I? Well, the house is still under police guard. Tell whoever's on duty that I sent you. And if Old Man Nicholson happens to be there and objects to your presence, you'll have to leave."

Gabriel gave Applegate a little bow and turned to go, but he was stopped in his tracks by Jack seizing hold of his wrist. "You're barking up the wrong tree, Father," snarled Jack, squeezing Gabriel's arm so tightly he could barely stop himself from crying out. "Charlie was not the victim here. He was a Nazi traitor. He got what he deserved."

11

Why do they always have to do that? raged Gabriel as he watched inspector and suspect walk away to the waiting car. There was something grotesque about the way a certain type of man seemed to take sadistic delight in teasing and provoking rather than doing the decent thing and just stating what he knew.

Not that Jack Harris had much reason to cooperate with Gabriel or the police, if Gabriel's fears had any foundation. Gabriel felt physically sick as he wheeled the bicycle to the path and steeled himself to climb aboard and pedal away. He had expected it to take some nerve to get back on a bicycle after his accident, but he had not expected to have to cycle for over a mile before he stopped looking over his shoulder every other minute. Lightning never struck in the same place twice, Gabriel told himself, and the person who had ordered the first convenient traffic accident was currently being driven to the local lockup.

The thought had been so horrible that Gabriel had put it out of his mind initially, telling himself that no man would do anything so dastardly. It always surprised Gabriel how much more despicable a betrayal of trust felt than significantly more serious sins, such as the taking of a life—though some might say that murder was the ultimate betrayal of trust. When Gabriel had studied Dante's *Divina commedia,* he had not understood as a young man why the deepest, cruellest circle of the *Inferno* had been reserved for Judas, Cassius, and Brutus. Judas was understandable, he had supposed at the time, but Brutus and Cassius? They might have been traitors and betrayers, but were they really worse than adulterers, murderers, cannibals, rapists, and liars?

At a moment like this, the answer felt painfully obvious. Betrayal was at the heart of so many acts of wickedness. Jack Harris' betrayal, if Gabriel's suspicions were true, would rank among the most horrific, with a young woman betrayed to her torturers and her unsuspecting husband battered to death before he could reveal the truth.

Jack Harris was an arrogant, self-seeking man if his treatment of Brigitte was any test of character. It was a popular prejudice to assume that the woman had provoked the unwanted sexual attention—Gabriel was not sure how many times he had heard such a lie bandied about. *She wears too much makeup; her clothes are too tight; she's always been a bit of a coquette. She was asking for it; she made him do it; she was playing with fire.*

But Brigitte's own actions had made it unequivocally clear that she had neither welcomed Jack's salacious behaviour nor expected it. There was something about that ferocious, almost feral response to Jack's dishonourable behaviour that suggested shock and panic more than mere disgust. What had Jack's exact words been? *She was French; they do things differently.* It was the sort of casual insult that had been directed at Giovanna during the early years of their marriage, the assumption that European women were shameless flirts who were game for a bit of adultery from time to time.

Gabriel held his breath as a bus roared past, causing him

to slow down almost to the point of losing his balance. He would have to learn to drive one day. Sooner or later, petrol rationing would come to a welcome end, and there would be far more vehicles on the road. If cycling was troubling Gabriel now, he had no idea how he would manage weaving his way through traffic. He could not remember how he had managed to ride a bicycle in London all those years ago, but youth had had something to do with it.

However much Jack Harris had justified his behaviour to Brigitte, what was not in doubt was that he had been seriously humiliated by the experience. He would have had to walk around with a visible facial injury for days, with half the village laughing at him. Even when it had healed, that jagged little scar would have been a bitter reminder of the encounter every single time Jack had looked in a mirror.

Would such a sense of humiliation have driven a man to betray the woman who had spurned him? Hell might have no fury like a woman scorned, but Gabriel was sure that, across the centuries, far more men than women had destroyed the person who had scorned them. But could a man like Jack Harris have been heartless enough to give Brigitte's name to the Germans?

Plantagenet was naive if she believed that only Charles could have known what Brigitte was doing. No one was completely discreet, even in times of extreme danger, and when Brigitte had left for France, it was likely that plenty of people would have seen through her story that she was returning home to rejoin her country in its hour of need. The work of the SOE was secret, but there had been many stories during the war years about daring resistance fighters working to overthrow the Nazi yoke from within. If Brigitte's nickname had indeed been Joan of Arc, she would have been cast in that role by those who had known her without ever having to encourage such ideas.

Gabriel remembered the wartime posters warning people to keep their mouths shut: Careless Talk Costs Lives; Tittle Tattle Lost the Battle; Keep Mum, She's Not So Dumb; Even Walls Have Ears. It was just possible that Brigitte's betrayal had been just that, a life lost through careless talk. It might have been a terrible mistake, some loose-tongued individual speaking out of turn; but even with his desperation to give humanity the benefit of the doubt, Gabriel could not make himself believe that Brigitte's capture had been unintended. Charles Nicholson would not have been murdered over an unfortunate error. Whoever murdered Charles Nicholson did so either because he or she knew that Charles had indeed betrayed his wife or that Charles had discovered the identity of the traitor.

Gabriel was appalled by how exhausted he felt by the time he reached Dilton Wylye. His damaged ribs made it difficult to take deep, regular breaths without pain, and as a result, Gabriel was in persistent danger of hyperventilating. He got down from the bike near the village shop so that he could get his breath back and rest for a moment before walking the last, short distance to the house. He contemplated leaving the bicycle near the shop, but he had already lost one contraption to crime and could not risk this bicycle being stolen. He doubted that anyone would be foolhardy enough to steal it from under the nose of the policeman on duty outside the Nicholson house.

Gabriel recognised the policeman standing to attention outside the front door as the young man who had had to deal with little Antoine when he had arrived at the house. "Good afternoon," said Gabriel, propping up the bicycle against the garden wall and walking up to the policeman as nonchalantly as he could. "Sorry to trouble you, but the inspector said that I might enter the house. There's—" Gabriel came to an abrupt stop, realising that he had no idea how to explain his errand in a way that would sound anything other than nosy. He had had a long cycle ride in which to consider the best ploy but had been too busy trying to decide whether Jack Harris was a murderer to think up his cover story.

"Have you come to bless the house, Father?" asked the policeman, inadvertently saving Gabriel's bacon. "I've always wondered what happens after a violent death in a house. Do you go round with the holy water? I shouldn't want to live in a house where someone had been killed if the ghost hadn't been sent on its way."

Gabriel smiled, wondering how much he dared take advantage of the situation. It was a commendable idea to say some prayers in a house where blood had been shed. He had never been asked to do such a thing before, but it was not an unreasonable request, even if the policeman seemed to think that ghosts and ghoulies were going to come flying out the chimney as soon as he started chanting Latin at them. "I certainly can bless the house," said Gabriel gently. "I actually wanted to take a look at the summerhouse. I was going to see if there was anything I might take little Antoine to remind him of his family. But I will pray before I leave."

The policeman stepped aside without further prompting, leaving Gabriel wondering whether he would need to do penance for deceit. He *could* pray and certainly would; he *might* find something to take the child to cheer him up while he was away from home. He still felt sneaky.

Gabriel instinctively crossed himself as he peered past the police cordon at the area where the body had been found. The door to the safe was still open on its hinges to reveal the empty interior, and there were brown flecks of dried blood on the rug where Charles had fallen from the force of the blow to his head. Gabriel made for the back door, stepping through the kitchen, where a cup, a saucer, and a bowl were stacked on the draining board from the last time a member of the household had eaten there.

Gabriel glanced back into the hall to ensure that the policeman had not followed him. He had returned to his makeshift sentry post, and Gabriel was in the clear. As quickly as he could, he began searching the kitchen, methodically opening drawers and cupboards until he found the medicine drawer. Every household seemed to have one, either in the kitchen or the bathroom, and he heaved a sigh of relief that this family kept their medical supplies in the kitchen. He knew what he was looking for and did not waste time inspecting the dusty, unused roll of bandage, the little box of safety pins, the unopened bottle of cod liver oil. It was evident that this was a household that seldom had recourse to medicinal remedies and in which the adults could not even bring themselves to dose up the child with cod liver oil in the mornings.

Gabriel could not recall who it was who had said that what we cannot see is sometimes more significant than what we can see. There had very definitely been something Gabriel had expected to see when he had first entered the house, and his brief skirmish in the medical drawer had convinced him that the absence required an explanation. For now, there were other mysteries to solve.

The kitchen door was unlocked, and Gabriel walked swiftly down the garden path, hoping that the summerhouse would also be open for him. It had been only a few days, but Gabriel was sure the garden already looked neglected, with no child running around the lawn and no one tending the unruly flower beds. It was his imagination, of course, as barely any time had passed since the death, but the before and after of a murder distorted time to the extent that it was impossible to measure the passing of the days with any accuracy.

The summerhouse was a beautifully maintained wooden structure that looked very like a life-size Wendy house. In many ways, it was in better repair than the main house. The walls gleamed with a coat of whitewash that must have been only months old, and the door and window frames were painted duck-egg blue. On the roof, there was not a trace of moss or lichen. Gabriel tried the door and found that it let him in easily, the blue door swinging silently open on well-oiled hinges.

Gabriel gave a low gasp at the sight that greeted him. He had stepped into another world, like one of H. G. Wells' time travellers setting foot in another dimension. The interior of the Wendy house consisted of a single, spacious room, decorated in an ostentatiously prewar style, and it seemed to have been planned down to the tiniest detail. The striped blue-and-white curtains were tied back from the windows with little blue satin ribbons; a rocking chair, decked out in immaculately laundered cushions, took pride of place, with a little cream-coloured rug in front of it, which looked as though no human foot had ever stepped on it. The walls were lined with shelves containing books, and also objects that belonged to another age: a rosewood jewellery box, a silver-backed hairbrush and mirror, a crucifix too intricate to have been made in this country, a set of pearl-white rosary beads. On the walls were several prints: a tall boat in the midst of a calm sea, a stylised painting of Paris at sunset, a print of Vincent van Gogh's *Sunflowers*.

Gabriel tiptoed around the rug, crouching down to look at the spines of the books on the shelves. They were almost all French titles, some of them classics Gabriel recognised, such as *Les Misérables* and *The Count of Monte Cristo*, alongside many others he did not know but which had obviously once been much loved and thumbed through.

"What do you think you're doing?" demanded an angry voice from the doorway, causing Gabriel to scramble to his feet so quickly, he only narrowly avoiding banging his head on the low ceiling. "How dare you come in here uninvited!"

Gabriel found himself looking into the enraged face of Roland Nicholson. It had not occurred to Gabriel to ask the policeman whether any member of the family was home; the crockery he had seen on the draining board was indeed recent. Roland Nicholson had returned home, whatever his initial plans, and he quite reasonably wanted an explanation as to why Gabriel had come trespassing onto his private property.

"Mr Nicholson," Gabriel began, trying to sound as though he invaded other people's houses on a regular basis and nobody minded. If Roland had been angry when he first noticed Gabriel walking around the summerhouse, he was disgusted now. "I didn't realise you had returned."

"Evidently," Roland retorted. "I am not staying overnight as yet, but I returned to ensure that the house was all right in my absence. It clearly was not, if every Tom, Dick, and Harry thinks he can march in here."

Gabriel cringed with shame. He wondered how he would have felt if he had caught a person picking through the charred remains of his house. At best, Roland must think him grossly insensitive; at worst, a macabre trophy hunter. "I was hoping to find something for Antoine," he said lamely, telling himself that this was no longer a cover story since the policeman at the door had given him the idea. "He must be homesick."

"If that were the case," Roland answered, "you might have found me at the pub and asked me to find some keepsake or other for him. I could even deliver it myself."

Gabriel brightened. "I'm sure he would love to see you, Mr Nicholson. He's being very well cared for and all that, but children crave their loved ones at a time like this."

Roland's features softened almost imperceptibly. He looked around the room as though for inspiration. "I've neglected him, I'm afraid. I don't know what to say to him."

"You will not have to say anything," promised Gabriel. "He will do the talking."

Roland nodded miserably. "I know, I remember that from last time. When I had to tell little Antoine that his mother would not be coming home, I had a whole speech carefully prepared. In the end, I never said a word. He climbed into my lap and burst into tears. By the time I'd calmed him down, there was no need to say anything."

"I'm so sorry you're having to go through this a second time," said Gabriel sincerely, though a nasty little barb of conscience was troubling him already. He was aware that he had used Roland's grief to diffuse a hostile situation, and it felt like manipulation on his part.

"One assumed the worst thing might happen in time of war. Not now."

It was unbearable to think about. It would be cold comfort to Roland that he had not been forced to break the news to Antoine on this occasion, but he clearly dreaded going to visit the boy. It would be difficult for him to have a conversation with Antoine ever again that would not veer back to the reality of his father's death. Both their lives would be dominated by the events of that terrible day, and sooner or later, Roland would have to face his grandson's grief and anger.

"I shall give him her statue of Saint Brigid of Ireland," said Roland after some consideration. "She was very fond of her patron saint. Brigitte's people gave Plantagenet the statue to bring back to England with her. They said it had been a baptismal gift and that Brigitte would have wanted her son to have it to remember her by. I should like Antoine to have it on his bedside table, watching over him."

The statue of Saint Brigid was a refreshingly unsentimental work of art. The face, framed by a modest veil, looked meditatively into the middle distance; her father's bejewelled sword in her hands pointed unthreateningly down at the grass-effect platform on which she stood. Beneath the rippled green plasterwork was a wooden platform inlaid with gold. "A fitting saint for your daughter-in-law," commented Gabriel, "and I think Antoine will find it inspiring. She looks like a warrior even if she did give that sword away to a poor man."

"I shall take it to him as soon as I feel able," said Roland, hanging his head. "You must think me a frightful coward, Father, but I will go to him as soon as I can trust myself to hold myself together."

Gabriel nodded, looking around the room in a final search for inspiration. "I don't suppose Brigitte kept a diary?" he asked hopefully, but there was nothing on the shelves that fitted the description of a lady's journal. "Or perhaps a notebook?"

Roland shook his head. "I'm not sure she would have had the patience to write a journal. In any case, she left strict instructions that on the event of her death, all her personal papers should be burnt."

"And you obeyed?" Gabriel could not hide his disappointment. It was not unusual for a person to leave behind such instructions before embarking upon a dangerous enterprise, but it always seemed such a waste.

Roland nodded. "I cannot pretend it was easy to drop all her letters into the flames; it felt as though we were burning her memory. But Charles insisted that we do as she had asked. He said we owed her that last kindness." Roland shuffled uncomfortably. "I have sometimes wondered whether Charles regretted it later, when he was trying to discover the truth about Brigitte's death. He knew there might have been some vital clue in amongst those pages."

"I suppose it's unlikely that she could have had any suspicions on that score, or she would never have risked going out there," said Gabriel, thinking aloud. "Did you put all her personal effects in here?"

Roland looked around the room as though drinking in the details of the place for the first time. "I hope you do not think it morbid of us, but we turned this summerhouse into a little shrine for her. We have no idea where her final resting place might be, or if she was ever buried. She loved this place. Used to sit here and sew when she needed some peace and quiet. We thought that it might be nice for Antoine, that he might feel close to his mother in here. But he could never bear to come in."

Gabriel tried to imagine what the room might feel like to a child. Now that he had got used to the idea, Gabriel was finding the room intriguing rather than anything more negative. To a small boy struggling to come to terms with the death of a mother he could hardly remember, it might be overwhelming or even a little creepy to be shut in a glorified shed filled with an eclectic range of memorabilia. "It might mean more to him when he's older," Gabriel suggested without conviction, "at an age when he will want to know more."

"Perhaps."

Gabriel could sense Roland's desperation for him to leave. He was encroaching on the most intimate territory, tantamount to stepping on a grave, and Gabriel could justify remaining here only with Roland's permission. "I know I have no right to ask this, sir," Gabriel began, "but would you mind awfully—"

"Take as long as you like, Father," said Roland kindly, sparing Gabriel the agony of asking. "I know you came in here because you wanted to look around, and you are welcome to, but please be respectful. Every object in this room is priceless, as far as I'm concerned. And with Charles gone, this is the only link I have to happier times."

"I promise I will not move anything unless I need to,"

Gabriel said. "I'm simply trying to clear up a few things in my mind. You won't know I've been here."

Roland gave a half smile, then stepped backwards out of the summerhouse, too polite to show a guest his back. "I shall be in the house if you need anything," he said. "Take your time."

Gabriel watched as Roland disappeared outside and closed the door before he scanned the room again, this time more carefully. He hardly knew what he was looking for and had to force back his discomfort at invading this hallowed space. It was even more uncomfortable than walking into a person's bedroom, which he had done many times before; but he needed to get the measure of this woman who was so adored and whose death had dominated the investigation from the start.

Gabriel began with the decor. It was cosy, rustic and a little girlish; the cream rug and the rocking chair almost felt as though they belonged in a nursery, along with the painting of the boat. Brigitte's books told of a cultured and intelligent Catholic girl with sophisticated literary tastes, but nothing more specific than that. Even the sacred objects fitted a familiar pattern—a statue of a patron saint, a rosary, a Bible. Gabriel wondered why Brigitte had not taken her rosary with her to France, but if it held a strong sentimental value, she might have chosen to take another with her and left this one behind for her son.

Gabriel sighed, sitting on the floor. He was clutching at straws. What was most transparently obvious about this summerhouse was that it revealed nothing. Roland had given Gabriel permission to look around—respectfully and carefully—but there was nothing to see. Brigitte's letters and papers had been reduced to ashes, and if Brigitte had had any suspicions that her mission had been compromised, Gabriel doubted that she would have risked going ahead with it.

With his new, lower eye level, Gabriel noticed a series of dolls in what appeared to be traditional French costumes: fetching little hats and shawls, brightly coloured frocks. He picked up one of them, a dark-eyed doll with long hair in thick black plaits, as immaculately clean as the day a young Brigitte had first taken it out of its box. These were either decorative dolls not meant to be played with, or Brigitte had been given them when she was too old to play with dolls. Roland's housekeeper must take good care of this room, as there was not a speck of dust on the doll despite it standing on an open shelf.

Why did this all feel so staged? The books looked genuine enough, and it was perfectly possible that the rocking chair had been Brigitte's favourite seat—many people did have a favourite chair that no one could bring himself to occupy after their death. Gabriel shifted position, suddenly unnerved by the row of glassy eyes staring at him in mute accusation. It might have been a specifically male problem, but he had never liked dolls with their cold porcelain faces and unblinking eyes, and their human hair styled in perfect ringlets. He had never even bought Nicoletta a doll, opting for gentler, safer teddy bears and cuddly toys, every single one of them lost with her.

Gabriel groaned and closed his eyes. Of course it was staged! Memorials to the dead were always staged! When a woman's life was cruelly cut short, her real self was quickly replaced by a fabrication no more human than these prim little dolls. There was no deliberate deception here, only the desperate desire to canonise the long dead, but it was little better than murdering a woman a second time, eradicating every detail about her, every idiosyncrasy that had made her the unique, never-to-be-repeated human individual she was. Gabriel knew that he had committed this outrage against Giovanna. Yes, she had been beautiful, talented, sweet-natured, fiercely intelligent, and outrageously funny, but she had also been stubborn, hot-tempered and sometimes pert to the point of rudeness. What right had he ever had to deny the existence of the traits of her character he had disliked? The Giovanna of his tortured memories was not the Giovanna who had dozed off to sleep in his arms, giggled uncontrollably, thrown a dinner plate across the kitchen at him during a particularly ferocious argument. An unidentifiable man had killed her in their home, and Gabriel had killed her in his desperation to keep her close to him.

Brigitte had had her faults too. She had had a temper like Giovanna's. Gouging at a man's face had been a passionate act of self-defence against a lecher. It could have been entirely justifiable under the circumstances, but it could also suggest a more deeply rooted anger, the origins of which only Jack Harris was in a position to reveal. Gabriel tried to imagine the stir that must have been caused by the arrival of a beautiful, passionate young French girl in the village—the heads she must have turned, the jealousies she might have provoked.

Gabriel could not remember, as he sat on the summer-house floor, who it was who had told him that there were only two motives for murder—money and love. For love, one might substitute the word "lust", as love in its purest form never provoked murder. Scorned love—or lust—had placed Jack Harris under suspicion. What of others?

Gabriel's eyes flew open. The man who had just come to mind had only been a boy, Gabriel calculated, perhaps sixteen or seventeen in those last few years before the war, but he was old enough to be drawn to Brigitte. And he was unscrupulous enough to make money on the black market, to agree to crash his van into a man's bicycle—and had been paid for that service. Gabriel did not believe for a second that Terry had been moved by a mere threat. Why would he not have sold a woman too if she had spurned him? Gabriel felt his heart thumping so violently that he had to pause for a moment to calm himself down before scrambling to his feet.

Gabriel stopped just long enough to say a quiet prayer for Brigitte's and Charles' souls, then he stepped out into the garden, relieved by the feeling of sunlight touching his face. If he had made the wrong call, supported the innocence of the wrong man, it was not too late to put things right. He could see Roland watching him from the house and made straight for the back door, trying—unsuccessfully as always—to look relaxed and in control. "Are you all right?" asked Roland solicitously as he held open the door for Gabriel. "I do hope that summerhouse hasn't upset you; it can be a little too much even for me on some days."

"Mr Nicholson, do you have a telephone?" asked Gabriel. "I need to make a call rather urgently."

Roland looked at Gabriel in embarrassment, as though he had let him down somehow. "I'm frightfully sorry, but I asked for the line to be cut. I knew I was going to be away from the house a little while, and I couldn't face arriving home to a bevy of people telephoning me to offer me their sympathy and then ask all sorts of ghastly questions." He gestured to the street. "There's a phone box nearby. I can take you there if you like."

Gabriel's hands went instinctively to his pockets. He doubted he had any change to make a call, but to his relief and embarrassment, Roland took a handful of pennies out of his own pocket and handed them to him. "No need to look so mortified, Father. I know you need to use the telephone to speak to someone about Charles' death. Consider it my contribution to justice."

Gabriel smiled gratefully. "Thank you. Don't worry about coming out. I know where the telephone box is. Perhaps we can talk again when I'm back?"

"I'm not going anywhere," said Roland. "Take your time."

Take your time. The one thing Roland Nicholson had in abundance now was time, thought Gabriel as he walked the short distance to the telephone box. When the investigation was over, Roland could at least occupy the hours with the care of his grandson; but childhood passed quickly, and in a few short years, Antoine would be grown up and gone away. If grief did not take Roland to an early grave, he faced the prospect of many lonely years watching the hours slowly passing.

Gabriel entered the telephone box and braced himself for yet another awkward conversation with Applegate. Antoine, Gabriel hoped, would grow up to be a fine young man and marry a nice girl, and Roland might live long enough to enjoy the blessing of great-grandchildren. He might even—

The voice at the other end of the line intruded upon his thoughts.

"Oh, I need to speak to Inspector Applegate," Gabriel blurted out. "It's urgent!"

"It always is with you, isn't it, Father?" came the cheeky response. "You're in luck. Half a mo."

There was the sound of what Gabriel thought was a hand being placed over the receiver, then the thump of the receiver being laid on the counter and picked up again. "What do you want, Father G?" demanded Applegate, not unkindly. "Made a citizen's arrest, have you?"

"You need to search Terry's place," said Gabriel. "It's urgent."

"We already have," answered Applegate dryly, "but thank you for telling me how to do my job. I'll tell you how to baptise a baby if you like."

"No, I don't mean just search, I mean—"

"Terry's place is a converted loft at the top of his parents' house," Applegate explained, as though he were trying to interest Gabriel in buying the property. "It's spacious, but it didn't take my men long to get round it. Funnily enough"—Gabriel braced himself for what he knew was coming—"the place was as clean as a whistle, legally speaking anyway. There were marks on the floor where there'd been some pretty big crates stacked, and a few little piles of mouse droppings. But nothing important. Nothing incriminating. Oh, and the miscreant himself had done a runner."

"Gosh, really?" Gabriel groaned. He had always been a hopeless liar; he could not even act the part of the surprised innocent. "Do we know where?"

"Miscreants evading the police don't tend to leave a forwarding address," snapped Applegate, the dry tone turning positively angry. Applegate was no good at acting the role of the coolheaded slightly sinister copper either. "Anyone would think that some interfering busybody had tipped him off. There was literally nothing to find, and Terry had apparently not even told his old man where he was heading."

Gabriel took a deep breath. He heard the pips sounding in his ear, warning him that he needed to put more money in the slot or the call was going to end. "I don't have much time, Inspector, but you're looking in the wrong place. You need to check the family safe. I think Terry is a blackmailer. I think he knows something."

"Why on earth would he put the money in the family safe? His parents would know about it."

"His parents do know about it. They may not know about the booze, but I'm sure they know that Terry's a blackmailer. They may even be—" There was a click signalling the end of the call, and Gabriel was left standing in the phone box, holding the greasy receiver to his ear, hoping against all hope that Applegate had understood what he needed to do.

12

Gabriel replaced the receiver and stood staring down at the encrusted floor of the telephone box. Part of him wondered whether he should leave the question of Jack Harris' innocence until after Applegate had searched Terry's parents' safe. If Gabriel's instinct was correct, and Jack Harris was the guilty man—or at least heavily involved in Charles Nicholson's murder—it might not matter what he had said about the dead man. Of course, a killer would try to besmirch the name of the victim. Or would he?

Jack's involvement with the Nicholsons troubled Gabriel because Jack Harris troubled him. Like the summerhouse, Jack Harris felt fake, reconstructed, lacking in all the normal idiosyncrasies of a man his age. He was a man who acted a part every day of his life, the part of the hearty, outgoing scoutmaster. He looked the part, and he acted the part as though the moment he put on that uniform, he became an entity of his own invention. Jack Harris had known that Antoine was not supposed to be at the camp; he was one of the few men who did. Just that piece of information might exonerate him, as who would be foolish enough to murder a man in his own home in the presence of his son? Unless it had been a double bluff, and Jack had known all the time that Antoine would attempt to inveigle his way into the scout camp despite having been banned. And would a killer have been so audacious as to make such an insulting allegation against his victim? There was no greater insult, no more terrible calumny than to accuse a man of having sympathised with Hitler, Britain's greatest enemy and perhaps the most hated human being in the world. Unless the allegation was true, and Jack had known that Gabriel would eventually find out.

A sharp rapping on the glass panel right next to Gabriel's head caused him to step back from the sound and hit his head on the inner wall. "You relieving yourself in there or what?" came the angry voice, and to his astonishment, Gabriel found himself looking directly into the twisted, unshaven face of Gordon Merriott.

"What are you doing here?" demanded Gabriel when he had removed himself from the telephone box. "You turn up like the proverbial bad penny!"

"Me brother lives here," answered Gordon, giving him a toothless grin. "I saw you the other day when I were waiting for the bus, so I might ask you what you're doing here. 'Cept, of course, I know why you're here, snooping around. There's been a murder, hasn't there?"

"There has." Gabriel could not suppress a grimace. Gordon's appearance always spelt trouble, and the last thing Gabriel needed at this most delicate moment was Sutton Westford's very own malicious gossip snapping at his heels. He began walking purposefully in the direction of the Nicholson house, but Gordon fell into step beside him. "Look, Merriott, this is a very distressing case. The victim leaves behind a young son and a grieving father. It might be best to leave well alone."

"Couldn't put it better meself," agreed Gordon, taking a packet of Woodbines out of his pocket. "You got a match?"

"I don't smoke," said Gabriel.

"More fool you then," answered Gordon, snatching the unlit cigarette out of his mouth and ramming it back into his pocket. "And you should leave well alone."

"I think I'll be the judge—"

"Old Charlie boy got exactly what he deserved. Filthy Nazi sold his own wife."

Gabriel stopped dead. He could feel his hands trembling with an unexpected surge of anger, and he clutched his fists behind his back. "Where on earth does that foul story come from? How many Nazis marry foreigners?"

Gordon guffawed with laughter as though he intended the entire village to share the joke. Gabriel noticed a few passersby turning to look at them, and winced with embarrassment. "So, a good Nazi can't fall for a good bit of skirt like the rest of us? You wouldn't be so daft if you'd seen her. Like a Hollywood film star, she were. Made Greta Garbo look dumpy."

"I don't care how beautiful Charles Nicholson's wife was, Merriott," Gabriel replied, determined not to be drawn into the conversation. Listening to gossip was like wading through an open sewer; the stench of calumny could never be entirely washed away. "Unless you have proof, you'd better keep your claims to yourself."

Merriott snorted. His being in need of a cigarette was evident in his attitude, which was more combative than usual. "I've plenty of proof if that's what you want. He were in with a bad crowd years ago. Got themselves arrested when a march turned nasty." Merriott dropped his voice to a conspiratorial whisper of pantomime proportions. "Bribed his way out of the army, didn't he? Another rich boy who paid to stay tucked up nice and safe."

Gabriel picked up his pace to try and shake off Gordon Merriott, but the man merely picked up his own pace. There were many men struggling with the stigma of never having worn a uniform, the majority of whom had had perfectly legitimate reasons for remaining civilians. Some were involved in reserved occupations—vets, doctors, policemen. Others suffered from illnesses, often invisible, that prevented them from joining up. Gabriel thought of poor Joseph Beaumont, kept away from the armed forces by a terminal heart condition. He had been baited and insulted mercilessly for his apparent cowardice, thanks to the ignorant judgements of his own peer group. Gabriel would not let Gordon Merriott persuade him. "You've no idea why Charles Nicholson was exempted from military service. And he's not from a wealthy family."

That much was at least certain. The Nicholsons were educated people, but a glance around their home had made it clear that they lived frugally. There were no modern conveniences; the house—apart from Brigitte's shrine—showed no sign of having been redecorated or refurbished in many years. Antoine had not been sent away to boarding school as might have been expected, and his idea of a treat had been a trip to the pictures and the chippy.

"You know why they've no money, don't you?" continued Gordon relentlessly. "Because secrets be costly to keep."

Gabriel spun round to look Merriott full in the face, determined this time to bring the conversation to an abrupt halt. "Mr Merriott, do you really have a brother living in this village, or did you come here out of ghoulish curiosity?" If Gabriel had expected Gordon Merriott to be embarrassed, he was swiftly put right.

Merriott looked coldly back at him. "You're quite the one to call me ghoulish, a man who causes misery wherever he pokes his nose in. How many folk died after your last investigation?"

Gabriel heard again the thud of the trapdoor opening and Florence Harding's final panicked gasp. He saw the chaos in that house, smelled blood . . . Gabriel marched away as quickly as he could whilst retaining his dignity, and Gordon Merriott at least had the decency to let him go without attempting to follow. He had drawn blood and knew it.

Gabriel was alarmed to discover that Roland was no longer at home. "It's all right, Father," said the policeman, indicating the pub. "He come over a bit upset and said he'd go back to the pub for a while. I think the sight of the house rather shook him."

"Of course, I should have thought of that," said Gabriel, giving the policeman a nod and a smile before walking away from the house. The difficulty of the situation presented itself, and Gabriel tried to think fast. He did not want Roland at the pub when Applegate's men came to search it. It would be needlessly humiliating for the landlord and upsetting for Roland, who most certainly did not need to see a swarm of policemen running around yet another building. More to the point, Gabriel knew he should not be seen on the premises either, as it was possible that someone would suspect that he was involved in Terry's sudden disappearance and the police search; if anyone asked Gabriel directly if he was involved, he would never be able to lie.

The pub was quiet when Gabriel entered, and the lights were on, reminding him that the day was trickling by yet again and he still had so much to do. Gabriel had hoped to come in without anyone noticing, find Roland—whom he had assumed would be ensconced in the snug—and persuade him to return to his house before the police arrived. It was too late for that. With the day waning, the pub was preparing for the first of the village regulars to appear for a pint, and an attractive woman in late middle age stood behind the bar, drying a glass tankard.

The woman clocked Gabriel immediately, but he was unable to gauge her reaction, as her professional smile of welcome appeared immediately, and she put down the glass. "Afternoon! You must be that Father Gabriel our Terry was talking about." She held out a freckled hand to Gabriel, which he shook automatically. "Abigail."

"How do you do?" answered Gabriel, noticing only when their hands touched that the woman was hot and a little flustered. "I was looking for Mr Nicholson, but please don't worry. I can find him. It looks as though you're busy."

Abigail let her smile drop at the tone of concern and folded her arms. She had the red hair and smattering of freckles that suggested Irish heritage, but she spoke in the warm, lilting Wiltshire accent everyone used in these parts. "It's all right, Father, he's in the snug having a nice cup of tea. I didn't think he ought to have any more to drink today; he's been that upset. We're just a bit shorthanded. My useless oaf of a son's gone walkabouts."

Gabriel hoped he was not blushing, but his face felt hot. "I see," he said noncommittally. "Does he often do that?"

Abigail held out her hands in a gesture of despair. "He's always been unreliable. Comes and goes as he pleases. No sense of duty."

Young people were usually disparaged by their elders, but a lack of any sense of duty was not usually associated with young men who had returned from the war. They had their faults, certainly, but they were seldom accused of being ill-disciplined. Gabriel said as much. "I'm sure he must have learned how to behave during the war. Perhaps he's still feeling demob happy."

Abigail gave a derisive snort. "He were never demob happy or whatever young'uns call it, 'cause he were never in the army, Father. Weak chest, asthma, wouldn't let him join. Not that he were exactly heartbroken to avoid getting shot at by the Germans. He had a nice-enough war."

Gabriel fled to the safety of the snug like a shell-shocked soldier diving for the dugout. There was no point in trying to get himself and Roland out of here before the police arrived, as Abigail had seen him and might make the association whether they left or stayed. It was quite possible that she might think that he had popped in on a pastoral call, though Gabriel was inclined to assume most people would think the worst of him given half a chance.

Roland was sitting in the snug, in exactly the same seat he had occupied when they had last met here. There was a tray in front of him containing a teapot covered by a quilted tea cosy made of red-and-white gingham. The fabric made Gabriel think of the pots of jam sold by the ladies of the Women's Institute on market day. There was a small enamel milk jug, and Roland had poured himself a cup of tea, which sat growing cold before him. The old man did not even look up when Gabriel entered the room.

Gabriel sat at the opposite side of the table and waited until Roland slowly raised his head to look at him. He did not seem particularly surprised or disappointed to see Gabriel there, wearing a look instead of weary resignation. "I am so sorry to have put you through that earlier," said Gabriel softly. "It was very kind of you to show me Brigitte's memorial. I know it must be very hard for you to talk about her, even after many years."

"You cannot possibly know how hard it is," said Roland, looking steadily through Gabriel. "Not a day goes by when I am not reminded of the day she left, and now I have two ghosts to haunt me. I can't stop thinking that if Brigitte had lived, my boy would still be here."

Gabriel wondered as always whether he should tell Roland that he did know something of how hard it was to live with that unrelenting sense of loss, but it never seemed to help another person to be told that his or her suffering was not unique. In some ways it was, as no two people ever felt exactly the same when faced with a bereavement. "I'm sorry to ask you this, Mr Nicholson, and believe me, I would never raise this if I did not need to, but there are some rumours I need to put to bed."

Roland's face did not flicker. Either he had slipped back into that lethargic stage of grief Gabriel remembered, or he genuinely did not care what Gabriel had to say. "I doubt you could put a rumour to bed; that's not the way it works. But you may ask whatever you like."

Gabriel made a show of moving his chair a few inches closer to the table to buy himself a moment. "I'm sorry even to say the word, but somebody told me that Charles was a Nazi." There, he had said it. He saw Roland flinch as though he had been slapped in the face, and Gabriel continued as quickly as he could. "I am not saying that there is any truth in the slur, but I need to know why anybody might say such a thing."

Roland made no answer. His hands were hidden under the tablecloth, and Gabriel suspected that he was clenching and unclenching his fists with the effort of remaining calm. Roland had the sort of complexion that turned purple rather than red in moments of anger, and Gabriel could see the tiny, grapelike clusters of blood vessels livid across his face. Still he said nothing, and the only sound in the tiny room was Roland's strained, rasping breathing. Gabriel was about to speak, simply to fill the silence, when Roland spoke in a strangled whisper Gabriel could only just make out.

"You should know better than to listen to tittle-tattle, Father. He was despised during the war because he was never a soldier. He had asthma. It wasn't his fault."

"I understand," said Gabriel, feeling an undue sense of relief that his first suspicions were correct. Charles had been unfairly labelled because he had never worn uniform, and someone had put it about that he had used his social status to worm his way out of the army. "It was mentioned before that he had asthma. Was that why Charles was so ill the morning he was murdered? I was told he was in bed with a cold."

Roland looked a little thrown by the question but nodded. "Yes, everything goes to a man's chest when he's like that. It was only a cold, but it was enough to lay him up."

Gabriel was tempted to leave the conversation there, accept Roland's explanation and go. It was perfectly plausible after all. Male civilians were targeted, sometimes quite nastily, in time of national conscription. Gabriel was old enough to remember the white-feather campaign of the first war, when suffragettes had done their patriotic duty by shaming young men in civilian clothes with their very public offerings of white feathers. There must have been many men dead on the fields of Flanders who had been humiliated into joining up to fight a war they did not believe in, and still others who had been haunted by the accusation of cowardice all their lives. And yet . . .

"Mr Nicholson, I need you to tell me the full truth," said Gabriel, and the words came out far more forcefully than he had intended. "Noncombatants might sometimes have been called cowards and even traitors, but I do not recall any being called Nazis. That insult was beyond the pale for most people, even the most malicious."

"I'm not sure I understand what you're getting at," said Roland coolly, but the telltale signs of panic in his face were unmistakable. "It was hardly Charles' fault what people chose to call him."

"Mr Nicholson, you must tell me the real reason why that slur was used against Charles. I'm not accusing him of anything, but your son's death has no apparent motive. It is quite obvious that no burglary was planned for that day; the whole thing was staged. It is possible that someone killed him because they believed him to be responsible for his wife's death, but it is equally possible that there was a more personal vendetta at work here. If there was anything in Charles' background that might have made him vulnerable—"

Roland stood up to leave. "I have no idea what you think you are talking about," Roland enunciated slowly, "but I have indulged you quite long enough."

"The police found a newspaper cutting," Gabriel blurted

out, but before he could continue, both men were startled by the sound of footsteps thundering through the pub, and Gabriel signalled for Roland to sit down again. "I think you'd better stay where you are," he said quietly. "That's the police."

The effect was immediate. Roland shrank back into his seat as though he expected Gabriel to strike him. "For pity's sake, Father, don't let them arrest me!" he pleaded, his eyes darting to the door. "It will kill me if I have to talk to them!"

"What is it you don't want to tell them, Mr Nicholson? We may not have very long."

Roland let out a pathetic whimper, and tears began to stream down his face. "Please, Father, my son has lost his life! He cannot lose his good name! It was a long time ago, and I don't believe it had anything to do with his death."

Gabriel listened intently. He could hear steps moving away from them, which suggested that the police were heading for the back room, where the safe was most likely to be kept, but he could also hear footsteps going up the stairs and the sound of raised voices, a male voice of authority and Abigail's angry protests. "Mr Nicholson," he said, "what did your son do? He may not lose his good name, but he will never receive justice if you try to lie."

"He was hardly more than a boy!" Roland said, sobbing. "When he went to university, the whole place was a hotbed of politics. Every student seemed to be a Communist or a Fascist or some kind of crank. It was not just him! He got in with a bad crowd, that was all. He was footloose, didn't know what he believed. His friends got him caught up with the lowest people, the worst type."

"The British Union of Fascists?"

"Mosley's men, yes." Roland took a handkerchief out of his pocket and dabbed furiously at his face, giving himself a moment to catch his breath. "I swear, it did not last long. They took him along to some rally. There was trouble; violence broke out. The next thing I knew, I was receiving a telephone call from the police to say that my son had been arrested. As you can imagine, I was mortified. Charles was always a good boy. I couldn't understand how he could have done anything so despicable that he'd ended up in prison."

"What was he charged with?" asked Gabriel. The question was already arising in his mind as to how Applegate had failed to discover Charles Nicholson's criminal record.

"He wasn't charged at all. He'd done nothing wrong!" exclaimed Roland. Grief was slowly turning to anger again, and Gabriel instinctively drew back. "The police said they were prepared to accept that it was all an unfortunate mistake. He had been in the wrong place at the wrong time, and that was the end of the matter. He walked away from that police station without a stain on his name."

No, he didn't, thought Gabriel. *He obviously did not leave the police station without a stain on his name because Charles Nicholson's dalliance with Oswald Mosley's men had not gone unnoticed.* "Who spread the story?" asked Gabriel. "I do not imagine that photograph was printed in a local newspaper."

"Who knows?" snapped Roland. "That report was in a London newspaper. I read the thing only because I was a member of a London Club at the time and saw the blasted paper in the smoking room. Most people here have never even visited London. For all I know, Charles may have confided in a friend and then regretted it."

"It's all right, Mr Nicholson," said Gabriel, though it was most certainly not all right. Gabriel needed a name. "If you really don't know, you don't know. It was a long time ago after all."

"It was a very long time ago, another world," agreed Roland. "And he never supported Hitler. Brigitte rid Charles of any remaining Fascist nonsense; I'm sure of that."

Silence again, quickly followed by softer footsteps outside the snug and the sound of indiscernible voices. Gabriel strained to catch any word that might warn him whether the police had found anything incriminating. When he heard the sound of the front door opening and closing, Gabriel got up and peered through the window in time to see the landlord walking away with Inspector Applegate, his shackled hands discreetly tucked into the belt of his jacket.

Roland was at Gabriel's side, but he was not looking at the understated drama going on outside. Gabriel could see Roland out of the corner of his eye, looking daggers at him. "You knew the police were coming," growled Roland, "and you knew they were not coming for me."

"In blackmail cases, the police tend to be more interested in the blackmailer than the victim," said Gabriel, keeping his eyes on Applegate and the landlord as they climbed into the waiting car. "Unless, of course, the victim is hiding a criminal past."

Roland pushed against the window frame as though trying to force his way out, then turned on his heel and moved towards the door. "I told you, Father, Charles was released without charge. I had nothing to do with it. There was no crime."

"Mr Nicholson, why don't you tell me the real reason

your family was being blackmailed? Charles is beyond harm now."

"With the greatest possible respect, sir," said Roland pointedly, standing in the doorway with more poise and dignity than he had shown since the murder, "go to the devil."

13

Behind the bar, a woman was sobbing. The few patrons who had been enjoying an early drink had gulped down their beers and fled at the first sight of the police arriving. Gabriel suspected that Abigail had forced herself to put on a brave face until she believed herself to be alone before going to pieces. He found her curled up on the damp, sticky floor, her head cradled in her arms like a child hiding from an angry parent.

"Abigail?" called Gabriel softly, leaning over the counter so that she would see his face as soon as she looked up. He did not dare venture behind the counter in case his actions were misconstrued, but he did not need to. Abigail looked up at him through streaming eyes, her mouth opening and closing as she tried to force out a response. "Abigail, why don't I close the pub for you? You're in no fit state to serve anyone tonight."

Abigail nodded, giving Gabriel a pathetic smile that stabbed at his heart. He busied himself with the tasks of turning the OPEN sign to CLOSED on the front door and bringing in the blackboard advertising a darts match on the following evening; then he came back inside, momentarily at a loss as to what to do next. "Blinds and curtains," whimpered Abigail, who had found the strength to stand and was wiping her face with a corner of her white pinny.

Gabriel's thoughts were still in a whirl as he pulled down blinds and snapped three pairs of curtains shut, letting off an odour of stale cigarette smoke. How on earth had he managed to make such a mess of everything again? He could not bear to think what Inspector Applegate would have to say about this sorry situation if he were ever able to prove that Gabriel had been the one to encourage Terry to go into hiding. But that had been then. Things had been different then.

Gabriel took his courage in both hands and turned back to Abigail, who had been watching him morosely as he went about closing the pub for business. "Abigail, where is your son?" he asked, cutting to the chase. "Do you know where he's hiding? It's important that you find him before the police do."

Abigail shook her head, her fingers still tugging at the corner of her pinny as though she were trying to tear it to shreds. "I didn't even know he were going!" she protested. "He never told me nothing. I went up to his room. I found it empty with just a little note saying that he needed to lie low for a few days."

"Where would he normally go if he was in trouble?" asked Gabriel. He had never had a son, but he had been a young man once and knew that every youth had some friend or brother to whom he could turn in a moment of panic. "Does he have a friend or a cousin? Someone who has always protected him when he's been in trouble?"

Abigail's shoulders were shaking again, but she looked him fixedly in the eye. "Father, even if I knew, I'm not sure I could tell you. You're friends with that horrible man Applegate, aren't you? If Terry knew the police were coming, he might at least have had the decency to warn us. We could have emptied the safe before the police turned up, and they would've been none the wiser. Anyways, how we make our money is our business."

"Abigail, Terry did not run away because he was about to be arrested on a charge of blackmail. I didn't know about the blackmail when I spoke to him. He was running away to avoid getting his collar felt over his black-market activities and because he deliberately tried to run me over. I didn't want him to get into trouble for hurting me, but I didn't know that you were all involved in hurting someone else."

Abigail's fists came down so hard against the counter that Gabriel flinched at the sound. "We hurt no one; it were payment!" she shouted. "And the old duffer were that stupid if he thought we'd grass him up. Our Terry's the one who'll be for it if they find out why we were taking his money."

Gabriel's look hardened, his worst suspicions realised. "Terry will certainly be 'for it' when this goes to court," he said, in a tone that caught Abigail off guard. She took a step away from Gabriel, her own face hardening into a glower, confirming yet another of Gabriel's suspicions. She had always known about Terry's criminal activities, and she was going to defend her family by any means necessary. "Madam, treason in time of war is a hanging offence. He may still hang. Do you understand?"

Gabriel saw the answer coming a second too late to avoid it entirely. Abigail snatched up a heavy glass beer mug from the counter and hurled it at Gabriel's head. He was able to move quickly enough to avoid the mug smashing in his face, but it struck him hard on his left shoulder, sending him staggering backwards onto the floor. "Don't do this!"

shouted Gabriel, but his back slamming against the wooden boards had partially winded him. "For pity's sake, Abigail, the police are going to find out, whatever you do!"

Gabriel's arm went up to his face in self-defence and he felt the harsh, dull pain of a shoe stamping on his forearm; he rolled onto his side to protect his head. He could taste blood in his mouth where the force of a kick had rammed his arm against his mouth, and he knew he had to find some way to fight off this furious, terrified mother before it was too late. He was far bigger and stronger than Abigail, but sprawled on the ground with her standing over him, kicking and punching him repeatedly, it was impossible to see how he could stand up.

"Bloody meddling, busybody priest!" she was shouting, every word accompanied by a kick. "Always poking your nose in other people's business! My boy won't hang for you!"

Gabriel made a desperate grab for Abigail's foot, shoving her backwards so that she was thrown off balance. She managed somehow to remain on her feet, but it gave him time to get up onto his knees. It was no good. His broken ribs, still in the early stages of healing, roared with renewed pain, and he could hardly breathe. He felt dizzy just with the effort of raising himself up this far, and knew he would never get to his feet before she came back for him. He heard a whooshing sound near his ear, then felt the overpowering sensation of something heavy striking the side of his head.

Somewhere far away, Gabriel heard a door being thrown open and an old man's voice shouting, "Stop it! What do you think you're doing?"

"My son won't die for yours, you dirty coward!" screamed Abigail. Gabriel could not move, and he listened helplessly as Roland struggled to restrain his attacker. Gabriel could hear screaming and swearing, then the total silence of defeat.

From where he was lying, Gabriel could see a mahogany tray on the floor near him that Abigail had used to knock him down. His head felt thick and fuzzy with the blow he had received. Roland was kneeling beside him, shaking him by the shoulders. "Father, are you all right? Can you hear me?"

Gabriel groaned, his eyelids suddenly very heavy. He needed to sleep.

"Oh no you don't! Stay awake!" shouted Roland in his ear. "You must stay awake!"

"Where is she?" murmured Gabriel. He was drifting in spite of himself. "Where has she gone?"

"It's all right, Father," came a stronger, younger man's voice. "She won't get far; I'll see to it."

The young policeman stationed outside Roland's house had seen the old man hurrying back in the direction of the pub. On instinct, he had followed some way behind Roland, arriving in time to see Abigail fleeing through the back door. "Sir, you'd better stay with the priest," the policeman instructed Roland. "My relief has just arrived. I'll tell him to come and help while I start a search."

Gabriel's body throbbed all over. He felt himself starting to shiver as the cool floor chilled him. Roland was still sitting beside him, begging him to stay awake. "Help's coming," promised the soft, sonorous voice. "Not long now. You're going to be all right, old man."

But the pain below Gabriel's ear was spreading into a powerful, suffocating sensation, and Gabriel simply could not do as he was told. He felt darkness slipping over him and the frantic sound of Roland pleading with him to stay awake. Then nothing.

Treachery. Betrayal. Deceit. So much deceit, so many attacks on the truth. Gabriel was an insect trapped in a cobweb of lies, and there were predators closing in on him from all sides. He tried to scream, but something was suffocating him, smothering the life out of him . . .

When Gabriel jolted awake, his first sensation was of being a good deal more comfortable than he thought he ought to be. He was lying, pinioned between starched white sheets, a soft bandage skilfully wound around his head. *Hospital then*, he thought. Roland had watched over him until an ambulance had arrived to bring him to this sanctuary.

A young nurse appeared at his side, an angelic vision in white pinafore and cap. "Good morning," she said brightly, taking his wrist carefully between her fingers. "Would you tell me your name, please?"

Gabriel blinked, wondering if this was a trick question. "Dom Gabriel Milsom, O.S.B."

"Good," she answered encouragingly, using her free hand to glance at the watch pinned to her front. "Do you remember what happened?"

The memory of being spreadeagled on the floor of the pub returned to haunt him. "I lost a fight with a woman," he said quietly. "I think."

The nurse laughed lightly. "You've had quite a time of it, I'm afraid," she confirmed, "and the doctor said you have some older injuries too."

"I came off my bicycle the other day," said Gabriel quickly. "Did I pass out?"

"Yes, you took a nasty blow to the head."

Gabriel looked past the nurse's slight frame and saw the door opening slowly to reveal a grim-faced Inspector Applegate. His heart sank. Part of him wondered whether he could pretend to faint again, just to avoid having to answer any unpleasant questions. "Nurse . . ."

The nurse turned around. "I'm sorry, sir," she said to Applegate, "you'll have to leave. Visiting hour is not until this afternoon."

The inspector took a tentative step into the room. "I just wanted to see how my old friend is getting on. He gave us quite a scare."

"You can see him this afternoon," said the nurse, her voice becoming steely. She was not the sort of professional to take any nonsense from anyone, especially from a man. "Please leave."

"I'm a detective inspector," Applegate persisted, "and this is urgent."

"I don't care if you are Clement Attlee," the nurse retorted, glancing coldly up at her prey. If the nurse bore any resemblance to an angel, it was of the Dantesque rather than the Romantic variety. "This patient is in no fit state to speak to anyone. Now please leave immediately, or I shall summon Matron."

The threat had the desired effect. Applegate gave an audible groan, turning to leave without even attempting to look at Gabriel again. The priest sank more deeply into the pillows, breathing a long, slow sigh of relief. "Thank you, nurse," he said softly, when he was sure that Applegate had definitely gone.

The nurse beamed at Gabriel, resting a hand on his bandaged head almost in blessing. "You're under strict instructions to rest," she said kindly. "Do you think you could manage a nice cup of tea?"

Gabriel heard his stomach rumbling loudly. "I don't suppose I could have a little something to eat?"

"I'll bring you some toast."

Toast and tea. Gabriel felt himself relaxing; then a jolt of panic struck him like an electric shock. "My community!" he cried, his hands pulling at the bedsheets, which stubbornly refused to budge. "They won't know where I am!"

The nurse put a hand firmly on Gabriel's hands to stop him. "Your abbot has been told of your accident. There's nothing to worry about."

Gabriel lay back again, wishing sincerely that there really was nothing else to worry about. He closed his eyes to keep out the picture of the sterile, white walls of his room and all the discomforting furniture of the hospital. He knew he should try to think about the best way to explain his actions to Applegate, but his head felt annoyingly clouded after the shock of two serious assaults in quick succession. Even Gabriel was not entirely sure what he had been playing at.

Ten minutes later, as he sat up in bed munching his way through two thick slices of hot buttered toast, the door burst open, and Applegate was standing beside him like the Penhill Giant. "It's not visiting hour," Gabriel mumbled, scattering crumbs across the red blanket.

"I went to Matron. I told her it was urgent police business and could not wait until this afternoon," Applegate explained, dragging an easy chair across to the bedside so that he could sit down at eye level with Gabriel. "Wonderful thing about nursing," he added sardonically, sitting down in the chair heavily enough to cause the springs to give a maddening creak. "Since nursing was built along the same lines as the army, there's this wonderful thing called a hierarchy. If the foot soldier won't give you what you want, you go to the sergeant."

Gabriel swallowed, but his mouth was dry, and he had already finished his tea. "I see," he said.

"It was fortunate for us that young Terry's mother led us right to him, as I'm not sure we would have found him—not quickly anyway. There are plenty of barns for guilty men to hide in, in these parts, and it might have taken us days to comb the countryside searching for a killer."

"He's not a killer; he's a blackmailer," said Gabriel, wondering too late at the wisdom of correcting Applegate in his current state of mind. "Amongst other things."

"Like traitor, for example?" asked Applegate. He leant towards Gabriel as if he were about to give him a racing tip. "Look here, Gabriel, before Matron decides you're about to die or something and changes her mind about letting me sit here, I think you owe me an explanation. What right did you think you had to tip off a criminal? You do realise how serious this is, don't you?"

"I'm not sure it is, actually," Gabriel retorted, breaking the last of his toast into tiny fragments. "I'm not obliged to help you with your investigations; I'm not the police."

"You knew he was a criminal!"

"I didn't know how serious it was at the time. I knew he was involved in the black market, and I knew about what he had done to me. I didn't want him to suffer on my account. What is that to you?"

Applegate snatched the plate from Gabriel's lap and placed it with a thud on the bedside table. Gabriel's tendency to fidget drove Applegate mad at the best of times, but he was explosively angry by now. "When did you realise how serious it was?"

"I knew he was blackmailing Charles Nicholson," said Gabriel, "and Charles' attendance at a Fascist rally wasn't reason enough. In any case, everyone seemed to know, so there was no secret for Terry to keep. Roland refused to talk to me about it, but Antoine had mentioned to me in passing that his father had asthma. I just couldn't get it out of my head that it was a bit of a coincidence to have two men—Charles and Terry—invalided out of the army because of asthma in the same small village."

Applegate sat back in the easy chair, crumpling his hat in his hands. Gabriel knew that Applegate was desperate for a smoke but would not dare light up his pipe and risk Matron getting a whiff of it. "It's suspicious but not conclusive," he said. "One of them might have given the other the idea of faking an illness."

"There's a lot more to it than that," said Gabriel, shifting position to make his own breathing a little less laboured. "I don't suppose you could pour me a glass of water, could you?"

Applegate got up, poured water into a glass from the carafe on the bedside table, and handed it to Gabriel with as much bad grace as he could muster. "Look, Gabriel, what I can tell you is that you were right about the safe. We found a substantial sum of money stored away, far more than a pub landlord could possibly earn through honest means."

"And the money came from the Nicholsons?"

"You were right about that too," answered Applegate testily. "Stacks of bank notes don't confirm blackmail—there are other ways in which money can be made—but based on what you told me, I paid Old Man Nicholson's bank manager a little visit while you were sleepy-bye here. Turns out that Roland Nicholson withdrew one hundred pounds in cash in November 1939."

"That's a lot of money," said Gabriel lamely. They both knew the significance of the timing.

"Exactly. It would have raised eyebrows, especially in time of war, but the bank manager in question went and died very bravely somewhere over Hamburg. All the current incumbent could tell me was the figure. To be honest, the bank manager's a bit of an idiot. He showed me the account records; substantial sums were withdrawn on a regular basis from that point. Seemed to think the old man was going a bit soft in the head, maybe stopped trusting the bank and had taken to stuffing his wealth under his mattress." Applegate watched in apparent irritation as Gabriel drained his glass. "Roland Nicholson insists that Terry's family were blackmailing him over Charles' flirtations with Fascism."

Gabriel thought back to Brigitte's little shrine and that nagging sense Gabriel had had that the contents of the room revealed everything and nothing about the dead woman; he thought back to the walls of the house and the family photographs he had briefly glimpsed; he remembered the suspiciously empty medicine drawer.

"Inspector, when I returned to the home to look at the summerhouse, I noticed there was no photograph of Charles in uniform," Gabriel began, immediately noting the sceptical look on Applegate's face. "Yes, yes, I know his father says that he had asthma and couldn't serve. I've known other men who had hidden conditions, and everyone called them cowards. My first thought when I couldn't see evidence of Charles' military service was that he must have been ill. Roland's claim that Charles had asthma made sense, except that it didn't. I'd already checked the family's medical drawer, and it spoke of a healthy family."

Applegate opened his mouth, evidently to point out that Gabriel had no business poking about without police permission, before remembering that he had agreed to his entering the house. "You wouldn't know what you were looking for; you're not a doctor."

"No, but one of the brothers at the abbey suffered from asthma," Gabriel persisted, determined to prove his case. "Old Brother Cuthbert. He was terribly poorly with it, particularly towards the end, and the winters were always a trial in a cold building. The infirmarian took care of him, but I was often in the infirmary too, helping out, especially in the winter when there was more sickness. Brother Cuthbert had medicines brought by the doctor, injections, tablets. I remember Brother Cuthbert marvelling at all the wonderful modern drugs there were when in his day they'd encouraged him to smoke to clear his airways." Gabriel looked at Applegate and realised he was losing him. "Inspector, there was no evidence in that house that anyone suffering from asthma lived there. Charles Nicholson was not asthmatic."

"So, you're saying that Terry was an asthmatic and therefore realised that Charles was faking it?" said Applegate with no enthusiasm whatsoever. "That was the secret, that Charles was a malingerer?"

"I'm afraid it's rather worse than that, Inspector," said

Gabriel apologetically. "I don't think Terry has the intelligence to guess something like that. The two men were not on close terms as far as I'm aware. I think Terry was paid by Roland Nicholson to pose as Charles at his medical examination. He's the sort of man who gets caught up in other people's sordid business."

Applegate's brow furrowed. "The money. Exactly one hundred pounds in November 1939. The time when Charles would have received his call-up papers."

"I've heard of such things happening before. If Terry went to the medical examination calling himself Charles Nicholson, the doctor would have signed an exemption letter for Charles Nicholson and not been any the wiser that he had examined the wrong man. Abigail more or less confessed the truth when she attacked me. She was afraid Terry would hang for treason."

"It was treason, and I don't fancy the lad's chances in court," said Applegate more softly than was usual for him when discussing the behaviour of criminals. "And he's made things about as bad for himself as he could have done."

"Greed, I'm afraid, Inspector."

"Greed. Once Roland had paid to save his son, Terry couldn't resist milking him for as much money as he could. And though it could be proved that Charles was not really asthmatic if it came to it, it would be much harder for the Nicholsons to prove that Terry had been behind the deception. The consequences would be horrific."

"Exactly."

Applegate stamped his feet on the ground and stood up, giving Gabriel a wry smile as he buttoned up his coat. "Well, you've certainly been thinking things through when you've not been putting yourself in hospital. Now you lie there with nursie tucking you up, and I'll seek out Charles Nicholson's medical notes."

Gabriel lay back, feeling suddenly bereft. He wondered whether he could persuade his doctor to discharge him or let him recover at his abbey's infirmary. At least there he would be surrounded by friends and could enjoy some company during daylight hours. He closed his eyes, wishing that he had spent more time chatting with Brother Cuthbert during his long, last illness. The days must have passed very slowly indeed, even for a wise old man who was used to spending hours lost in meditation. Cuthbert had had an incredibly rich life as a merchant seaman; he had travelled all over the world like a veritable Odysseus. *He saw the cities of many peoples, and he learnt their ways*. Cuthbert had been born in a land of crinolines and horse-drawn carriages; he had died in the age of petrol engines and the atomic bomb. What memories must have whispered through old Cuthbert's mind through those long, weary, wakeful nights, and Gabriel had never thought to ask him about them.

Gabriel flinched at the sound of the door opening, but it was only the nurse come to take away his tea tray. Gabriel did not like to admit it, even to himself, but he wanted to return to the abbey not only because he longed to return to his community but because he would feel safer there. Gabriel doubted that much would get past Matron, but nothing whatever would get past Abbot Ambrose, and after being attacked twice, Gabriel felt the need of an infallible guardian. Unbeknownst to Gabriel at that precise moment, rescue was coming, but it was not in the form Gabriel would ever have expected.

14

Gabriel found it impossible to concentrate. The different characters involved in this sorry drama went round and round his head like incongruous figures on a carousel: Plantagenet, Roland, little Antoine, Terry and his family, Jack Harris, and the ghostly figures of Brigitte and Charles, who knew the truth but could never tell it. There might even be others—in fact, there almost certainly were. If Gordon Merriott had his sticky fingers all over the story, others would know about the family's woes and might have reason to want to do the Nicholsons harm. Grudges ran deep in old villages, as Gabriel had learnt to his cost. They ran deep and exploded into violence at the most unexpected moments.

When his head began thumping with pain, Gabriel reached for his rosary beads and began to pray, but even the ancient prayers brought him back to his present troubles. *The first sorrowful mystery, the Agony in the Garden*. The loneliness of Christ's vigil, the sleeping disciples, the traitor waiting to betray his master with a kiss . . . betrayal, betrayal everywhere, the treachery of false friends . . . Gabriel slipped into a troubled sleep, the beads still wound around his fingers.

It was late afternoon by the time Gabriel opened his eyes again, woken from a deep, drug-induced sleep by the sound of footsteps entering the room and the murmur of conversation. Gabriel felt the queasy sense of disorientation brought on by having slept at the wrong time of day, and he could taste acid in his mouth. A bleary glance to his right caused Gabriel to start in surprise. He was not sure whom he had expected to visit him, but Dr Paige stood beside him, not a sign of a white coat anywhere, very definitely an off-duty doctor visiting a friend. "Good afternoon, Father," said Dr Paige cheerfully, sitting himself down without further ado. "You have been in the wars."

Gabriel cringed at the doctor's tone, which he suspected was reserved for little boys who had fallen off their bicycles or sprained their wrists playing cricket. "I've felt better, if that's what you mean. Have you come to spring me from jail?"

Dr Paige chuckled softly. "You're not my patient, I'm afraid."

"I want to go home."

Dr Paige slipped an envelope out of his pocket and handed it carefully to Gabriel. The envelope was sealed but not stamped or properly addressed, with just Plantagenet Nicholson's name written in neat black letters on the front. "Regardless of whether you are my patient, I may need to get you out of here, Father," said Dr Paige seriously. "I'm not sure I should be giving this to you, but Antoine was so frightened, I didn't think it wise to give it to the police."

"Should it not go to the intended recipient?" enquired Gabriel, but he was already tracing his finger along the sealed edge, looking for a way in which to open the envelope without damaging it.

Dr Paige took the envelope back, indicating the name as though Gabriel could have failed to notice it. "Antoine said that his father had given this to him to deliver on his way to the scout camp, but in his excitement, he forgot all about it. By the time he remembered, he was afraid to tell anyone about it." Dr Paige looked almost embarrassed on behalf of the child. "Look here, this is going to sound silly, but Antoine seems to have got it into his head that his aunt did it. He thought the note might be important."

"You should probably hand it to Inspector Applegate in that case," suggested Gabriel halfheartedly, but his curiosity was getting the better of his moral judgement. He had learnt to take the intuition of children more seriously than most adults deigned to do, having known children who had been ignored with disastrous consequences. "This all feels a bit grubby, frankly."

Dr Paige threw Gabriel a look of comradely defiance and opened the envelope in two deft movements. "I don't think I owe Inspector Applegate anything," he said tartly. "I'd rather have you as the arbiter of the truth than a man who looks like he did his police training with the Gestapo."

Before Gabriel could answer that this was a little harsh—Gabriel was hopeless at picking his battles—Dr Paige had looked into the envelope and brought out a flimsy piece of folded notepaper. He handed it to Gabriel, who refused to take it. "There's no need to be so pious about it, Father Gabriel. If it turns out to be an olive branch for an estranged sister, I can find some way to get it to her without her knowing I intercepted the letter."

"I really don't—"

"Read it!"

"I can't help feeling you're bullying a sick man," answered Gabriel desperately. "There has to be something against this in the Hippocratic oath."

"There isn't," answered Dr Paige with a smile. He gave a shrug, unfolded the notepaper, and read: " 'Since you have not deigned to answer my last letter, I am writing to you again. You know perfectly well who betrayed my wife to her torturers; you have always known. I know the truth now too, no thanks to you, and I will settle the score. Brigitte has a right to justice.' "

Gabriel reached out for the note and took it from Dr Paige. The terse message was written in the hand of a man who would normally have had impeccable handwriting but was too agitated to take much time over the formation of the letters. The lines of script were not straight, and Charles had blotted the paper twice. "And this was his second letter?"

"Yes," confirmed Dr Paige. "I knew that before reading the note. Antoine told me that the previous week, his father had sent him to put another envelope through Plantagenet's letterbox. Though of course he had no idea what it was about."

"Did Antoine say anything about how his father had appeared when he gave him the second letter to deliver?" asked Gabriel.

"He did say that his father had seemed out of sorts, but Antoine assumed it was because his father had had a falling out with Plantagenet and was finding it a strain to write to her. He was very insistent that the envelope had to be delivered through her door immediately, which was why Antoine was so upset when he realised he had forgotten the second message. I gather his father had been quite insistent about the first one as well. Father, what are you doing?"

Gabriel was attempting to remove the bandage from around

his head, but the doctor who had applied it had been determined to ensure that it remain in place. "Help me get this thing off," he demanded. "I can't go walking around looking like the ghost of Jacob Marley."

"I'm not sure you should do that. I don't know how bad the head wound is," said Dr Paige, grasping Gabriel's wrist to stop him poking his fingers under the layers of crepe.

"Well, check for me!" exclaimed Gabriel. "It can't be that bad; she only bashed me with a tray."

Dr Paige sighed, gave a quick glance back at the door and began carefully unwinding the bandage. It came away easily in his skilled hands, and he gave a nod of satisfaction at the sight of Gabriel's exposed temple. "There's some colourful bruising and a largish scab behind your ear where the edge of the tray must have cut you, but it's not as bad as I expected. You can do without the dressing."

"Good," said Gabriel, rubbing his head with relief. His fingers strayed to the large tender place where the tray had slammed into him, and he could not help wishing that he had been attacked with a less ridiculous weapon. "Now get me out of this bed and get me out of this hospital. I need to speak to Miss Nicholson."

"That's easy," said Dr Paige, reaching under the bed. There was the rustle of paper, and he handed Gabriel his clothes, neatly parcelled up in a brown paper bag. "Get dressed and we'll go."

Gabriel looked nervously at the door as Dr Paige turned his back to allow his friend some privacy to change. "Are you sure about this?" he asked. "Don't I have to fill out a form or something?"

It did not help Gabriel's confidence in his escape that,

when he slipped off his hospital gown, he saw his mottled skin for the first time: grey-blue bruises competing with fresher, darker patches from the battering he had received the day before. "Can I really just walk away?"

"This is hospital, not a prison," said Dr Paige, taking the opportunity to open the door a fraction and cast a cautious eye on the corridor outside. All was quiet for the moment. "But all the same, I think it best if you slip out without having to confront any of the doctors or nurses here."

"Won't they be a bit alarmed when they find the bed empty?" asked Gabriel, imagining the sweet nurse having to tell Matron that one of her patients had absconded. "I don't want to get anyone into trouble."

"They'll probably phone the abbey to find out where on earth you've gone; then they will write on your medical notes that you were released against medical advice. After that, they will leave you alone. You're a grown man, and you're entitled to discharge yourself." Dr Paige risked turning round and saw Gabriel struggling to raise his arms enough to fit his Roman collar. "Having said that, if you were my patient, I'd do anything to get you back into hospital, where you belong. Is there no other way to deal with this?"

"None that I can think of. Either we confront Plantagenet Nicholson ourselves or we go to Applegate with the evidence. Either way, I need to be up and about. I can't stand hospitals."

"You don't have to like them," said Dr Paige, but he would have to save the lecture about the importance of trusting the medical profession for another day. He had enough trouble convincing his own wife to trust doctors at the best of times, and she was married to one. Gabriel was dressed and almost ready, apart from his shoes, which were unlaced. "You can't bend down far enough to tie your laces, can you?" asked the doctor.

Gabriel felt himself blushing as he shook his head and waited whilst Dr Paige got on his knees and tied Gabriel's laces for him. He could almost hear his father: *It's really very simple, my boy. Right over left and under . . .* "Thank you," mumbled Gabriel. He hesitated for a moment to pick up his knapsack, then realised that, of course, he had brought nothing with him.

The two men tiptoed into the corridor like a pair of thieves from a Charlie Chaplin picture, giving an already nervous Gabriel the urge to laugh. "Now walk out with me as though you own the place," Dr Paige instructed under his breath. They walked, backs straight—or as straight as Gabriel could manage—down the corridor and out of the hospital via a side door, with Gabriel daring to catch his breath only when they were safely outside. "Not so bad, was it?"

"It's all right for you," said Gabriel, following Dr Paige to his car. He was already having to force himself not to limp, as there was a tenderness across both his knees from having fallen heavily onto them. "You're used to hospitals."

Dr Paige helped Gabriel into the car, sensing that any change of posture was going to be painful for him. "I'll drive as gently as possible," promised the doctor, closing the door to the passenger seat and walking round the front of the car to get in behind the wheel. "If it helps at all, I used to get very nervous visiting Marie in hospital after the liberation."

Gabriel looked at him in confusion, bracing himself as the car lurched forwards. "But you were working in that hospital!"

"Yes, but you have no idea how ill Marie was when I carried her out of that hellhole. As a doctor I probably knew better than she did how bad things were looking. Every time I was free to visit her, I prayed I would not find another patient in her bed."

"I don't think I'd realised quite how serious it was. Of course, I knew that she must have been starving, but one forgets how many of those prisoners died after being liberated."

"Too many to count; it was heartbreaking," said Dr Paige. "It's not just the starvation that's a problem in those cases. She had open wounds that had become infected, and her body was ill-equipped to fight infection. She managed to avoid typhus, thank goodness; it was endemic in the camp. That really would have finished her off."

"I'm sure a lot of it was down to you," said Gabriel, hoping he was saying the right thing. The very mention of the camps caused people to talk in hushed tones, if they could bring themselves to talk about them at all. "You saved her life."

"She was pretty determined to live," said Dr Paige modestly, but they both knew that Marie would have been unlikely to survive if he had not found her that day. "Do you know the only thing she asked me for when she was recovering? A covering for her head. She said she wanted her dignity back, and it would help her to feel more like her old self. So I paid a woman to sew her a little hat. I thought it made her look like a nun, but she was delighted with it."

Gabriel glanced at Dr Paige's wristwatch. As always, Gabriel was anxious about the time and the many hours wasted in the hospital bed. Plantagenet might be long gone from the village by now. If her brother's previous note to her had carried virtually the same message, Plantagenet must have had some idea that the finger of blame would eventually point at her. For all Gabriel knew, she might have left the country by now, and no one would be any the wiser. There was no warrant out for her arrest, no reason why she should have been detained at any port from which she chose to travel. "I wonder if you should drop me off at Plantagenet Nicholson's house and go in search of Applegate yourself," said Gabriel, sitting forwards in his seat. "There may be little time, but I feel the inspector should know about the latest turn of events."

"Father Gabriel, I'm not leaving you to confront anyone on your own," said Dr Paige firmly. "Even if I weren't so unwilling to go near that old bully, I'm not prepared to risk your safety. A third assault might be one too many."

"Plantagenet Nicholson is many things, but I can hardly imagine her braining me with a frying pan," answered Gabriel. But then he had hardly imagined that Abigail would fly at him in the way she had done. Gabriel never saw a threat coming; it was all too easy to imagine Plantagenet turning on him if he gave her cause. And he was about to give her every possible cause to do him harm. "I'm not sure you should come into the house," Gabriel added, trying to imagine Plantagenet's face if two men appeared uninvited on her doorstep. "You could stay in the car, and if I don't come out within ten minutes, you can join me."

"I'll say I'm here in my capacity as your doctor. You are

too unwell to be left alone," suggested Dr Paige with calm authority. "She can't object to that."

"She certainly can, and she will," said Gabriel. "She's not at all fond of men, and I need her to trust me. She'll see through a ruse like that immediately."

"I'm not so sure about that; you should see what you look like."

Gabriel ignored the observation and gestured to a nearby grass verge. "Pull over here and let me walk around the corner to Plantagenet's house. Don't drive round; the car will be too conspicuous in a narrow country lane. Walk round after me and wait out of sight."

Gabriel hoped that he was not getting too above himself, issuing orders like someone out of a James Cagney picture, but he knew from painful experience that this was the most sensitive moment, and—if Plantagenet were still to be found—he must do nothing to frighten her or arouse her suspicion. *Jesus, mercy*, he whispered, but Gabriel could do nothing to prevent the familiar tightening of his chest as he climbed the steps to the door.

The door opened swiftly before Gabriel could alert anyone to his presence, revealing Plantagenet's housekeeper, whom Gabriel remembered was known as Mrs B. "Can I help you?" said the lady in question without further niceties, but almost immediately, her already harried face took on a look of shock. "Whatever's happened to you? Are you all right?"

Gabriel looked away, running a hand over his face. "It's nothing; I fell off my bicycle." This was not entirely untrue; he had fallen—after he had been rammed into by a van and before he had been attacked by an enraged landlady. "Is Miss Nicholson at home? It's quite urgent."

Mrs B looked positively exasperated now. "No, she went out about an hour ago."

"Do you know where?" Gabriel felt a small stab of hope. If she was here just an hour ago, she could not have fled far.

"She said something about going to her father's house," said Mrs B. "Took some jars of jam for him, said he must want for a few things." To Mrs B's immediate annoyance, Gabriel failed to take the hint to leave. "I hope you'll not think me rude," she said, "but I've to pack Miss Nicholson's bags, and I've not got long. Was there anything else?"

Gabriel gave Mrs B an apologetic smile. "No, not at all. Thank you for your time."

Mrs B prevented Gabriel from taking up another second of her time by closing the door in his face, just quietly enough to avoid an obvious insult. Gabriel turned around and noticed Dr Paige making an embarrassingly poor show of discretion by standing by the gate with an open newspaper covering his face. Gabriel strode over to him and poked at the newspaper, causing Dr Paige to crumple the edges of the paper in his fists. "You'll blow my cover," hissed Dr Paige.

"She's not at home. We need to go round to Roland Nicholson's house. The housekeeper thinks she went there, and she's planning to go away shortly." Gabriel glanced back at the house as they walked away, troubled by the sense that something was amiss. Glimpsing at the downstairs window, Gabriel noticed a partially concealed face, impossible to recognise through the net curtains.

"What do you want me to do?" asked Dr Paige, making an awkward attempt at rolling up his paper and succeeding only in crumpling it further.

"Keep Roland Nicholson talking," said Gabriel. "I want him to know as little as possible for the moment."

The Nicholsons' house looked very much as it had done the day before, except Gabriel did not recognise the policeman on duty, which he took as a bad sign. Before Gabriel could consider his next move, the policeman noticed the two men walking towards him and gave them an appraising glance.

"Good afternoon, constable," said Gabriel, trying to imitate Inspector Applegate's air of confidence. "I'm looking for a Miss Plantagenet Nicholson. Her housekeeper mentioned that she'd come to see her father."

The policeman recovered from the sight of Gabriel's face and gave a mischievous smile. "So, you're the famous priest who thinks he's Hercule Poirot," he said, speaking with an accent Gabriel did not recognise. It was too harsh to be Wiltshire; it might almost have been Cornish, but likening Gabriel to the little Belgian detective with his little grey cells made a refreshing change from comparing him to Sir Arthur Conan Doyle's drug-addicted, ungentlemanly creation. "The old dear's here all right, but her daddy don't want to talk to her. He's in the house, sulking. She's in the summerhouse, probably also sulking."

Gabriel did not ask permission to enter, pushing past the constable in a way that he would normally have regarded as the height of bad manners. He would make his apologies on the way out. "Go and find Roland; I'll talk to Plantagenet," Gabriel told Dr Paige. "It may make our job a little easier if they're keeping themselves separate."

Dr Paige nodded, making his way through the narrow hallway whilst Gabriel hurried through the now-familiar kitchen and into the garden. The first thing he saw was that the sweet little curtains of Brigitte's memorial had been drawn across the windows. He could hear movement inside and hurried to the door, pushing it open and entering immediately to prevent the occupant from hiding whatever she was doing.

Brigitte's beautifully preserved shrine was being plundered by a distraught woman almost unrecognisable as the restrained, orderly Plantagenet Nicholson. She was not so completely absorbed in the task of taking the place apart to fail to notice that she had company, but it took several destructive seconds before she stopped what she was doing and turned to face Gabriel. Plantagenet's face was flushed scarlet, and she stood in the midst of piles of books she had dragged from the shelves. "What are you doing in my house?" she shouted in Gabriel's face, recovering her nerve enough to play at just indignation. "How dare you barge in here!"

"Miss Nicholson, this is not your house," said Gabriel, forcing himself not to take a step back. He rather wished he had asked Dr Paige to accompany him in here, but it was too late now; he comforted himself that there were three people within screaming distance if the situation turned ugly. "You have no more business barging in here than I have. What are you doing?"

"Get out!" she shrieked, thrusting her face so close to Gabriel's that he could feel flecks of spittle on his skin as she shouted at him. She was determined to force him to step back out of the summerhouse, but he stood his ground. "This is none of your business! None of this was *any* of your business!"

Gabriel took a risk and placed the palm of his hand

on Plantagenet's shoulder, nudging her away from him. "Madam, murder is never a family affair. The truth was always going to come out sooner or later; it was simply a matter of which of us got to it first."

Plantagenet raised her hand as though she meant to strike him, causing Gabriel to twist away from her, but she covered her face with her hand and let out a muffled scream of anguish. It was a sound so horrible, Gabriel could feel it piercing him like barbed wire. "My brother should never have died! None of this should ever have happened. Oh, God!"

Gabriel helped Plantagenet pick her way across the littered floor to the rocking chair, where she could sit and catch her breath. "Miss Nicholson, why did you betray Brigitte?"

Plantagenet was shaking her head like a wounded animal, gulping and sobbing in utter despair. Gabriel heard the whimpering noises of a woman desperately trying to speak and failing, the words refusing to form themselves. Her weeping went on and on; Gabriel knew better than to try to comfort her. Plantagenet had been fighting this guilt since Brigitte had first disappeared, and nothing Gabriel said could take away the raw, toxic force of emotion she was experiencing.

Eventually, as exhaustion began to creep over Plantagenet and her cries became softer, Gabriel attempted to speak. "Was that why you went out to France after VE day? Did you hope somehow that it had not been you who had condemned her?"

Plantagenet nodded miserably. "Father, I swear on all that's holy, I never meant to do that poor dear girl any harm. I meant every word when I said I loved her, that everyone loved her. I'm afraid I did something very foolish." Plantagenet pulled a handkerchief out of her pocket and blew her nose. Her efforts to speak failed her again, and she put her head down.

"Careless talk costs lives," said Gabriel, "or so the wartime propaganda told us. And it does."

"Don't I know it," said Plantagenet between sobs. "My careless talk cost Brigitte her life. She died a terrible death, and it was my fault. When I told you that she was killed in her own town, that wasn't the half of it. Her family told me that her teeth had been knocked out, that her fingers were bleeding because she had no fingernails, that her face was so swollen she could barely open her eyes. No one deserves to die like that, especially not Brigitte, and she died because I couldn't keep my mouth shut."

Gabriel cleared some space on the floor, carefully stacking the dropped books in a pile by the shelf before sitting down, so as to avoid standing over Plantagenet as they talked. "The argument that separated you from your brother, Miss Nicholson, was not caused by you accusing him; it was the other way round. He knew that Brigitte had confided in you and that you had betrayed her trust."

"I never meant to betray anyone; you have to believe me, Father!" Plantagenet burst out. "I swear to you there was no malice in my actions whatsoever. I would never have let anyone hurt her! I'm afraid I'm one of those who loved not wisely but too well." Plantagenet looked searchingly at Gabriel, as though trying to discern how much sympathy she could expect from him. "How did you know?"

Gabriel looked directly back at her. He knew she had the

right to know everything he had discovered. "Charles sent you a second letter through Antoine, but in all the excitement of the scout camp and then the drama of what happened next, the child forgot all about it and found it this morning in his pocket."

"You opened a letter intended for me?" exclaimed Plantagenet, a ripple of anger rallying her strength for a moment. "What right had you to do that?"

"I didn't open the letter myself, Miss Nicholson, and it merely confirmed what I had already guessed about you." Gabriel took a deep breath, knowing that he was slipping into very dangerous territory now. "If you'll forgive my saying so, Miss Nicholson, you struck me from the start as rather an indiscreet person. I do not mean to insult you, you understand, but you were very quick to share details of your family's life with me."

"You are a priest!" Plantagenet blustered, stung by words of criticism she had almost certainly heard before. "I believed I could trust you."

"People are often very open with me for exactly that reason," Gabriel confirmed, "but you went a little beyond that. Most people are not keen to divulge the intimate details of family disagreements to complete strangers, even a person they believe they can trust. I usually have to try quite hard to find out information, but you told me far more than I could ever have thought to ask."

Plantagenet was glaring fixedly at Gabriel, causing him to stand up slowly, preparing himself for a confrontation. "You set traps for me," she said in an undertone that was more unnerving than a raised voice. "You betrayed my confidence."

"I assure you I did not," said Gabriel gravely. "I would never do such a thing, and I had no reason to believe that you were in any way caught up in your brother's death at that point. I merely listen to what I am told. Brigitte confided in you, and you repeated her secret to your brother."

"He was her husband; I thought it couldn't possibly matter!" Plantagenet protested, repeating a justification she must have told herself hundreds of times.

"If Brigitte had chosen not to tell her husband, she must surely have had her reasons," said Gabriel. "It is a serious matter to keep secrets from one's own husband."

Plantagenet gave Gabriel a smile that still managed to be patronising even in the midst of her distress. "I'm afraid you men have a very inflated view of yourselves. There are plenty of things a woman will tell her closest female friend that she will not tell her husband. There's a bond between women that men do not always understand." Plantagenet rocked back and forth in the chair, her eyes wet and shiny. "To this day, I've never really known why I felt the need to tell him. I suppose that, because it was Charles, it didn't seem important. He adored her, or so I thought. He would never betray her, and I knew he'd be tickled by her choice of code name."

"That was what she told you—her code name?"

"Yes. Her code name was Darnay, after—"

"The hero from *A Tale of Two Cities*," Gabriel interrupted, remembering seeing a copy of the book on the shelf and then on the floor just a moment ago. "The Frenchman who starts a new life in England only to return during his country's greatest peril."

"That's correct. Those agents had to learn a poem or a

passage from literature to identify themselves to their minder, I suppose. She took the last lines of the book as her text. 'It is a far, far better thing that I do, than I have ever done; it is a far, far better rest that I go to than I have ever known.'" Plantagenet stumbled over the Dickensian quotation but succeeded in preventing herself breaking down again. "We were the only ones who knew Brigitte's identity, Charles and I. I blamed him; he blamed me."

"Miss Nicholson, what were you trying to find when I came into the room?" He cast a hand around the cluttered space. "You've turned the place upside down, and I do not believe you would have been so disrespectful unless you were quite desperate."

Plantagenet rose to her feet. She no longer stood up straight, and her hunched shoulders and defeated figure made Plantagenet look many years older than she truly was. "Brigitte asked that all her letters and personal writings be burnt if she did not return from the war. It was desperately hard to do, but my brother insisted that we should do as she had asked. But she also said that if she were captured, she would find some way to expose her betrayer."

"Most people who were captured by the Gestapo must have been betrayed by trusted friends or associates," said Gabriel. "She knew the—but this makes no sense!"

It was Plantagenet's turn to step away from Gabriel. "What's the matter? You've a face like thunder; what is it?"

"What you have just said. How could she possibly find a way to expose her betrayer when she had already been captured? None of this makes sense! Even if you did betray Brigitte's secret to Charles, why should Charles have given his own wife's code name to the Nazis when everyone seems to agree that he adored her?"

Plantagenet was backing towards the door, trembling with panic. "I don't know! It made no sense to me either, but there was no other possibility. The only person Brigitte told was me, and the only person I told was Charles. Perhaps he was careless too!" She paused for breath. The emotional upheaval of the meeting was beginning to tell, and Plantagenet sounded like a swimmer struggling to stop herself from being swept out to sea after wandering into a cross current. "Father, help me. I didn't kill him. I have Brigitte's life on my conscience, not his."

"That is not how the courts will see it," said Gabriel as gently as possible. He was unsettled by his own confusion, and he fought to focus his attention on Plantagenet's predicament. "If the prosecution can dispense with the idea that Charles was killed by burglars, you are the obvious suspect. The counsel for the prosecution will argue that you killed Charles either because you believed him to have betrayed Brigitte to the Germans or because he was threatening to expose your own treachery. Either way, they will make the case against you stick."

Plantagenet was pale but calm now, though it felt more like the resignation of the damned than a sense of peace, which she would never enjoy. "I cut myself off from my brother because I believed that he had used the information I had given him to condemn his own wife. I didn't kill him, and there is no one else who could have done."

"Miss Nicholson, I have to ask you this: Are you absolutely certain that you told nobody else?"

She groaned in exasperation. "I may be indiscreet, but I am not a malicious gossip. I told Charles, and only Charles!"

"Was anyone else within earshot when you talked to him? Your father perhaps?"

Plantagenet shook her head. "We were alone in the house. I would never have talked to my father about Brigitte anyway; he was too upset about her leaving. I tried to avoid the subject as far as possible."

Gabriel looked at the almost empty bookshelves, and his heart gave a start. His eye kept being drawn to the same empty space. "What happened to that statue? The Saint Brigid?"

Plantagenet looked back at Gabriel as though she thought he had lost his mind. Gabriel did not wait for Plantagenet's answer. He hurtled out of the summerhouse and back in the direction of the house, with Plantagenet calling desperately after him. In the kitchen, Gabriel almost collided with Dr Paige, who was in the process of making a pot of tea. "What are you doing?" exclaimed Gabriel, looking past Dr Paige in the hope of seeing Roland. "Where is he?"

"Mr Nicholson's just popped out for a minute," Dr Paige explained, looking Gabriel up and down in surprise. "What's the matter? I didn't think you'd mind as long as he was well away from his daughter."

"But where did he go?" demanded Gabriel. "Did he say where he was going? Was he . . . was he distressed at all?"

"No, not at all. We had a perfectly nice chat. Then he mentioned something about having a parcel to deliver and went off to the post office. He'll be back in a minute."

Gabriel gave Dr Paige a shove in the direction of the hall. "We need to get to your house immediately."

"But why? What on earth—"

"There's no time to explain. Just go!"

They rushed out of the house, passing the astonished policeman as they hurried out onto the road. "My car!" exclaimed Dr Paige, pointing at the empty street. "I parked it over there!"

Gabriel felt his hands trembling. Making decisions under pressure had never been Gabriel's greatest talent, but he had to think of a solution. "Dr Paige, go to the telephone box and ring Marie. Tell her to lock the doors and let nobody in the house."

Dr Paige blenched. "What's going on? Is Marie in some kind of danger?"

"I'm so sorry, my friend. This is my fault. Tell her absolutely nobody is to enter the house until we arrive. Nobody at all. Do you understand?"

Dr Paige needed no further explanation and hurried in the direction of the telephone box whilst Gabriel turned back to the house and called out to the policeman. "Constable, do you have a car?"

The policeman looked incredulous. "Of course not. Why?"

"Then you're going to have to requisition one," answered Gabriel. "Go now; we need a car."

Incredulity turned to horror. "I can't go just taking some poor chap's car!" he protested. "The guv'nor will have my neck!"

"No he won't; he'll have mine," Gabriel assured him, hustling him away from the door. "Do it now. The next car you see."

"But I'm not supposed to leave my post!"

"Young man, if you delay, a life may well be lost,"

said Gabriel, "and you don't want that on your conscience." He knew he was putting the constable in an unenviable position; if there had been any easy way to do so, Gabriel would have tried to warn Inspector Applegate, but he had no way of knowing whether the inspector could be located in time. "Please do this. I shall take full responsibility."

Gabriel watched to ensure that the young constable had hurried off along the road in search of a suitable vehicle, before rushing over to the telephone box to find Dr Paige. He was replacing the telephone receiver, visibly agitated. "She's not answering the phone," he said, looking to Gabriel for an explanation. "Father, answer me honestly. Is she in any danger?"

"I don't know," Gabriel replied. "All I know is that we have to get to your house before Roland does." Gabriel heard a screech of brakes and what sounded like a violent argument being conducted just around the corner. "Quickly!"

The policeman had certainly excelled himself. He had requisitioned the first vehicle to drive past him, which happened to be a bus. The constable was now engaged in a shouting match with the furious driver, who not unreasonably resented having his passengers turfed out onto the road so that he could be forced into some fool's errand. "When your guv'nor hears about this, you'll never wear that uniform again!" shouted the driver. But Dr Paige and Gabriel were already mounting the steps onto the bus, and the driver was too shocked to continue berating the policeman. "What the hell is this? Some kind of practical joke?"

It ought to have been the most ludicrous joke imaginable: *A policeman, a doctor and a Catholic priest hijacked a bus . . .*

"I'm so sorry about all the trouble," said Gabriel, as though he had mislaid his ticket, "but this is an emergency. There's a killer at large, and we need your help to stop him."

Gabriel had doubted his words would have any effect, but the driver pulled away immediately, causing his three passengers to be thrown back into the aisle like a trio of drunks. Gabriel and the policeman hauled themselves into seats whilst Dr Paige stood next to the driver, giving him directions to his home. The thought crossed Gabriel's mind momentarily that he might have got everything wrong, that this whole misadventure was going to look absolutely ridiculous when it was reported in the county rag at the end of the week, but fear quickly focused his mind on the dangers about to descend upon Dr Paige's welcoming little home.

Gabriel had wondered at first whether they might intercept Dr Paige's car on the way, but it was much too far ahead for that. The bus bounced and thumped along the road, causing the three men to rattle about like rag dolls. The bus was not meant to be driven at this sort of speed, and Gabriel shielded his face from the incredulous and indignant passersby who watched openmouthed as the lumbering village bus revved dangerously along the winding roads like a thing possessed.

Please, O Lord, don't let us be too late. I beg of you . . .

The bus lurched down the familiar main road through the town, past Saint Patrick's Church and Gabriel's old home, past the bookshop and the pub and the civic hall. As they hurtled past a side road, Gabriel heard the angry parp of a car horn as the bus narrowly missed a collision. Then to Gabriel's eternal relief, they began to slow down as the surgery and the Paige home came into sight. "Stop here," Dr Paige commanded the driver, who immediately slammed on the brakes without troubling to pull over onto the verge.

Gabriel, Dr Paige and the policeman had barely descended the bus steps before it pitched forwards and disappeared down the road in an outraged cloud of smoke. The policeman staggered towards the hedge and vomited copiously, but Gabriel and Dr Paige had no time to assist him and ran in the direction of the house. "Will you for pity's sake tell me what's going on?" demanded Dr Paige. They both registered the presence of Dr Paige's car directly outside the house and made a last effort to reach the front door.

The door was locked. "The statue was missing," said Gabriel between strained breaths. "He said he'd take it to Antoine. I knew he was coming here. The statue . . . it would be a distraction. The child would—"

Dr Paige gave up rattling the door handle and began hammering on the door. "Marie!" he shouted. "Open the door!"

Gabriel heard the faint smash of glass breaking round the corner a split second before Dr Paige registered what had happened, and the priest tore round the side of the house in time to see a flutter of floral print cloth as Marie disappeared inside through a broken window. "Marie!" Gabriel called. She had already noted that she was being watched and looked back through the broken window in alarm. Marie had been so desperate to get into the house that she had not bothered to knock out the remaining shards of glass from the frame, and her hands were bleeding from the many little cuts she had received as she had scrambled through. "Marie, what's happened? Open the front door!"

"I have to find them; he locked me out!" she replied, terrified and gasping for breath. Gabriel watched Marie hurrying away through the sitting room—scattering droplets of blood as she ran—driven by a primordial maternal instinct to come to the defence of a child in trouble. Dr Paige was pushing Gabriel to one side, clearing the remaining glass with his gloved hand before climbing through the empty window frame. He ran through the sitting room and out into the hallway to find Marie, not stopping to wait for Gabriel.

Gabriel was in the house a moment later. He could hear shouting and the sounds of a scuffle nearby, and he knew that Marie had got there first. Shouts, not screams, he told himself, though it was the weakest of reassurances. People shouted when there was hope; they screamed in despair. Marie was shouting. She was shouting with the anger of an avenging angel.

Gabriel could barely remember how he made it into the room, but he was greeted by a scene of such confusion and panic when he entered the kitchen that it was impossible to process what was happening. Dr Paige stood behind an enraged Marie, holding her arms in an apparent attempt to restrain her; Roland sat slumped against the far wall, clutching his shoulder, oblivious to the blood seeping between his fingers. Antoine stood as still as a tree, eyes blazing, the fingers of his right hand smeared with blood. His hair was soaking wet and plastered against his forehead, beads of sweat running down his face. On the floor lay a vegetable knife, a poor weapon snatched from the knife block at random by an unskilled hand.

For a moment nobody moved. They all seemed to be stricken by the shock of being caught in a nightmare without knowing which of them was dreaming it. Then Marie broke the impasse. Without any apparent effort, she shrugged off her husband and stepped towards Antoine, putting her arms around him. He stood frozen to the spot, not looking at her or even facing her, his gaze—too angry and haunted to come from a child—continuing to rest on his grandfather. Then childhood took over. Not for the first time, Antoine fell into Marie's arms and burst into tears.

Dr Paige and Gabriel moved over to Roland, the doctor moving Roland's hand away so that he could take a look at the cause of the bleeding. "He stabbed me," said Roland pathetically. "The child stabbed me with that knife."

It was then that Gabriel noticed the water on the floor, and the washing-up basin in the sink, half-full of water. He looked back at Marie, who was gesturing to Antoine and mouthing the words "He's soaking wet." The knife block was within easy reach, even of a child, from the sink. As Roland had been forcing Antoine's head into the water, Antoine had reached out desperately and grabbed the first weapon he could find. "Darling, you'd better take Antoine into another room," said Dr Paige, without looking back at her. He was busy unbuttoning Roland's waistcoat and shirt to reach the knife wound.

"I'm sorry," said Antoine, sobbing, as Marie propelled him gently but determinedly out of the kitchen.

"Is it bad?" asked Gabriel, avoiding looking at the damage. He had seen worse, but there was something ghastly about a man sitting wounded in the middle of a domestic kitchen, waiting passively whilst a doctor stripped off his upper clothes, shaking his head in a gesture that could mean almost anything.

"Barely a scratch," said Dr Paige, sounding almost disappointed. "The child would not have had the strength to force the blade in very deep. As it is, the knife had to get through two layers of cloth before puncturing the skin."

"But I'm bleeding!" wailed Roland like a little boy trying to convince the grown-ups that he really is very poorly. "Look at me!"

"There's nothing to concern yourself about," answered Dr Paige coldly. "The tip of the knife has cut into a blood vessel, that's all." Doctor Paige brought a clean white tea towel out of the kitchen cupboard and handed it to Gabriel. "Press this against the wound, would you, old man? I shan't be a moment."

Whilst Dr Paige went over to his consulting room to gather whatever he needed to dress a wound, Gabriel sat beside Roland, pressing the folded tea towel against a wound that did indeed look quite small now. "I meant him no harm, you know," said Roland, still sounding like a whining child. "It was very naughty of him; he was a naughty boy."

"Mr Nicholson, you were trying to drown him," said Gabriel, struggling to keep his own anger out of his voice. "No naughty boy deserves that."

Roland hung his head. "I would never have let him drown, even if that's how it looks. I would never have hurt him."

"You have hurt him more horribly than any man could," said Gabriel with deliberate slowness. "You killed his mother; you killed his father. He will always live with the wounds you have inflicted upon him."

"I never meant any harm," murmured Roland. What strength remained in him had dwindled away. "I never meant any of this to happen. I've lost everything."

The man's outrageous self-pity sickened Gabriel, but in many ways, Roland was right. He may not have lost everything, but he had thrown away everything, including—almost inevitably—his own life. Gabriel knew that there was no way to sugarcoat it. "You have not lost anything; you threw away the lives of those who most loved you, and it's over now," said Gabriel, noting Dr Paige standing at the kitchen door, unwilling to interrupt them. "You had best spend what little time is left to you atoning for what you have done."

Dr Paige stepped across the floor, kneeling opposite Roland. "I'm just going to clean the wound," he said, holding out a bottle of iodine. "You shan't require stitches."

"How did you know?" asked Roland listlessly. He had the air of a man who does not greatly care how he became ensnared but cares only that there is no longer any way out. "How did you—" The rest of the question was silenced as the iodine stung Roland into a gasping silence.

"I never quite believed the story about Charles dabbling with Fascism," Gabriel explained. "Somehow, it did not fit well with the image I was also given of a young man falling in love with a beautiful French girl, going so far as to convert to her faith in order to marry her. His actions flew in the face of generations of bigotry to do so. The fact that it was you, not Charles, behind the scheme to dupe the War Office made me even more suspicious."

"He was furious with me when he discovered what I had

done," said Roland glumly, turning his head away from Dr Paige as he dressed the wound with perfunctory professionalism. "It put him in an impossible position. If he had admitted what I had done, he risked putting a noose around his old friend's neck, not to mention disgracing his own father. The shame of being forced to stay at home whilst his own wife went away to fight was almost unbearable."

"And the Nicholson who was arrested at that Fascist rally was you, not your son, wasn't it?" Gabriel pressed him. "The newspaper article said merely 'Nichols', meaning 'Nicholson', but it was you who attended that rally. It was you who had the dubious connections."

Gabriel thought of that incriminating photograph accompanying the news report, the older man reaching out to an angry son in the hope of saving him from the snares of Oswald Mosley's empty promises. The old adage "The camera never lies" was nonsense, of course; even when there was no deliberate intent to deceive, a photograph snapped without any relevant context could give a false impression of events. Roland might have been calmly appealing to an angry son, or Charles might have been angrily remonstrating with a sullen father. Gabriel had interpreted the picture incorrectly thanks to an erroneous but all-too-common assumption that it is always the younger generation who go astray. The claims about Charles' alleged bad character had cemented that false view.

"You'd better stay where you are until the police come for you," said Dr Paige, standing up and stepping away from Roland. His manner was not exactly hostile, but Dr Paige had refined the great British art of exuding disapproval without doing or saying anything specific. He turned to Gabriel. "I'd better attend to Antoine and Marie."

Roland did not wait until Dr Paige had left the room before he began protesting again. "I never imagined that Brigitte would be killed, Father; you must believe me. They said she'd only be detained."

Gabriel's mind flashed back to the courtroom, with Marie describing the evils of the Nazi penal system to a horrified gathering of lawyers, reporters and friends. "Ask Marie what it was like *only* to be detained by the Germans," he said softly. "No good man would condemn his own daughter-in-law to a fate like that."

"I didn't want to do it; I had no choice!" Roland spluttered. "Terry's family were bleeding me dry; it started as soon as Terry had arranged to impersonate Charles for me. If Brigitte's blood is on anyone's hands, it's on theirs. They knew I was not a wealthy man."

"Mr Nicholson . . ."

"And then Antoine went and blurted out his mother's code name to me. Thinking himself so clever, putting temptation in the way of a desperate man."

It was always somebody else's fault. The more serious the offence, the more determined a man would be to convince himself that culpability lay elsewhere. It was Terry's fault for taking Roland's money; it was a little boy's fault for innocently divulging the details of an overheard conversation. "And Charles?" asked Gabriel. "Was his murder also his fault?"

"There was nothing to be gained by exposing me!" shouted Roland, his voice rasping with strain. "She was dead! It was too late! Brigitte would have forgiven me; she was a good girl! I told him I was sorry!"

And there it was. The world was so simple for men like Roland. The moral responsibility belonged to others, including a child and a man seeking justice murdered by his own father. Roland should apparently face no penalty whatsoever, no shame, no censure, because he said he was sorry. Gabriel suspected that Roland would still be protesting that it was not fair as they placed the noose around his neck.

Gabriel heard the sound of the front door being unlocked and footsteps approaching. The policeman they had left vomiting outside was standing before them, looking pale and uncertain but surprisingly dignified. He cleared his throat. "Am I supposed to be arresting anybody?"

Roland actually rolled his eyes, reaching up an arm for Gabriel to help him to his feet. "It's all right, young man," he said. "I'll come quietly."

It was farcical, watching a nervous young constable fumbling the formal words of arrest to a man who might have been his grandfather. Dr Paige was standing in the doorway, waiting for the appropriate moment to speak. "I telephoned the constabulary. Inspector Applegate is on his way."

"Is there somewhere Mr Nicholson could sit with PC . . ." Gabriel hesitated, realising to his shame that he had not asked the policeman his name.

"PC Castle," said PC Castle, as though reporting for duty. He had slipped handcuffs onto Roland's wrists and looked expectantly at Dr Paige. "We could sit at the table if you prefer, Doctor, well away from the knives and things."

Dr Paige nodded. "Very well. If I know Inspector Applegate, he'll be here in a jiff." He looked at Gabriel. "I need to look after my wife; she's hurt. Perhaps you could come with me and talk to Antoine? I'm afraid he's in a state of shock."

And that was how murders were resolved, it seemed. After all the drama of stolen cars and locked doors and blood and tears, the hours that followed seemed to belong to another time and place altogether. Roland, predictably, made no fuss when Inspector Applegate arrived to transport him, and the constable to whom he was shackled, back to the station. Gabriel noted Applegate praising young PC Castle for apprehending a dangerous man and assured him that his exemplary conduct would be remembered. The exchange reminded Gabriel of what a decent man Applegate was, despite the many disagreements they had had over the past year.

Gabriel tried to encourage Antoine to go out into the garden, as he knew it was a place where the boy felt safe, but Antoine refused to be parted from Marie and sat in stony silence whilst Dr Paige cleaned and bandaged Marie's lacerated arms. Perhaps to reassure Antoine that all was well, or simply through force of habit, Marie made no sound as her husband applied the harsh disinfectant and warned her that some of the wounds were likely to scar. "I shall remember that when I take part in my next beauty contest," said Marie, her laughter only a little forced. "Scars are battle trophies."

You know that more than most, thought Gabriel, noting the difference in Dr Paige's behaviour towards his own wife compared with the criminal to which he had so recently attended. No surprises there, but there was something endearing about the tenderness with which he cared for Marie, finishing the whole process by kissing her lightly on the forehead. "You don't need any more battle trophies," he chided. "Next time you feel the need to hurl yourself through a window, do make sure you've cleared away all the glass first. Or perhaps remember your door key?"

At this, Marie stuck her tongue out, causing Antoine to giggle. The laughter died as quickly as it had come, but it was a start. Antoine would live and thrive. Despite everything—the loss of his mother, his father and now his grandfather, the shattering of childhood trust—somehow or other, Antoine could recover. And a woman who had been broken herself when she was little more than a child might be the one to help him put his life back together.

Marie offered Antoine her hand, which he took without hesitation. "Let's go and put the kettle on," she said, leading him out of the room. "I think there might be some flapjacks hiding somewhere in the kitchen."

Gabriel watched her go, aware that Marie was doing something very deliberate that went beyond distraction techniques. By leading Antoine back to the place where he had so recently been through the most traumatic experience of his life, Marie was stopping fear from taking root. They would sit together at that table, drinking tea and eating flapjacks, keeping one another company, so that Antoine knew he was not alone.

15

Dr Paige had work to do, and Marie was busy attending to Antoine. Gabriel knew when it was time to make a quiet exit, and he made his way to the constabulary, hitching the slowest and most uncomfortable ride of his life on the back of an empty hay cart. He hoped to talk further with Roland, but when he arrived at the police station, he was greeted by a beaming but uncooperative PC Castle.

"Thanks ever so, Father," chirped PC Castle from the desk. "The inspector's very pleased with me. I'm hoping I might get a posting to the city, see some real police work."

Gabriel shook PC Castle's hand in congratulations. He was a young man who had no intention of walking a comfortable beat among Wiltshire's green hills. Gabriel could not quite imagine him dealing with armed robberies and gang warfare in the dark alleyways of London's East End—he was not sure the lad would even cope with pickpockets in Salisbury—but stranger things had happened. "I don't suppose I could speak to Mr Nicholson?" asked Gabriel, banking on PC Castle's gratitude translating into active assistance.

PC Castle shook his head emphatically. "He won't talk to nobody, not even Inspector Applegate. Just sits there, staring into space. Won't even say 'No comment' when he's asked a question."

Gabriel hesitated, unwilling to abandon Roland to his own brooding silence. He knew from experience that killers were intensely vulnerable themselves in the hours and days following arrest, with the enormity of their crimes weighing down on them and the bleakest of futures—or the lack of a future—rising before them. "He might talk to me," Gabriel said.

PC Castle squirmed visibly. "I'm sorry, Father. I'd help if I could. I owe you one. But he said he'll talk to nobody ever again. Especially not you."

Gabriel sighed. There was the smallest possibility that Roland would relent at the last minute, acknowledge his guilt and express his sincere repentance, but Gabriel had learnt not to rely on the threat of a swift if violent death to jolt a man's conscience. Plenty of men and women were forced into self-reflection by an imminent meeting with the hangman, but many more went to the scaffold cursing and protesting until their last strangled breath.

"I don't suppose Inspector Applegate might be—" Gabriel stopped abruptly at the sight of PC Castle shaking his head. "No, I suppose he must have his work cut out now." *But my work is done*, thought Gabriel, giving PC Castle a little bow as he turned to leave. The inspector and a small team of lawyers would be occupied with Roland Nicholson's case now for months; Marie Paige had the task of caring for Antoine. It was time for Gabriel to return to the abbey and to work for the Nicholson family on his knees.

"Wait a moment," said PC Castle to Gabriel's retreating back. Gabriel turned around to look at him, hope soaring that he might be given the chance to approach Roland after all. "I was just about to put the kettle on. Why don't you stop for a cuppa before you go? You must be exhausted."

Gabriel gave a weary smile and nodded gratefully. He was not sure how he felt about being an object of pity, but a cup of tea and friendly company would do Gabriel no harm. "That would be splendid, thank you."

PC Castle led him to a back room, where a tiny kitchen lay tucked away, complete with a hob, a water-filled sink and a shelf containing tins of what looked like tea and biscuits. As PC Castle filled the kettle and lit the gas, he visibly relaxed. "Actually, Father, I'm dying to know how you worked it all out," he said. "Stevens says it's your little angel voices, but I told him that's daft." He looked uncertainly at Gabriel. "I am right, aren't I? You don't really have little voices in your head telling you who done it?"

Gabriel paused in astonishment before bursting out laughing. "Is that what people say?"

PC Castle reddened. "Oh yes. Hercule Poirot has his little grey cells; Father Gabriel has his little angel voices."

Gabriel leant back against the doorframe. "Oh dear, oh dear. I certainly pray for guidance, but I've never had my archangel namesake whisper the name of a murderer in my ear."

"But how did you know?" PC Castle persisted, lining up a chipped brown teapot and two grimy-looking mugs on the work surface. "We were all looking at the same things!"

Gabriel was grateful for the whistle of the kettle boiling, which gave him time to gather his thoughts. "Well, I don't think anyone was fooled by the attempt to make the murder look like a robbery gone wrong. Not for long anyway.

Someone told me once that the commonest motive for murder is love or money. Sometimes both. If Charles Nicholson's murder was not the unfortunate act of a frightened burglar, there had to be a motive."

"Love and money this time."

"In a manner of speaking. Brigitte's memory was so omnipresent in that house, it was not difficult to sense that her story was caught up in the mystery somehow, especially as guilt had divided the family. People are most frequently betrayed by those closest to them—well, Judas was very close to Jesus, wasn't he?"

PC Castle looked bemused by the sudden biblical reference but hid it by handing Gabriel his tea. "Yes, well . . . yes, I suppose he was."

"Politics can certainly drive a person to betrayal," Gabriel continued. "I have noticed that Communism and Fascism have one thing in common: they demand loyalty to the state above everything else. Family ties mean nothing. But even when I considered that Charles Nicholson had flirted with Fascism, it somehow did not ring true. It was abundantly clear that he and his family loved Brigitte, truly loved her. Even when I realised that Roland was the Fascist in the family, I knew he would never have betrayed Brigitte willingly. The love in that family was so obvious that I thought it might be a smokescreen at one point, but there was no getting around it. Brigitte was loved."

"So, you went chasing the money," said PC Castle, helping himself to a biscuit after Gabriel had waved away the tin. "You know, you should have been a policeman."

"I'm not sure your Inspector Applegate would agree with you on that point," said Gabriel with a smile. "Now that I think about it, perhaps there are three motives for murder: love, money, and fear. When a person is truly frightened for his life, his reputation, his security, he becomes vulnerable. All sorts of unspeakable possibilities suddenly arise." Gabriel leant back and closed his eyes. "That was always the difficulty. I suspected Roland, but when he came to my rescue, I doubted myself. And then I could not see how he would have had either the contacts or the information to betray her even if he had wanted to."

"He knows he's going to hang," said PC Castle without emotion. "That's why he's gone into himself. A lot of them do that, I gather."

Gabriel stared into the uninviting contents of his cup. The milk was slightly sour, and little white specks swirled around on the surface of the brown liquid. "I can't understand how I failed to see what was going on in that picture. We always blame the young for everything, but we should know better than that. It was the older generation who took the world to war—twice—and the young who were the victims." Gabriel put down his cup, hoping PC Castle would not notice that it was still full. "And then, of course, I should have realised that Antoine might have found everything out from the start. Children are very good at overhearing things and sneaking about undetected because no one is looking for them in the first place."

PC Castle cleared away the tea things, noting Gabriel's untouched tea. "You know, Father, if you don't mind me saying, you're awfully glum for someone who's just solved a murder. Most coppers would be bouncing off the walls by now, going down to the pub to celebrate."

Gabriel stood up sadly. "I suppose I can never get it out

of my head that nobody wins. A man is still dead, a woman was still betrayed and killed, an old man is going to hang, and a little boy has lost everything."

"But the truth is out," said PC Castle, "and that has to count for something."

Gabriel nodded, murmured his thanks and left.

Early the following day, as Gabriel was clearing up after saying his Mass, he saw Abbot Ambrose walking purposefully towards him. His heart always sank a few inches whenever Abbot Ambrose approached him, and Gabriel followed him out of the chapel with a familiar sense of impending doom. "No need to look so crestfallen," promised Ambrose as soon as they reached the narthex. "Dr Paige is here. He needs you to accompany him to his home, and I have assured him that you will come."

"What's happened?" demanded Gabriel, all manner of terrible scenarios flashing through his mind. "Is everything all right?"

"I'll let him tell you," said Ambrose noncommittally, raising his hand in blessing. Gabriel lowered his head, listened to the whispered words and then took his leave.

Dr Paige was standing in wait by the door, looking as though he had barely slept. "Father Gabriel, I'm sorry to burst in on you like this," he said, offering his hand in greeting. "I didn't know whom else to ask. Could you come with me, please?"

Gabriel followed Dr Paige out to his car. The priest waited until they were both settled and Dr Paige had driven away from the abbey before asking the obvious question. "What's happened?"

"We have a visitor," said Dr Paige bleakly. "Antoine's ghastly Aunt Plant has arrived. I'm busy with my patients, and Marie is occupied with Antoine. I'm going to be desperately behind all day as it is, but I wouldn't know what to say to her even if I did have the time to talk to her."

Gabriel felt a familiar knot of anxiety tightening in the pit of his stomach. His behaviour towards Plantagenet on the previous day had been appallingly rude and probably extremely distressing for her, but he had had no time to explain what he was doing. He had left her alone in her dead brother's house, and Gabriel had no idea who had broken the news to her of her father's arrest. "Of course, I'll talk to her. The poor woman deserves my time after the events of yesterday. How much does she know?"

"Everything. After the arrest, Inspector Applegate went back to the house to find Miss Nicholson sitting on the floor of the summerhouse in a state of some distress. Apparently, she was too upset to make her way home after we all left, and she just sat there all that time."

When they arrived at the house, Dr Paige indicated the kitchen door before disappearing upstairs to check on Marie and Antoine. Gabriel walked through to the kitchen and found Plantagenet sitting in a catatonic daze at the kitchen table, too stunned by recent events to so much as turn her head to look at him when he entered the room. There was something spooky about a living, breathing human being slipping into statuesque stillness, so much so that Gabriel would have liked to have waved his hand in front of her face or given her a gentle shake to nudge her out of her somnambulism. Then he remembered slipping away like that in the sickening aftermath of his own tragedy and knew he had simply to sit down at the table and wait until she came round.

Dr Paige tiptoed through the room as quiet as a mouse,

but Gabriel doubted that Plantagenet would have noticed if he had come crashing into the room in gum boots. Dr Paige sat down gingerly next to Gabriel and whispered, "Antoine's a little calmer this morning. Marie is sitting with him. She's made up a little bed for herself in his room for the next few nights; she doesn't think he should be left alone."

Gabriel nodded. "Thank you," he said, though it sounded so inadequate considering the care that the Paiges had lavished on a child they had only very recently met. "Thank you."

"I'm going to take up some tea for Marie," said Dr Paige, getting up as quickly as he had sat down. Gabriel might be able to sit in silence watching Plantagenet, but there was no way Dr Paige was going to be able to cope with the oppressive silence for more than a few minutes. "I'll take some milk to Antoine while I'm at it and see if I can coax him into drinking it."

Dr Paige picked up the teapot on the table, filled a cup and set it on a tray before retreating to the larder to fetch some milk. Plantagenet moved in her chair almost imperceptibly, waiting whilst Dr Paige picked up the tray and left the room before she looked up slowly to face Gabriel. "How am I ever to bear this?" she said weakly, her eyes half-closed as though she barely had the strength to stay awake. "I accused my own brother of betraying his wife to the Gestapo; I stormed out of his life and gave him no opportunity to defend himself. I *knew* I was wrong! Deep down, I knew it was not his fault, and now it's all too late."

"Miss Nicholson," Gabriel began, but he was lost for words. The fact was, it really was too late. Like so many family estrangements, time had run out for the Nicholsons;

Gabriel could not pretend to her that her hurtful words of accusation would not have been as devastating as she had intended them to be at the time; he could not lie to her and pretend that she had not made the two most catastrophic errors of judgement of her entire life. However well intentioned she had been, Plantagenet had made the wrong deduction when she had tried to investigate her sister-in-law's disappearance and death, and there was no way back. Plantagenet could have made that short journey from her home to her brother's at any time she had wanted, but she had stubbornly refused to see him, convinced beyond reason that he was little better than a common murderer.

"You have no idea what it was like, Father," said Plantagenet in the same exhausted tone. "To go back to France and see the home where Brigitte had grown up, to meet her family—what remained of it. The Germans shot her in the middle of the market square, Father! They watched her die!"

"I know they did."

"Her old school friends, her father, everyone in that little town who had seen her grow up . . . imagine if it had happened here! Imagine what it must have been like. Most of us would run mad watching any innocent person die like that in cold blood, but somebody one knew and cared for? To have to watch her die and be powerless to do anything to help her . . ."

Gabriel reached across and placed a hand on Plantagenet's clenched fist, but the comforting gesture came a moment too late, and tears began to course down her waxen face. Even Plantagenet's grief felt unnatural. Tears traced their way along the contours of the woman's sunken cheeks, pattering onto the table top, but Plantagenet's expression did not alter at all. Her voice became breathless and even quieter, but she somehow managed to continue to talk. "Her brother, Henri, said that he thought Brigitte wanted to say something at the end, but she couldn't speak. He said she was trying and trying to talk, but the words wouldn't come out. Because her hands were tied she could not make the sign of the cross. She couldn't do anything, and they wouldn't let a priest come." Plantagenet's head slipped down onto her folded arms, muffling the words that followed. "It was my fault! All my anger against Charles was pointless; it was I who gave away her secret!"

"Miss Nicholson—"

"For pity's sake, my name's Plantagenet!" she snapped, covering her face as though suddenly embarrassed by her loss of control. "Whatever is the point of all these niceties when you know every disgusting secret of my family? You know that my father betrayed his own kin to conceal his grotesque little secrets, that he killed his own son. You know that I maligned an innocent man!" She looked at Gabriel in inexplicable fury. "Do you enjoy raking up the dirt about everyone?"

Gabriel swallowed hard. It was not the first time he had found himself on the receiving end of misdirected anger, and he knew it would not be the last time. He shook his head slowly. "It gives me no pleasure whatsoever, madam, but with murder there are no niceties. There is little respect for secrets." He hesitated, wondering about the wisdom of what he was about to say, but he thought it was worth the risk. "Many years ago, I was living—"

But Plantagenet was not remotely interested in Gabriel

and where he had once lived. The only grief about which she had any interest was her own, and she stood up, walked over to the sink and splashed water on her face. The result made her look, if anything, even more distraught, tears replaced by rivulets of tap water which did nothing to cool her swollen eyes and nose. "I should like to see my nephew now, please."

It was a perfectly understandable request, but Gabriel hesitated, wondering what sort of a state Antoine might be in by now. Marie might only just have settled him, and this distressed, agitated female was planning to march up the stairs and engage him in conversation. "I'm not sure if he'll be awake," Gabriel began cautiously, but Plantagenet's look of undisguised exhaustion was almost harder to resist than her steely confidence had been. "Dr Paige may have—"

"I very much doubt he's drugged that milk, if that's what you are insinuating," said Plantagenet with something of her old acerbic tone. "Antoine is all I have left now, and I owe it to Brigitte and Charles to take care of him. I don't know what they would have thought if they had known that their son would end up in the hands of strangers."

Gabriel was about to point out that thousands and thousands of parents had handed over their children to strangers in London, Berlin, Czechoslovakia, Warsaw—anywhere where the desire to protect a child was strong enough to force a woman to part with a beloved son or daughter. Brigitte would have understood better than most that the greatest act of love can sometimes be to place a child in the hands of strangers. As always, he was given no chance to say anything. Plantagenet pushed past him out of the kitchen, into the hall and up the stairs. Gabriel hurried after her.

Antoine was sitting up in bed, sipping the glass of milk with little enthusiasm, whilst Marie read to him from a well-thumbed-through copy of *Just William*: "William had received specific instructions. He was not to come into the house till the tea-bell rang, and was to go out and play in the garden again directly after tea . . ."

Marie noticed Antoine looking towards the door and followed his gaze, the book falling unobtrusively into her lap. "We're just having a story while Antoine has his milk," Marie explained. "I thought William's antics might be a nice diversion."

Gabriel smiled. "I missed the *Just William* stories," he said. "After my time, I'm afraid. I'm sure they're very entertaining."

Antoine nodded, but that was the extent of his contribution to the conversation. He was watching Plantagenet with a combination of anxiety and dislike, which Gabriel hoped Plantagenet had not noticed.

"Antoine, my dear," said Plantagenet with a hesitance Gabriel would not have expected even after the emotion she had shown in the kitchen. Whatever Plantagenet was, she was normally decisive to the point of being brusque. "Antoine, I am so very sorry about everything that's happened. I know you must think very ill of me indeed because of the things I said about your father, but I want you to know that I was wrong. Your father was a good man, and I was a fool not to realise that."

Antoine blinked in apparent surprise but did not look away or turn to Marie for assistance. "I know he was a good man," replied Antoine with a coldness Gabriel suspected he did not intend. "Everyone told me he was a good man except for you. Grandpa was the bad man, but he didn't seem so bad to me."

Plantagenet nodded, giving a sad smile that did not suit her. "It's all so complicated, isn't it?"

Gabriel looked at Marie this time, feeling the need to gauge her reaction; she looked as awkward as he felt. Poor Plantagenet was entirely out of her depth. She had no idea how to talk to a child at the best of times, but there was no easy way to apologise to a child for maligning his dead father and no way at all to try and explain why a beloved grandpa should have turned out to be a traitor, a betrayer, and a murderer. In the end, Plantagenet was given no chance to say anything else, as Antoine had something he wished to say. "Don't make me leave this house," he said, with the same calm tone. "I want to stay here."

Plantagenet's brow furrowed, but she regained her composure and remembered to smile. "I'm sure Mr and Mrs Paige have been very kind to you," she began. "Very kind and—"

"Doctor and Mrs Paige," Antoine corrected her, causing Plantagenet to step back a pace. No one had imagined that this conversation was going to be easy, but this was turning into a disaster. "But I'm allowed to call them Uncle Dickie and Auntie Marie."

Plantagenet flushed; Antoine's last comment had crossed an invisible line between them. "Look here, Antoine," she said, visibly flustered. "I've no doubt that these people have been very good to you indeed, and I am grateful. Truly grateful. But the fact of the matter is, you are *my* nephew and I have a duty to look after you. Families should stay together."

"Why?" answered Antoine in a manner that was either guileless or impudent; Gabriel was not sure which. "Why should families stay together?"

Plantagenet was lost for an answer and simply moved the conversation on. "I've spoken to my solicitor, and it should be very straightforward for me to adopt you. You can come and live with me as soon as you are better."

"I want to stay here," said Antoine relentlessly, and Gabriel saw that he had slipped a trembling hand into Marie's, and Marie squeezed it affectionately. "Please."

Plantagenet, like a born soldier, knew the best moment to retreat, and she walked backwards to the door, her smile never wavering. "It's all right, Antoine. We can talk about this when you are feeling a little stronger. It will seem strange at first, but it's what your father would have wanted."

She never gave Antoine the chance to respond, slipping out of the room and closing the door a little too loudly behind her. Gabriel was about to follow her when he heard a whimpering noise from the bed and turned round in time to see Marie starting to cry. He hesitated, wondering whether he should attempt to comfort her, but Gabriel knew that he was surplus to requirements in the room. Marie and Antoine clung together, comforting one another, while the truly lonely figure in this drama hurried down the stairs.

Gabriel found Plantagenet in the kitchen, gathering up her hat and gloves with the air of cold determination he remembered from their first meeting. To begin with, Plantagenet appeared not to have noticed Gabriel standing in the doorway, but without looking back at him, she began talking. "I said once that no man is an island, but a woman may be if she chooses," she said in a choked voice that did not seem to be hers. "Well, I lied. No woman chooses to be an island. No one desires to walk through life alone; it's nonsense. I'm a ridiculous old spinster for the happily married to pity and for children to mock."

"No, you mustn't—" Gabriel began, but he stopped dead when Plantagenet held up a hand as though he were an omnibus charging down the road.

"I know what people say about me behind my back," said Plantagenet, carefully pinning her hat on her head, her fingers feeling deftly along the brim. "I know what Antoine thinks of me, but he's all I have left."

Gabriel followed Plantagenet into the hall, watching as she buttoned up her coat with unwarranted care and attention. "Miss Nicholson, was there a will? It may be that your brother—"

"I have already consulted my solicitor," answered Plantagenet. "My brother died intestate, but I have been advised that there will be no problem with my plan to adopt Antoine. England is full of orphans, so the state is unlikely to interfere with the adoption of an orphan by his next of kin."

Gabriel watched miserably as Plantagenet walked to the front door and stepped outside, leaving the house without a backward glance. He thought of Plantagenet's house, neat, tidy and so very cold. He tried to imagine Antoine's life in such a home and had to concede that there were worse places in which a child could grow up. He would be well fed and go to sleep at night in a comfortable bedroom. Plantagenet would ensure that Antoine received the best possible education, probably packing him off to a Catholic public school such as Stonyhurst or the Oratory to fulfil the obligation to bring him up Catholic without having to go through the embarrassment herself. As Plantagenet had said, there were plenty of orphans in Britain with no one to claim them, and Antoine would be expected to be grateful.

Grateful. That was the word that always jarred. Antoine would want for nothing except for affection, excitement and all the giddy abandon of childhood, not to mention a father figure, which he so desperately needed after losing his own father and grandfather. Plantagenet would be a dutiful, diligent guardian, and Antoine would be miserable; but if the adoption case came to court, Gabriel doubted that a judge would see things the way he did.

Gabriel walked slowly back up the stairs, hoping to give his two friends time to compose themselves before he intruded again. He could hear the murmur of conversation from the landing and knocked on the door, waiting until Marie called, "Come in!"

Antoine was lying down in the bed, the crocheted blankets tucked up to his chin as though he were in hospital. He was quiet, but his face was moist with tears, as was Marie's, though she had made more of an effort to tidy herself up.

"Has she gone?" asked Antoine balefully. "I thought I heard the door."

"She's gone for now," said Gabriel, standing at the foot of the bed. "You know, Antoine, she really is very, very sorry about your father. She knows she was wrong about him now."

"I don't care; I don't want to live with her," answered Antoine emphatically, closing his eyes as though Aunt Plant were a nightmare vision come to spook him. "I want to stay here with Auntie Marie." Antoine reached out from beneath the bedclothes and clasped Marie's hand as though afraid she would slip away. "You won't make me go away, will you?"

Marie disentangled herself from Antoine's desperate grip and tucked him back into the bed, ruffling his hair as though she had put him to bed every night of his life. "You're not going anywhere until Uncle Dickie says you're well enough. And whatever happens, we will never be far away."

"If she comes back for me, I shall lock myself in the lavatory, and I won't come out!" promised Antoine with passion. "I can be a fighter too."

"I'm sure you can, *mon petit chou*," said Marie, kissing the top of Antoine's head before rising to her feet. "Leave the fighting to me for now. You get some rest."

Downstairs, Marie and Gabriel took a walk around the garden to avoid the possibility of Antoine overhearing their conversation. Gabriel had often noted that the outdoors was a good place to have difficult conversations; there were so many opportunities for little distractions when the topic became too painful and one or other party needed an excuse to look into the distance or show his appreciation for the beauty of the place. Marie, ever the practical soul, had brought out some scraps for the chickens and stood with her fat brown feathered friends all around her as she engaged in what must have been one of the hardest conversations of her life.

"Father, I never meant to cause any distress to Miss Nicholson or to Antoine," she said, glancing absently up at Antoine's bedroom window, where the sky-blue curtains were unmoving. "I had always assumed he would go home with his grandfather once this terrible ordeal was over, but the first thing he said after . . . well, after it all happened . . .

the first thing he said was that he wanted to stay with us. I'm afraid I was rather foolish and said that we'd adopt him if it was possible."

"It was very good of you to say that, Marie," said Gabriel sincerely. "It's in your nature to welcome everyone, so of course you offered him a home. And the fact that you did not think twice about welcoming him into your family is commendable. You have nothing to apologise for."

Marie shook her head. Gabriel tried not to notice that when Marie was upset, her fingers drifted to the tattoo on her opposite arm and pinched at the flesh as though trying to rub it away. "But I've got his hopes up now," she said. "And of course his aunt will adopt him. I should have known she'd want to do that; he's her own flesh and blood. I could see she'd be heartbroken if he didn't come to her."

The thought occurred to Gabriel—and not for the first time—that Marie might be unable to bear children herself. The starvation and mistreatment she had suffered during her time in the concentration camps might have damaged Marie so much that her body might be incapable of conceiving or carrying a child now. Gabriel knew virtually nothing of such matters, but even as Marie appeared so much healthier than when he had first met her, she still looked too frail to bear the rigours of pregnancy. "Marie, are you . . . do you wish to adopt because—"

"Father, I can't have children!" Marie burst out, sparing Gabriel the embarrassment. "I don't know what they did to me back then, but I'm . . . well, I'm fairly sure I am not fertile. But I think you guessed as much, didn't you?"

"I suspected that it might be the case." It had hardly been difficult to guess, but the confirmation saddened Gabriel.

Marie and Dickie could never be parents of their own offspring, but there were children in England in desperate need of a happy home, and the couple—very generously—wanted to adopt children who had lost their own parents, starting with Antoine. Marie was right that Plantagenet would be heartbroken if she lost Antoine, but so would Marie. "I'm sorry. Are you sure?"

Marie nodded, blinking away tears. "The SS doctors injected me with drugs. I don't even know what they poisoned me with, but I'm not . . . nothing is as it should be."

Gabriel remembered Dr Paige telling him that Marie was frightened to death of hospitals and became hysterical at the sight of hypodermic needles, and how much of a battle it had been to give her iron injections, so much so that her screams had made nosy neighbours think she was under attack from a violent husband. "Mengele?" he asked softly.

"He wasn't the only one," said Marie, and Gabriel wondered whether she had had this conversation before. "He got away, didn't he? The doctor who attacked me was hanged for his crimes, and I am still afraid of him."

Gabriel would never cease to be astounded by how much people concealed as they went about their everyday lives. As a priest, Gabriel had the privilege to share in the darkest moments of the human experience that others never saw or even suspected. It was a position of trust he could never take for granted. To look at Marie, blushing with embarrassment as she tried to tell a priest that she could not menstruate, the telltale tattoo hidden from view as she hugged her arms to herself, it was impossible to think of her as the same woman who had endured arrest, interrogation, torture, rape, starvation and the horror of the Nazi medical experiments. "Marie, I am so very sorry," said Gabriel gently. "Can anything be done?"

Marie shook her head. "No one knows. That's why we want to adopt. We never thought of Antoine, of course, because we thought he would return home, but when he asked if he could stay, I was overjoyed."

Gabriel sighed. His every instinct told him that Antoine should remain here. From the way Marie was talking, it was likely that she and Dickie would adopt other children. Antoine might even have some brothers and sisters before long, a big, lively family in which he would learn to play, to quarrel, to forgive, to love. "The trouble is, Marie, that if Antoine's aunt insists, the law will be on her side as the next of kin. Even without a will . . ." He stopped, aware of a dull metallic sound behind him; Marie stepped aside to look at who it was who had entered her garden. Gabriel turned around to see Applegate coming through the garden gate, making straight for them. Gabriel had never seen Applegate with such a grim expression. "Inspector? What is it?"

"Is the boy here?" Applegate asked Marie, pointedly ignoring Gabriel's question. "Can I speak to him?"

"Antoine is resting," said Marie quickly, fear written all over her face. "He's in a bad way, Inspector; I can't disturb him now."

Applegate's manner was unusually gentle as he removed his hat and looked Marie directly in the eye. "I'm afraid things are about to get a good deal worse for him, Mrs Paige. I'm here to tell him that Roland Nicholson took his own life in his cell two hours ago."

Gabriel felt the blood draining from his face. This was the worst ending of them all. Roland Nicholson had died with the lives of two innocent people on his conscience.

Making his peace with his grandson was now impossible. As for his peace with God, who could say for certain what might have happened in his final moments? Gabriel had no time to muse further on the matter; Marie was shaking so violently that Applegate had taken hold of her arm, thinking that she was about to faint.

"Please don't tell him, Inspector!" she pleaded. "This is too much; he won't be able to bear it!"

"I'm sorry, Mrs Paige, but he's going to have to be told sooner or later," said Applegate, glancing around for somewhere for Marie to sit down. He noticed a garden bench and led her towards it, but she shrugged him off, looking back at Gabriel in mute appeal. "Mrs Paige, if he does not hear it from me, he'll hear about it from someone else, and it will be much harder for him."

Gabriel looked up at the window and saw a small pale face staring down at them. "Marie, I'm afraid Antoine is watching us," said Gabriel in a low voice, as though he honestly feared that the child could hear him. "I suspect he already knows what the inspector has come to say."

Marie's eyes darted upwards to the window, but Antoine stepped away, the curtains slipping back into place. "Inspector, let me tell him," said Marie. "He'll take it better from me."

Applegate nodded in evident relief. Any policeman was used to the unwelcome task of breaking bad news, but no amount of experience could render it easy, especially when the recipient of the news was a child. "If you feel able to, I'd be much obliged."

"Would you like me to come with you, Marie?" asked Gabriel. Marie shook her head.

"I think it's best that he doesn't have an audience," said

Marie. "That way he won't feel the need to put a brave face on it."

She was right, of course, thought Gabriel, watching as Marie walked back to the house with an air of stoic resignation. They both knew that it was possible to fall into the deepest valley and live to see a better day. There would be a better day for Antoine Nicholson—Gabriel was sure of it—but there was no knowing when it would come.

EPILOGUE

The weeks that followed were a trial for Gabriel in ways he had not expected. His nightmares continued to be filled with images of nooses and crashing trapdoors and a hooded woman falling; he was not sure whether he would ever stop reliving that horror. Now, however, his daydreams were tormented by the thought of what had happened to Roland. Applegate had made the mistake of telling him that Roland Nicholson had had a razor blade concealed under the insole of one shoe, suggesting that he had always intended to commit suicide if he found himself cornered. Roland had written a long letter to Antoine, which he had left folded on his mattress, before sitting in the corner of the cell where it was hardest for him to be seen through the spy-hole. He had made no sound as he had cut his throat, and a young police constable had made the grisly discovery just minutes too late.

Abbot Ambrose sensed Gabriel's distress and gave him the lightest duties, making sure that he spent as much time as possible outside, as it always had the effect of calming him. It was with some trepidation, therefore, that Ambrose allowed Gabriel to see the woman who had arrived at the abbey gates, determined to speak with him.

Minutes later, Gabriel was seated in the parlour, rising to his feet as Plantagenet walked in. She held out a hand in greeting, which he took without hesitation. "Good morning, Father," said Plantagenet in a brisk tone Gabriel was grateful to hear from her again. She might be dressed from head to foot in black, but Plantagenet had started the long road to recovery. "You look as ghastly as I feel."

Gabriel gave a wan smile. "You look well, Miss Nicholson," he answered, waiting until she had seated herself before returning to his chair. "How are you?"

"Soldiering on, Father," she answered, "as one must at such a time. I must say, Father, you certainly have the intellect of a detective, but I'm not sure you have the constitution."

"I'm well, but I . . . I suffer somewhat from nerves at times," said Gabriel, wondering whether he was being entirely truthful. It would probably have been more honest to say that he suffered somewhat from nerves when his life had been turned upside down by a murder, but this would have felt like stating the obvious. "How is Antoine bearing up? You have both been much in my prayers."

"It is about Antoine that I have come to see you, Father," said Plantagenet, the brisk tone vanishing abruptly. "I'm not sure why, but I felt you had a right to know where things stand with him."

Gabriel braced himself, though part of him was surprised that Plantagenet was confiding in him at all, after his part in the destruction of her family. "Miss Nicholson, I know you care very deeply about your nephew, and I'm sure you will look after him in every way you can."

Plantagenet looked at Gabriel as though he had insulted rather than expressed respect for her. "I'm afraid you do not understand me, Father," she said softly. "I've come to let you know that I have made the decision to let Dr Paige and his wife adopt Antoine."

Gabriel could not hide his astonishment, but he did not need to. Plantagenet got up and turned abruptly to look out the window, not quite in time to hide the flicker of emotion that crossed her face. "I thought long and hard about the situation, and I could not avoid the belief that he would be happier with a mother and a father. The Paiges are young and in love, and Mrs Paige must remind Antoine a little of his mother with her background. In a way, I almost feel that Brigitte might perhaps have turned out a little like Mrs Paige if she had returned safely from the war. I do not have many virtues, Father, but I am capable of being honest with myself; and I knew I could never make Antoine as happy as they could."

Gabriel stood up, speechless for a moment. "You're quite a woman, Miss Nicholson," he managed to say eventually, "worthy of your name."

Plantagenet turned slowly round to face Gabriel. Her eyes were dry, but she looked so sad, it was impossible for Gabriel to imagine that she had ever known joy in her life. She looked like the sort of person who had missed an appointment with happiness long ago and spent the rest of her life distracting herself from the thought of what might have been. "I admired Brigitte because of her courage," said Plantagenet. "I still do. She was not the sort of woman who became a fighter when she had no alternative, when the Germans were beating on the door and her neighbours were being dragged out into the street and shot. She chose danger over safety because she knew that freedom was worth fighting for, perhaps dying for. She was not prepared to sit back while men died on battlefields all over Europe on her behalf."

"She was a true heroine."

Plantagenet nodded, screwing her eyes tight shut. Gabriel suspected that she had done a great deal of crying in private and was too exhausted to express any more grief. "I have never really had to be brave before, Father, but letting Antoine go has been the hardest decision of my life."

"Miss Nicholson, I meant it when I said that you are worthy of your name," said Gabriel. "You have behaved like a queen. And Antoine will always be grateful to you. You have shown that you really do love him, and that is something precious."

Plantagenet looked resignedly at Gabriel; she did not sit down again and gave every signal that the conversation was nearing its end. "The Paiges have been most kind to me. They have told me that they wish me to remain close to Antoine. They have been courteous enough to tell me that I will always be welcome in their home. I should like that very much indeed."

With that, Plantagenet made for the door, turning back to Gabriel almost as an afterthought. "I want to thank you for getting to the truth of things, however painful it has been for all of us. I heard why you were hounded out of your parish. It seems to me that you are a brave man too."

Gabriel stood alone in the parlour for a long time after Plantagenet had left, unable to bring himself to move. As so often happened at these moments, Gabriel found himself wishing that the puzzle could have ended differently, that Charles Nicholson's death could have been a horrific mistake on the part of a contrite stranger, that Antoine could have rebuilt his life in his own home, with the benevolent guidance of a blameless old man, but there were no happy endings in the aftermath of a violent death. There were only broken lives to be rebuilt as the survivors took those uneasy steps on the road to life's next adventure. There had been wise and kindly friends to help Gabriel once; there were wise and kindly friends to help Antoine—and Plantagenet—now.

Gabriel snapped himself out of his dreamlike state and made his way to the chapel, where he would pray for the souls of Charles and Brigitte . . . and offer a prayer of thanks for welcoming homes, and the love of friends and strangers in a grieving world.